Don't Fade Away

A Ghost Story

by

Natalie Pearce

This is a work of fiction. Names, characters, and descriptions are either products of the author's imagination or are used fictitiously. Any resemblance to actual persons, living or dead, is entirely coincidental.

1. Edition, 2023
Copyright © 2023 by Natalie Pearce

All rights reserved. No part of this book may be reproduced in any form without permission from the author except for the use of brief quotations in a book review.

ISBN 9798371627926

Cover design by Natalie Pearce
www.nataliepearceauthor.com

Dedicated to Huw Pearce
I couldn't have finished this book without your support

Chapter 1

It really was such an undignified way to die.

In fact, if there was anyone she could actually talk to, she would probably be too embarrassed to tell them.

Hi. My name's Elle, and I'm so clumsy I managed to kill myself.

Not that she remembered what happened. Not really—just the end result. Her crumpled form lying at the bottom of the goddamned stairs.

She sat on that bottom step quite often these days, pondering her fate. Or sulking, as someone else might have called it, that is, if someone else could see her.

She wondered if all ghosts were like her, constantly drawn to the very spot they met their demise. The fact that the step remained solid beneath her was also a plus. Unfortunately, she couldn't say the same about the couch to her left in the outdated lounge room. At least not the one there these days.

The trusty old couch she and Amelia rescued from the side of the road when they first started university was long gone. Not that Amelia took it with her when she moved out after Elle died. No, she left so quickly that she hardly took any of the cheap furniture or knick-knacks they accumulated during their student days.

The poor old couch survived a couple of subsequent tenants before Michelle? Melissa? consigned the good old 'solid' couch back to the side of the road. Of course, the horrible pea green thing she replaced it with was also long gone along with… Melissa? Yes, it had been Melissa.

Elle actually quite liked the bright red leather couch that now took pride of place in the lounge room. It was just a pity she couldn't sit on it. It looked comfy even if it did clash horribly with the kitsch wallpaper and yellow bottle glass in the entry hall in front of the staircase.

The red couch arrived along with Dean two years ago, and Elle hadn't missed Melissa or her ugly green couch for long. Not for the couch's sake, since she quickly discovered that trying to 'sit' on any new furniture resulted in her butt making contact with the ground, but because Melissa spent a lot of time with her own butt on that couch watching television. And while Elle could quite comfortably watch from the bottom step, she hadn't always appreciated her former housemate's taste in crime shows with their plethora of dead bodies.

Entertainment options were hard to come by when you were dead, but as it turned out, Dean managed to put his couch to much better use on a fairly regular basis. While it may have felt a tad voyeuristic to start with, Elle quickly got over her prudishness once she realized watching Dean make his own entertainment with his frequent guests, was a hell of a lot more interesting than CSI reruns.

What could she say? This was still her house—was she supposed to leave the room? It's not like she followed them into his bedroom (okay, she may have followed them into his bedroom once or twice) but come on, what's a ghost to do with so much spare time?

Over the past four years, many people had moved in and, before long, out of the house. Dean was the only tenant of the admittedly dated seventies split story who bothered to stick around for longer than a year. One guy lasted all of three weeks. Sometimes Elle wondered if it was her. Not that she got up to any spooky hi-jinks, she was more of a watch from the shadows type of ghost.

When it came down to it, haunting a share house proved far less glamorous than haunting one's ancestral family home. But it's not like she had any say in the matter. Or an ancestral home to haunt.

When she shuffled off her mortal coil, there hadn't been a light she didn't go into, nor any familiar faces waiting to guide her to the other side. Not even a strange disembodied voice. Just a very confused ghost at the bottom of the stairs. And Amelia, crying over the loss of her friend.

She remembered Amelia crying a lot in the beginning. But she didn't like to think about that. If she were still alive, she'd say focusing on her death—her past—gave her a headache. Now, though, it made her feel…fuzzy, dazed, like trying to focus after waking up in a strange place. Except her mind never cleared, and the more she tried to remember, the worse it got.

Sometimes she wondered if that block was why she was still here. If she could remember her death, would she become so fuzzy she'd just fade away?

It had happened before—it just never stuck. Sometimes long periods went by when she wasn't really there anymore. But sooner or later, she came to again, usually on the bottom step or lying on her bed staring up at the ceiling. The bed was still her old one, thankfully. Although she had found herself sharing it with a parade of students and nurses over the years, those who did their time in the house before moving on to wherever it was living people moved on to.

It was a good bed. The only new piece of furniture she could afford when she moved into the house a year into her nursing degree. At times she worried someone would replace the mattress, and she'd sink straight through and end up lying on the slats in the midst of someone else's brand-new mattress. She'd made an unwritten deal with herself that if it came down to such an undignified circumstance, there was truly nothing left for her in this world, and she'd move on. Or try to. That is, if she could just work out how, she would try to…

Ghosts didn't need to sleep, but Elle drifted off sometimes while lying in her bed. Not to sleep, of course, more like into the ether. It felt a little like falling asleep, unlike when she got fuzzy, which was more akin to passing out.

At times, it scared her, but other times it came as a welcome relief. She had no reason to still be here, but it felt like the alternative was…well, nothing.

It was quite the letdown after an entire lifetime (albeit a short one) of wondering what mysteries lay beyond the great unknown. The answer to the burning question of what happened after you died, so far, for Elle, was in fact a long stream of tedious boredom broken up only by these occasional episodes of nothingness.

What if she fell into one of her fuzzy states and never 'woke up' again? Would she make it to the other side, or would she just be gone?

It wouldn't be so bad if she could leave the house, but apparently everything beyond the front porch was out of bounds for ghosts. Or at least for her ghost. Most of the time she couldn't even see out of the windows properly. The glass appeared foggy or frosted over like a bathroom window. Not all the time, though, just when she was feeling a little…fuzzy.

Still, it could be worse. It's not like she was suffering endless torment in the depths of hell. Not that she would have expected to. She thought she'd been a good person, always wanting to help others. That's why she became a nurse.

The only good thing about haunting a share house was that something interesting was usually happening with at least one of her housemates, although lately things were quiet. Dean had been on his own for a while now. The two girls he'd shared with for the past year both moved out within the span of a couple of months with little notice.

One was a country girl who, once she got a taste of city life, transformed into a party animal. To no one's surprise, her new lifestyle had an unfortunate effect on her grades. After failing two of her courses last semester, she'd dropped out and moved back to the family farm. Elle doubted much partying went on there, but as mummy and daddy were paying the rent, she had little choice once they worked out what she was spending their money on rather than textbooks.

Hailey had been the sweet and innocent type. Unfortunately, she also turned out to be a hopeless romantic who bought into the idea that the good girl could tame the player in the end, and it wasn't long before she set her sights on Dean.

Once the country girl moved out, she'd seized the moment. Dean was up for it, at least for the first couples of weeks, and they barely left the bedroom. But after another couple of weeks of bickering, recriminations and tears she was out the door. Elle didn't know whether she ended up running back to mummy and daddy as well, but she wasn't too disappointed to see the back of Hailey.

It was frustrating enough to watch Dean with the normal parade of girls he had no trouble picking up every weekend, but someone who might have been serious? Well, maybe that would have been enough to tip Elle over to the other side. Who knows? Judging from Dean's quick resumption of his previous weekend activities, it wasn't something she needed to worry about anytime soon.

He might not be able to see her, or even be aware of her existence, but as long as Dean remained single, Elle liked to fancy herself the woman in his life. He just didn't know it. Talk about unrequited love.

Having Dean to herself, however, grew old quicker than she expected. Watching someone surf the net (mostly for porn), try to take the perfect selfie, and do their laundry, proved a hell of a lot less interesting when they didn't have someone else to talk to. Not to mention that he was hardly ever home. Perhaps that's why she drifted off for so long this time.

But things were about to change. She could sense it. Someone else was in the house. She could always distinguish a new housemate from a visitor. It's like the air shifted slightly, and a new scent diffused throughout the entire house.

She sat up and surveyed the room. Shit! Someone else was definitely here. She'd drifted off in her bed again, and now, judging from the overlarge suitcase next to the door, it appeared the new person had chosen her room.

Elle frowned, lips tightening as she took in not only the bedroom but the whole house, her ghostly senses extending outwards.

It wasn't really a scent (she didn't have a working nose, for one thing), more of a sixth sense type of feeling. The one that told you whether anyone was awake when you got home in the middle of the night, or that someone had left the room right before you entered. At least that might be how a living human would describe it. As a ghost, she was pretty much all sixth sense.

Usually. Not only had this new person decided on her bedroom over the third actually vacant bedroom, but she hadn't even noticed them move into the room in the first place.

It left her uneasy. It's not like she thought her ghostly body stayed in the bed when she drifted off there, but surely she should have known when someone entered her room!

The suitcase was empty, the wardrobe door wide open.

At least it's not on the bed, Elle thought as she shifted off the edge and strode to the wardrobe to take a closer look.

A man, and not a very stylish one from the look of it. Her gaze landed first on a bunch of t-shirts haphazardly stacked on a shelf, the topmost emblazoned with some comic book character she didn't recognize. A handful of checked long-sleeved shirts in several shades of blue hung lopsidedly from bent wire coat hangers. Nothing like the muscle T's, bold shirts and leather jackets Dean tended to wear.

Elle huffed. This was hardly the first time she'd ended up sharing her room, of course, since no one knew it was already occupied, but it always felt like an invasion, especially at the start.

On the other hand, if someone stayed in her room, they could hardly blame her if she, you know, watched them sleep and...stuff. It's not that she got off on just being a voyeur, though. Even the most unimaginative people could still be interesting when they thought no one was watching. Sometimes at least. She'd seen some truly creative dance moves over the years.

A loud thump, followed by a string of curses, distracted Elle. She headed for the door as a much louder bang vibrated throughout the house.

"Holy shit, that's a heavy goddamn chair!" Dean exclaimed as she made her way through the door and to the landing of the staircase. She barely repressed the shiver that always struck her when she passed through a solid object.

"Well, thanks, but I can manage the rest myself," an unfamiliar voice replied. It sounded a touch out of breath. And like he was speaking through clenched teeth.

"Nah, it's all right, man. You'll pull a muscle if you try to carry too many boxes up the stairs with those skinny arms!" Dean countered with what Elle could tell, even from the top of the stairs, was a smirk, albeit a relatively good-natured one, she was sure.

Dean hardly had a mean bone in his body. Plenty of inconsiderate and downright oblivious ones, though, as she could certainly attest to.

The new guy huffed out a laugh. "Well, not all of us have time to hit the gym as often as you obviously do." He might be trying to match Dean's banter, but from the strained tone in his voice, he was a little out of his depth.

As Elle reached the bottom of the staircase, she got her first glimpse of the new guy, lips pursed and glaring slightly at Dean's back as he headed out to the small rent-a-truck idling in the driveway.

Other than the sour expression, there wasn't anything too interesting about him. He had short, somewhat floppy, light brown hair. Not floppy in a trying to be fashionable way, more of an 'I don't use any product' kind of floppy. The most notable thing about him was a pair of thin-framed black glasses that didn't suit the shape of his face.

Of course, everyone looked a little less attractive next to Dean. He was a six-foot-two gym junkie of the tall dark and handsome set. To be fair, that wasn't Elle's type either. Or it hadn't been before she died. She struggled with the uneasy feeling that a guy like Dean would have looked straight through her, even when she wasn't a ghost.

For her part, she probably would have dismissed him as exactly what he appeared to be. The girls Dean came home with were usually flashy and drunk, and Elle never saw herself as the one-night-stand type. But over the years she'd seen how kind and easygoing Dean could be, and even if he swam a little in the shallow end of the pool, it wasn't like she could have a deep and meaningful conversation with him anyway. So all in all, that felt like a moot point.

"Hey, Ethan!" Dean called from outside. "I don't mind helping, but I'm not going to carry all your shit by myself!"

Ethan winced. He'd been busy stretching out his shoulders as he pouted at the admittedly heavy-looking leather recliner. He muttered something that sounded like 'for fuck's sake' under his breath before intercepting Dean as he tried to maneuver a coffee table with a box precariously balanced on top of it through the front door.

Elle made her way further into the lounge room to get a closer look at the new guy and anything else he'd moved into the house while she was 'sleeping.' She darted out of the way as the box slid off the end of the coffee table and spilled its contents across the entryway. A biology textbook came to rest on the floor at her feet.

Instinctively, she reached down to pick it up, only to curse herself as her hand passed straight through. She started to straighten, feeling foolish, but came to a sudden stop when she found herself face to face with Ethan as he bent down to retrieve the book.

The annoyed expression on his face transformed to one of confusion. He faltered, fingers fumbling as he tried to grasp the book while his eyes darted around the room.

If Elle had any breath left to hold, she would have been doing so as part of her waited for his eyes to settle on her own. A yearning for recognition welled up from deep within as she watched his face for the slightest sign he could sense her right there in front of him.

The glasses really were a mistake, and not just because the shape was all wrong. No, they hid his eyes as well.

They were quite startling this close. If only there were more light in the room, she might be able to tell if they were blue or green. But pretty as they were, all that concerned her right now was whether those eyes would actually see her.

No one had since the day she died. She'd reasoned to herself more than once during her loneliest nights that if ghosts were real, then psychics and ghost hunters and bloody mediums must be too, damn it! Someone had to see her eventually, didn't they?

Intense disappointment flooded through her when, after a few more seconds of darting eyes, he gathered up the textbook and a couple of others that hadn't made it as far and stood. He turned to Dean, leaving Elle with a view of his back.

"I told you I can do the rest myself!" he snapped, dropping the books back in the box after he righted it on the floor. He took the small coffee table from Dean and headed towards his recliner.

"No pleasing some people…" Dean grumbled as he nudged the box out of the way with a scuffed boot and walked past Elle into the adjoining kitchen.

Elle felt numb as she stared into the box, absently noting the titles of several textbooks. They were all medical ones. She recognized the one on top from her boyfriend, Adam. Or should she think of him as her ex-boyfriend? Not that they broke up, she just died. Perhaps she should refer to him as her former boyfriend. Somehow, she didn't imagine he sat around thinking about Elle as his girlfriend anymore.

She shook her head as Dean called out from the kitchen, offering Ethan a coffee. She smiled. The man couldn't hold a grudge to save his life. It was one of the things she loved about him. Ethan, on the other hand, appeared to have the opposite problem. As Elle turned to watch him, she saw narrowed eyes glaring in the direction of the kitchen.

Shaking her head once more, she decided to return upstairs when she noticed his eyes peering furtively around the room yet again. *Huh.*

She made her way to the couch instead, somehow resisting the urge to wave her arms about like a madwoman hailing a taxi. She had spent so long jumping around in front of the first few newcomers that it became downright embarrassing, even if no one else would ever know how desperate she looked.

"Ethan..." Elle said, not much louder than a whisper. Not that yelling ever made a difference in the past. She'd tried that repeatedly too.

"Coffee?" Dean called again.

Ethan frowned. A hand brushed his hair out of his eyes as he took an indecisive step toward the kitchen.

"Wait!" Elle exclaimed, desperation rising up from deep inside. The intensity left her disoriented. This guy was moving in—there would be plenty of opportunities to work out what was different about him, but at that moment, it felt like she'd lose her last chance to ever connect with another person if he left the room.

"Please wait," she begged.

Ethan opened his mouth like he was going to make an abrupt comeback, but he paused as his eyes darted around the room one last time before taking a long deep breath.

"No thanks, maybe later!" He shook his head twice, then proceeded to gather the rest of the contents of the spilled box from the faded rug in the entryway.

Elle gazed on, wondering more than anything else, how he could not hear her non-existent heart. Because to her, it was beating harder than it ever did while she was still alive.

Natalie Pearce

Chapter 2

Elle lounged on the bed, one arm propping her head up as she watched Ethan dig through the wardrobe.

Typical man, he hadn't bothered to unpack properly and instead had more or less shoved everything into the relatively small wardrobe. Nothing was folded, and even the shirts on hangers were wrinkled.

He pulled out a faded t-shirt depicting some cartoon character that seemed vaguely familiar from long ago Saturday mornings spent in front of the television. He shook it out, gave it a sniff, and threw it on the floor.

"Oh, come on!" she complained. "Didn't you even wash your clothes before you packed them?"

It had been three torturous days of this since he moved in. After unsuccessfully trying to get his attention again, or at least trip his spooky meter or whatever the hell she had done in the entryway, she'd started up a running commentary on his day-to-day activities. And it was becoming increasingly uncomplimentary.

Another t-shirt landed on the bed next to her. She shifted to take a closer look, but this one was too crumpled to determine the image printed on it. She let out a disgusted sigh and leaned back to stare at the ceiling instead.

It was some weird stucco effect that had been popular in the seventies. She'd hated it while she was alive, but found it strangely soothing now. Sometimes she thought if she had to stare at a completely blank ceiling these days, she might go mad.

She played with the sash on her dress absentmindedly. A fancy red cocktail number that was apparently to die for. Or perhaps that had been the killer heels. Not that she needed to worry about them anymore. She might be stuck dressed up for a night on the town for the rest of her existence, but somehow the heels hadn't made the cut, which was something to be grateful for. They had been Amelia's and half a size too small. The blisters forming on both of her feet were part of the reason she came home early that night.

Elle wiggled her bare toes now—blessedly stiletto and blister-free. Although she supposed the shoes wouldn't hurt anymore if she still wore them. They would just be ghost heels, like her ghost dress and her ghost hair, which was still a mess of brown waves rather than the straight boring style she had worn most of her life.

She still remembered the pang of worry as she stared at the broken heel lying at the bottom of the stairs. Ridiculous, the things one's mind fixated on at a time like that. She had already been dead. Still, Amelia loved those shoes.

She was starting to drift off again. It hadn't happened since Ethan moved in, but she could feel it creeping in now. She didn't have the energy to fight it, nor any desire to. The incident in the lounge room had given her some kind of bizarre hope, and now everything felt anti-climatic. Ethan hadn't so much as twitched an eyelid at even her rudest comments.

Admittedly, he did seem a bit clumsy. He spilled his coffee yesterday morning when she asked if he was going to offer her one, but then all he did was carefully put his cup down, grab a cloth and mop up the spill before tossing it into the sink. He'd finished the coffee while leaning his hip against the counter and sipping like he didn't have a care in the world.

And he stopped scratching his balls on the couch last night when she made some comment about men being nasty, but there was none of the furtive looking around the room from the first day. He'd just continued channel surfing for another fifteen minutes, yawned wider than a bear ready for hibernation, and headed to bed. Leaving Elle to wallow alone on the bottom step.

She wasn't even hanging around Dean much. Although that was partly because Ethan seemed to be avoiding him. Not that avoiding Dean was hard.

He worked shifts at the hospital most days, was barely home on the weekends, and preferred working out at the local gym rather than watching the sci-fi channel in the evening. He also had a second job supplementing his somewhat underwhelming orderly wage, serving barely legal students at the university bar.

Dean, for his part, didn't appear to notice the cold shoulder. Much as Ethan didn't seem to notice her.

To make matters worse, most of the time, Ethan wasn't even remotely interesting. As she'd suspected from the textbooks, he was a medical student—which meant study. And then more study.

It was the mid-semester break now, so he had no classes, but Ethan still spent most of his time on his laptop at the tiny desk next to the bedroom door. Generally with at least two medical texts open, one precariously balanced on the edge of the desk and another on his lap.

Elle had spent more than enough time in another life (or rather her actual life) watching a med student study. Put simply—it was boring. Which she told him. Repeatedly.

She even told him about Adam and how he always came over to study because his housemates were too loud and how he made her quiz him constantly. So much so that she started toying with the idea of switching from nursing to medicine. But she never had the grades for it, as Adam was quick to point out the one time she voiced the thought out loud.

The only mildly diverting thing that happened during one of these study sessions involved Ethan knocking a textbook off the desk and then, in a desperate attempt to save it from falling to the floor, spilled his glass of water all over the other one on his lap. Like she said, clumsy.

Suddenly Elle felt herself flicker, and then she was staring at the ceiling again. She'd been almost gone, she knew it, but something had pulled her back. She propped herself up and surveyed the room. Ethan wore a new t-shirt. No cartoon character this time, just a plain blue that brought his eyes out.

His eyes... Elle followed their gaze to yet another discarded t-shirt on the bed. Or rather, on her foot. Not that it was actually *on* her foot—that would be impossible. Things just went through her when she wasn't careful enough to move out of the way first, because that was always a little too weird for her. Had that brought her back? Something touching her ghostliness?

But that didn't explain why Ethan was staring at a simple piece of clothing like that. In fact, he wasn't just staring. His hand was shaking.

Feeling wide-eyed herself, she shifted to take a closer look. Her foot wasn't visible at all, but that was just the way the t-shirt had bunched up...wasn't it?

She flicked her eyes up to Ethan again. His hand wasn't shaking anymore, but his lips had thinned and...was he about to turn around? Leave? Panicked, Elle pulled her foot away, and the material fell flat against the bed.

Well, it was still wrinkled, Elle reflected as she stared at it. She swore she almost felt her pulse racing.

She glanced at her hands, at the bedding beneath her. It was smooth, showing no sign anyone rested on it at all. She wasn't sure whether to be disappointed or relieved by that as she moved her hand over the bedspread. She stretched her foot out to toe the limp t-shirt and...nothing. It went straight through the fabric.

Ethan's ragged breath swiftly drew her attention back to him. He stood right at the end of the bed now. Eyes still fixed on the offending piece of clothing. Elle shook her head in confusion. He reached his hand out, only to snatch it back. He took another shaky breath, and...there it was...the eyes. They darted around the room even though he barely moved his head.

What was wrong with this guy? It was just a stupid t-shirt!

Dean wouldn't even notice if that happened to a piece of his clothing. Most people wouldn't notice. And even if someone thought something looked weirdly foot-shaped under the material, they wouldn't think twice about it, but this reaction? Was it the t-shirt landing on her foot that brought her back or the way he fixated on it?

She got off the bed and approached Ethan. By now, he'd gathered enough courage to pick up the t-shirt. He frowned as he turned it over and over in his hands, brow furrowed and a tremble in his left hand. She leaned closer. She *felt* different now. It might just be her imagination, but she felt more…real.

"Boo," she whispered into his ear.

He jumped. He opened his mouth, then closed it and exhaled deeply out of his nose before dropping the t-shirt from limp hands. He didn't look around the room this time. No, he backed up two steps, nearly fell over when he hit the open wardrobe door, then abruptly turned and fled the room. The bedroom door bounced against its frame before it swung shut behind him.

If Elle thought she could feel her pulse racing before, now it felt like her stomach was in her throat. She sat back down on the bed.

"Well, well, well," she murmured. "Fancy that."

***

Elle didn't see Ethan for the rest of the evening. He hadn't just run from the bedroom. He'd fled the house.

At first, she felt a touch guilty about that, but guilt soon turned to frustration, then anger, when he didn't return until nearly 2am the next morning.

"Finally, where the hell have you been?" she exclaimed. "Don't you understand how important this is?"

Elle wasn't surprised when no response was forthcoming from Ethan, but it still pissed her off.

"I've been here—like this—for years! Do you have any idea how boring that is? How frustrating?" Elle continued as she followed him into the kitchen.

"Look..." she slowed down. "I'm sorry. I wasn't trying to freak you out but if you can hear me...please—" Elle's desperate words cut off as she watched Ethan gulp the glass of water he'd just poured from the sink, then lean down to rest his cheek against the kitchen counter. It didn't look comfortable.

"Are you...all right?" Elle asked. She approached the sink and lowered her head to better see his face.

His eyes were closed, and his mouth slack. Elle straightened up and sniffed before cursing Ethan, cursing herself and the whole goddamn house. He was drunk as a skunk. If her nose worked, she would have smelt it on him as soon as he opened the door!

"Shit..." Elle leaned back against the counter, her mind whirling.

Would he be more or less likely to hear her when he was drunk? Generally speaking, he would be a lot less aware of anything while he was this out of it. On the other hand, his inhibitions would be down.

Before she could second guess herself, Elle approached Ethan again and reached out with tentative fingers to stroke his face. Or as close as a ghost could get, since she couldn't actually touch him.

She had lost count of the number of times she made a similar gesture with Dean. He never so much as flicked an eyelid, and eventually, she gave up as the ache of disappointment left her feeling hollow for days afterward.

She immediately regretted trying to touch Ethan too, but the second she moved her fingers away, his hand darted up to brush against his own cheek as if shooing away a fly.

Elle imagined she could feel her heart beating in her chest again and instinctively stepped back. She reversed another couple of steps as Ethan groaned and pushed himself up from the counter. It looked like it took quite an effort, but he wasn't scared, apparently he was tired. Elle almost saw to the back of his throat as he yawned before running his hands through his still messy hair.

"Well," she said. "Occasionally there are times when I'm glad I'm not still alive. I can practically see the fumes pouring out of your mouth."

Ethan's only response was another yawn as he vaguely looked around the room. Not like he was wondering who was talking though, no, more like he wasn't sure what he was doing there in the first place.

"Completely wasted," Elle murmured, this time more to herself than to him. "And completely oblivious."

He somehow made it up to his bedroom before crumpling face-first onto the bed. It had been touch and go at a couple of points there on the stairs. Drunk and clumsy were a deadly combination. For a minute, Elle worried another ghost would end up joining her on the bottom step.

That was how she ended up there. Apparently. Or so she gathered from Amelia and Adam's lamenting of it after the fact.

She didn't remember having more than a few drinks that night, although she supposed it would explain why her memory of the night was out of reach from the moment she stepped through the front door until she 'woke up' as a ghost.

Still, whatever the case back then, she didn't think she'd ever been as wasted as Ethan appeared to be right now, and he managed to make it all the way to the bed.

A low groan interrupted Elle's thoughts as Ethan rolled over. He gasped in a couple of rough breaths now that he wasn't smothering himself, and started to awkwardly toe his shoes off as Elle watched on, thoroughly unimpressed.

"You're going to get cold," she observed.

Ethan snuffled before rolling over again and grabbing the other side of the quilt, which he awkwardly folded over himself. Like a cocoon. One shoe still dangled from a foot. Elle's hands itched, wanting to take that shoe off like the proverbial missing limb.

Biting her lip, Elle approached him, keeping a careful eye on his face as she reached out. She hesitated, fingers hovering above the quilt. She couldn't see his foot, just the shoe at an unnatural angle, dangling precariously. Taking a deep breath to steady herself, she lowered her hand right through the quilt. She had no way of knowing if she'd reached his leg, or his foot, or into his foot!

She told herself she was being stupid, but she couldn't help but hold her breath as the tension built. She watched his face for any sign of...well, anything. A loud snuffle made her snatch her hand back so quickly that she almost lost her balance. Then he started twitching.

Elle's brow furrowed as she watched his legs shifting under the covers. But the shoe remained. He flopped onto his back with a huff, and off it popped. Elle stared at it—was he just a restless drunk, or did he actually feel her touch?

Her gaze returned to his face. His mouth hung slightly open, and he was out cold. Cute as he looked now (kind of) Elle had the feeling she would be even more grateful for her lack of smell by the morning. There was no way that much alcohol was staying down, and while she wouldn't have to breathe it in, she also really didn't want to see it come back up.

Another drunken snort followed her as she left the room. Well, it looked like a night on the step again for her. As she settled down, she reflected on the strange nature of ghostly existence. Why was it that she couldn't smell, but she could hear?

Because right now, considering the buzz-saw snore that had just started upstairs, it did not seem fair.

***

You could have knocked Elle over with a feather, figuratively speaking and also possibly literally, when she came to herself the next morning as Ethan half stumbled down the stairs.

"You really should be more careful where you're putting your feet on these stairs," Elle called out. "Trust me."

He paused halfway, one foot hovering over the next step for a second too long, before he grabbed the handrail and continued down much quicker, eyes on his feet. She scooted out of the way just in time as he reached her step.

It was instinctive, not wanting someone to walk through her even though she knew they could. She couldn't sense anything when it happened, but the idea was like someone walking over her grave. Figuratively speaking. Although, for all she knew, someone was doing that too, now that she had a grave.

She followed Ethan into the kitchen. Her eyebrows shot up as she caught sight of the clock—it was only 7am. He must still have alcohol in his system. Did he forget to turn his alarm off? To say he looked the worse for wear would be putting it mildly, and there was no way he wasn't still at least a little drunk.

Head hanging and eyes fixed firmly on his feet, Ethan made his way around the kitchen. He flicked the old coffee maker on and opened the fridge, blinking rapidly for several long moments before retrieving some bread and butter.

"You might want to pour some more water into that and, you know, coffee." Elle pointed out.

He stopped short in front of the toaster, staring at the bread bag in his hand like he didn't know what to do with it. The sound of gurgling soon interrupted his deep thoughts.

"The coffee maker's nearly empty," he mumbled to himself with a furrowed brow.

Elle's brow was equally furrowed as she watched him top it up with water and grab the coffee tin.

Dean rarely got up this early, so this was her best chance to find out what the hell was going on here. Ethan's behavior had her baffled. Could he hear her now or not?

She was so distracted she absentmindedly sat on a chair that had been left pulled out from the table.

"Shit!" she exclaimed as she fell straight through and hit the floor in a ghostly sprawl.

Bloody Dean, she cursed, as she blinked up at the ceiling—it was that weird stucco effect in here too. He never bothered to push his chair under the table when he got up, and it drove her crazy for this precise reason.

Really, she should have learned by now. She'd only been falling on her butt for four years whenever she tried to sit in a kitchen chair. If she was still alive, she would have cried.

Strangely enough, once she gathered herself together, she saw Ethan wasn't staring in her direction as she'd half expected. His eyes were still fixed on the coffee maker. He'd dropped a teaspoon on the floor, though. Like she said, clumsy.

Not that she should judge at the moment, although, one good thing about being a ghost was that no one could actually *see* you when you fell on your butt.

The coffee maker finished brewing, for real this time. As Ethan moved towards it, he caught the end of the teaspoon with his foot and sent it skidding halfway across the kitchen, clattering against the floorboards. He flinched like it was machine gun fire.

"You've got to be kidding me," Elle said in disbelief as she watched him. His face bright red as he ran both hands through his hair.

Going out for a coffee would be a lot less trouble than this.

He put a mug down on the bench and bent over to pick up the spoon, only to send it skittering under the kitchen table this time as his toast popped up. The toaster really seemed to do him in, and before Elle could even make a snarky comment, he was out of the kitchen and grabbing Dean's leather jacket from the back of the couch.

The front door slammed behind him as Elle reflected that, one: Dean was going to be pissed off when he saw his favorite bomber jacket was missing and, two: Ethan probably wasn't going to get far in just his socks, boxer shorts and of course the ubiquitous comic tee. Oh, and three: At this rate, Dean was going to be looking for another new housemate by the end of the week.

The thud of a car door slamming drew Elle's attention to the front window. As Ethan's car pulled out of the driveway, it occurred to her that he might get a bit further without those shoes than she gave him credit for. Certainly a hell of a lot further than she ever would. After all, she couldn't even make it out the front door.

With a dejected sigh, Elle turned her back to the window and glanced around the empty room.

Hopefully, it wouldn't be too long before Dean got up. She liked to watch him wake up in the mornings. At least when he was alone, which was currently not the case. His stretching routine was truly something to behold.

Oh, come on! What else was a ghost to do? There had seemed no harm in it before, plus he was so cute when he was all sleepy!

Now, as she gazed up the stairs, she couldn't help wondering how he would react if he sensed her there with him. Would be freak out like Ethan? Would he move out? She couldn't imagine being in the house without Dean.

Mind whirling, Elle sat down on the bottom step once more and tried unsuccessfully to fade away.

Chapter 3

Ethan laid his head against the steering wheel.

Now that his heart had finally slowed down from a bass drum beat to something resembling its usual dull thumping rhythm, he realized he wasn't wearing any shoes. Unfortunately, the bright green bed socks his big sister gave him for Christmas last year wouldn't exactly cut it out in public.

It reminded him of nightmares he used to have as a kid where he would be at school and suddenly notice he had no shoes on. His sister, Julie, said it was a sign of anxiety, like dreaming you were naked in public.

Sighing, Ethan lifted his head and looked around the supermarket car park he'd ended up in this morning. It was still early enough that not many people were about. He could sit here and sober up more until it was a decent hour to turn up at Julie's place.

He wasn't too keen to visit his big sister in his current state, but he didn't have any friends nearby, and his mother's place was out of the question. Not that he didn't want to see her, he did love her, but he couldn't think of a single plausible reason for turning up so early wearing little more than his socks and a smelly t-shirt. The truth would definitely not go down well—it never had with her.

His stomach rumbled loudly, and he thought regretfully, and with a rising flush, of the toast that spooked him this morning. He leaned over and punched his glove box. The catch was stubborn and only popped open after several more tries. He was pretty sure he'd stashed some emergency rations in there. It took a bit of rummaging, and half a dozen empty wrappers tossed into the passenger foot well, but he finally held up a lone yogurt-covered muesli bar in triumph.

Julie's house was usually chaos in the morning with an eight-year-old to get off to class, but it was school holidays now, and if he interrupted even the smallest sleep in, she wouldn't hesitate to remind him how annoying little brothers could be.

Not that big sisters were much better, although Julie had listened to him when they were kids. She even told their mother he didn't need to see that kiddie shrink when he was twelve. After grandpa died.

Of course, if he told her he freaked out at a toaster, a spoon, and oh! Let's not forget the t-shirt…well, she might just decide he'd been crazy all along.

***

An hour later, Ethan felt even more ridiculous. The expression on Julie's face when he knocked at her door in boxers and a black leather jacket that probably cost more than his entire wardrobe combined was bad enough, but the deliberate and patient way she questioned him about his morning was almost enough for Ethan to have himself committed.

"So you just left…in your Christmas socks?" Julie asked, with her head nodding slightly and eyes downcast as though she could see them now under the kitchen table.

"Ah…" Ethan started, lost for words.

Maybe he should have just made up some story. Now that he was sitting here, plenty of plausible explanations for his early morning outing came to mind. Like he accidentally locked himself out of the house getting the morning paper. Not that he ever read a newspaper or had one delivered for that matter. But he might have had a fight with his new housemate. In fact, that one was good. That's what he should have gone with since it would also explain why he might need somewhere to stay until he found a new place. He blamed the lack of caffeine as he took another sip of the black coffee Julie had handed him without question soon after he sat down.

The problem was this wasn't exactly his first rodeo. He should have been out the door on day one. The place had a funky vibe, but he'd told himself it was an older house, and it wasn't unusual for there to be some kind of…history.

It was just his bad luck that the 'history' seemed to be hanging around. And had attached itself to him. He'd barely unpacked before he felt barraged every time he turned around. It was all he could do to keep it together with the almost constant…tension…in the air.

"Are you sure it's some kind of...spirit?" Julie asked in that same deliberate tone. "A rundown place so close to the university, well, you know what they're like. Student after student going through a share house with only the bare minimum in maintenance ever being done. The electrics are probably not up to code or—"

"Faulty wiring doesn't talk!" Ethan snapped and immediately regretted as his sister's eyes widened.

Shit. What was he thinking? Julie was better than their mother, at least. She never actually *said* he was crazy, although perhaps that was about to change. He had never actually told her that he could talk to ghosts. Not that he did. No, definitely not. He'd learned that lesson young. It was like not feeding the monkeys at the zoo. If you ignored them, then they'd go away.

"Talk?" Julie repeated faintly. She leaned back in her chair now, eyes troubled and a wariness evident from the stiffness of her shoulders.

Ethan ran his hand over his mouth. If the coffee wasn't so damn good, he'd be out the door, even with a ghost waiting for him at home. He sighed and rubbed his eyes. There was only so much running a man could do in a day and still call himself a man.

"Not...talk exactly." He looked straight past Julie and focused instead on the print of Munch's *The Scream* on the wall opposite. It seemed an appropriate choice right now, although a little ironic for Julie. Then again, she'd been an art major before she'd dropped out of university when she fell pregnant with Levi.

Julie cleared her throat, but Ethan continued to avoid her eyes, shifting his own to his nearly empty coffee mug.

"More like...trying to talk," he said, quieter now. He felt Julie leaning towards him. "But sometimes the meaning comes through." He sighed, took a deep breath and continued. "And this one doesn't like me."

He finally met his sister's eyes as he finished speaking. She opened her mouth, then closed it again, clearly at a loss.

"Uncle Ethan!" a high-pitched voice exclaimed, saving them both from their impasse. Levi stood in the hallway rubbing bleary eyes and clasping a worn teddy Ethan was pretty sure he wasn't supposed to see.

"Good morning, little man!" Julie held her hand out to beckon him over. After another rub of his eyes, Levi pouted and confirmed Ethan's theory about the bear by hiding it behind his back.

"I'm not little anymore, mummy," he complained as she coaxed him in for a one-armed hug.

"You know," Julie started with a sly tilt to her mouth. "I'm always saying you boys should spend more time together, and since you," she gestured vaguely in Ethan's direction, managing to encompass the whole of him from his brightly socked feet to his still mussed hair, "have found yourself at a bit of a loss today...well, I have just the thing!"

***

The hour was late by the time Ethan found himself back at his own front door. Whatever else she thought, apparently Julie considered her little brother was still sane enough to babysit, and she'd wasted no time jumping in the shower and getting ready for an impromptu shopping trip. She'd even come home with some decent clothes for him and a cheap pair of sandals, so he could make it back to his place without looking like a vagrant or having to explain his state of undress to Dean.

But there was still the small matter of the jacket. Perhaps he hadn't noticed it missing yet? Dean wasn't alone last night, and judging from how loud the girl had been, they must have been drunk too. Or...you know...Dean was just really good at what he did. Good enough that they woke him up with round two this morning in any case.

Luckily the man in question wasn't in the lounge room when he slipped quietly through the front door. Ethan stripped off the jacket and placed it halfway under a cushion on one of the lounge chairs. The chairs were a mismatched bunch, as were the cushions, so he picked the darkest one and hoped for the best.

As long as Dean hadn't turned the room over trying to find his favorite going out jacket, all would be well. Somehow Ethan couldn't imagine pulling off a feigned, 'sorry, but I thought it was my jacket.'

The black polo shirt and khaki shorts Julie had bought him today were close to the highlight of his wardrobe. Of course, it's not like he had cash to burn. If he did, he certainly wouldn't be living here. The only thing the place had to recommend itself, besides the view from upstairs, was its proximity to the university.

Strangely enough, Ethan had been so distracted by the jacket situation that he hadn't thought about the spirit since he walked through the door. Suddenly he stilled and found himself *listening* before he realized what he was doing. Shaking his head, he forced himself to stop.

"No feeding the monkeys," he mumbled to himself.

This spirit was far stronger than any he'd encountered before, and he needed to be more careful. He almost heard actual words this morning, and that hadn't happened since he was a kid.

The spirit even managed to partly manifest in his bedroom yesterday. That was terrifying enough in itself, but he doubted it would have been strong enough to do so if he wasn't so focused on trying to ignore it. He'd tried so hard to deny its presence, but it was too persistent.

Before he got wasted last night, he spent hours at the library researching manifestations. A spirit could only do that if it absorbed the energy from something in the living world, and right now, he was pretty sure that *something* was him.

***

Elle watched Ethan arrange Dean's jacket on one of Amelia's old lounge chairs. It was the only one she could still sit in since it had been a fixture in the room before she died.

She'd been waiting all day, determined to make him speak to her, and then all of a sudden he froze. Was the cocked head for her, or had he heard Dean upstairs?

He seemed awfully concerned about hiding the jacket. He and Dean hadn't hit it off, but this was a bit of an overreaction. Dean was a nice guy. Sure he wasn't always what someone might call tactful, but he was hardly petty. He would have gotten over it. He also hadn't emerged from his room until near lunchtime, although his guest snuck downstairs not long after Ethan fled and helped herself to his abandoned toast and a coffee before tacking a cheery pink post-it up on the fridge for Dean. He had given it a fond smile this morning before promptly tossing it in the bin.

Elle felt inexplicably nervous. Worrying about what anyone else thought of her hadn't been an issue since she died. In some ways, that had been a relief. She'd never been that good with people even when she was alive and could, you know, actually communicate.

Amelia was her only close friend, and sometimes she wondered if they would have drifted apart too if it wasn't for this house. Once Adam arrived on the scene, Elle never seemed to have the time for other friendships. Not that Ethan was a friend, of course, although she already knew more about him than most of those he probably called friends. One lesson Elle learned the hard way after she died—you never really knew anyone as well as you thought you did.

Ethan had calmed down. His head was still tilted, but he was looking towards the stairs now and the telltale squeak of the second to the top step announced Dean's descent. Somehow Ethan seemed to simultaneously relax and tense up. For god's sake, he was still worried about the jacket! He even walked back to the front door, carefully opened it and pulled it firmly shut again. It made a satisfying thump as Elle's eyebrows rose at his paranoid behavior. She couldn't help but shake her head.

"For god's sake, Ethan, the man's a pussycat!" Admittedly very much of the tom cat variety.

Ethan took two steps back into the lounge room, but the third one faltered for a split second. Just long enough for Elle to raise an eyebrow. He plastered a strained smile on his face as another creak announced Dean's arrival on the second last step of the staircase.

Elle huffed in frustration but backed off. With how jumpy he seemed between her and Dean, Ethan certainly wouldn't appreciate it if she made him flinch in front of his housemate and the last thing she wanted was him running off again. What if he never came back? Could she cope with being nothing to anyone again?

Well, she supposed that wasn't true, she wasn't *nothing*. She was sure her mother and little brother still remembered her, missed her. They probably still had her graduation photo up in pride of place. But while she struggled with guilt at the thought of the pain her death must have caused them, rather than haunting her family, she was stuck here haunting a share house full of a bunch of strangers.

Even Amelia hadn't stuck around long, although it was plenty long enough considering the short amount of time it took poor heartbroken Adam to move on. A bunch of strangers were better than having to watch those two 'miss' her so much!

A sudden gasp drew Elle away from her thoughts. She looked at Ethan and saw his eyes were fixed on Dean, who was scratching his designer stubble as he studied the ceiling. A strange low level buzzing filled the room, and the light flickered. Elle looked upwards too, just in time to hear a muffled bang before darkness shrouded the room.

"Well, shit," Dean swore. "I only replaced that bulb a few days before Hailey moved out." He threw a sheepish look at Ethan. "I reckon that was the last bulb. I've been meaning to buy more, but…" he finished with a shrug as if to say 'what can you do?'

Elle could see relatively well in the dark, far better than she ever had as a living person. The whites of Ethan's eyes stood out in particular as he stared, speechless at Dean's nonchalance.

Dean clapped Ethan on the shoulder a tad harder than Ethan might have expected judging from the way his mouth fell open. Dean didn't notice.

"Don't worry, the shops are still open. I'll pick up some spares too, this time."

Dean laughed when Ethan didn't respond.

"What's wrong, man? Afraid of the dark or something? I just need to get my wallet," he continued before turning around and walking to the couch. Finally, Dean seemed a little at a loss as he looked around in the dark. "Have you seen my jacket?"

Ethan blinked rapidly. His breathing was rapid too, but in the dark Dean couldn't see how frazzled he truly was.

Elle felt quite frazzled herself. Nothing like this had ever happened before. Not even close. It was like a scene out of a horror movie. Only she hadn't been trying to do anything. She didn't even know she *could* do anything! If Ethan didn't clearly think this was a supernatural occurrence, she might have doubted she was responsible for the light globe, but...well, maybe he did have good reason to be scared.

Somehow she managed to keep her mouth shut as she watched Dean continue to quash Ethan's freak out without ever realizing it was happening.

"It's all right," Ethan managed to interject as Dean started patting down the couch in the dark looking for his jacket. "I just got in, so I can easily pop out again and ah…"

He fished his keys out of his pocket and held them up. He gave them a sad little jingle when Dean didn't immediately stop his pat down of the couch.

Surely he wasn't still worrying about the jacket, Elle thought incredulously. Somehow she had managed to change something in the living world. There were far more important things to worry about now.

***

Ethan disappeared for a lot longer than a trip down to the local supermarket warranted, leaving Elle to wonder if Dean would be left in the dark all night.

Not that he seemed too concerned. After another round of patting down the furniture, he'd found the remote and promptly switched the television on and settled in to watch some show about a man who just had a premonition of the day he would die. By the time Ethan reappeared, Dean and Elle were both engrossed.

Ethan had regained his composure, such as it was, and now balanced a half dozen light bulbs and a six-pack of beer on top of a large meatlovers pizza.

He brandished his offering awkwardly with a mumbled explanation about how grateful he was that Dean had welcomed him to the house. Dean waived his words off with a grin, swiftly reached into one of the boxes before Ethan could even make it to the kitchen, and somehow folded an entire slice of pizza into his mouth in one go. He wasn't too far behind in liberating a beer from the six-pack either, opening the twist top with his elbow and chasing the pizza down with a good third of the bottle.

At least this time, Elle reflected, Ethan's mouth was hanging open in shock for some reason other than her supernatural hi-jinks.

At some point, they actually got around to changing the light globe. This was preceded by a good few minutes of arguing over who would get the honor (Dean won because he's taller).

Elle watched from Amelia's chair, now free of Dean's jacket, which hung over the back of the couch again in its usual spot. As unlikely as it seemed, they were bonding!

She shook her head fondly. Everyone liked Dean in the end. He was just one of those guys. He'd give you the shirt off his own back. That is, if he actually noticed you needed it, or you know, that you existed… It also didn't hurt that he was pretty damn gorgeous and didn't mind taking said shirt off for pretty much any other reason. Although Ethan possibly found those traits less endearing.

It took a couple of beers for Ethan to lose the hunted look on his face. At least until Dean announced he needed to break the seal. He sat stiff as a board on the couch, eyes fixed on the television and hand clenching the remote so tightly that Elle managed to restrain herself. Barely. He wasn't such a bad guy. Hopefully if she played it cool for a few days, his curiosity would get the better of him.

The last thing she wanted was him to move out. Dean wasn't exactly fast on the uptake, but Elle had eavesdropped on their conversation closely enough to pick up on the hints, and Ethan seemed to be trying to work out whether anyone else was interested in moving in.

It was a three-bedroom house. Ethan might be hoping another new tenant would distract the troublesome ghost, but from the furtive way his eyes kept flickering up to the light while he spoke, Elle thought he was really looking for an excuse to move out.

The thought was enough to make her ghostly heart stop beating. The chances of someone else like Ethan moving in were slim to none judging from the last several years, and she couldn't go back to being nothing. Something left behind.

She couldn't even claim she'd truly been 'haunting' this house since no one before Ethan had the slightest awareness anything was going on in the house other than their own lives.

Ethan was different. He might be a nervous wreck half the time, and he clearly had no idea what he was doing, but Elle felt more…real…just from him being able to sense her presence.

And real was a heady feeling for a ghost who was used to not feeling anything.

Chapter 4

Over the next week, the life of a med student suddenly involved a lot less time at home studying and a lot more time absolutely anywhere else.

Elle quickly lost track of how often she found herself glaring at Ethan's unsteady stack of textbooks. They stayed in their pile on the corner of the desk, even though his battered laptop generally went wherever he did.

There were no more light globe blowing incidents to scare him off, and his toast popped up at the right time when he actually stuck around long enough for breakfast. Elle even managed to refrain from commenting on the Transformers t-shirt he wore two days in a row last week. Barely.

When Ethan was home, he did a pretty convincing job of playing dumb, but there was no fooling Elle now. She knew Ethan wasn't like the other people who had moved into the house for a year or so before moving on. Her resolve to 'be nice' was wearing thin. Seriously thin.

After a week of being MIA whenever he wasn't sleeping, Ethan gradually started to make an appearance earlier each evening. Unfortunately for Elle, he had apparently made it his mission in life to befriend Dean and proceeded to stick to him like glue whenever they were both home.

This important male bonding process was facilitated by a concerning amount of fast food brought home by Ethan, all high in saturated fats, she noted disapprovingly (and somewhat enviously) from her perch on Amelia's old chair. More beer also proved instrumental, although now Dean was the one supplying it. Presumably, in gratitude for all the free food.

"You know, Dean, you're going to have to be careful or, at this rate, you'll lose *your* six-pack," she commented idly as she watched him help himself to yet another chicken wing.

Neither of them twitched so much as an eyelid. Not that she expected a reaction from Dean. If he possessed anything like a sixth sense, it would have been evident long before now.

"As for *you*," Elle directed at Ethan, "you would need to actually have some muscles first before you could lose them."

No reaction. Again.

She shook her head, fingers impatiently tapping away on the armrest. As soon as Ethan's butt made contact with the couch, his focus was on Dean or the food or whatever lame action flick they found on TV. Tonight it was James Bond.

She had no idea which one. She'd never seen more than a handful of Bond movies in her life and had no interest in upping that tally now.

If Elle could fade out, she would in a heartbeat. It would be far less frustrating than being ignored. But she'd been trying for days, and no matter how long she stared at the ceiling or sat on her step, she couldn't switch off.

How many nights had she lain awake while she was alive, worrying instead of sleeping? It was the same thing now except her earthly worries had been replaced with one concern. Connecting with Ethan. But whenever Dean was around, she felt like she was being ghost-blocked.

Finally, Dean was the one to call it a night, finishing off the last of his beer and leaving the empty bottle on the kitchen bench before bidding Ethan goodnight.

Elle's feet shifted restlessly as she watched him head up the stairs. The impulse to follow him both familiar and tempting, but she'd been waiting too long to get Ethan alone for more than a few minutes.

Her attention snapped back to the man in question at the sound of glass clinking. He awkwardly gathered the rest of the empty bottles from the coffee table and headed into the kitchen. She was on her feet in an instant.

"Are you drunk?" she asked as he swayed a little.

He managed not to drop any of the bottles, though, and carefully lined them up one by one on the bench next to the bin. A far cry from the bleary eyes and heavy head he'd sported the first time she'd seen him drunk.

He gave a wide yawn before making his way upstairs. Elle noted Dean's closed bedroom door as Ethan headed straight to the bathroom. She let out a long breath as she waited on the landing and watched him disappear behind the closing door.

After she heard the toilet flush and the water turn on, she gave up her hallway vigil and entered the bedroom through the open doorway. She settled in to wait, cross-legged on the bed. The last few nights, Ethan had stripped down to his boxers and jumped into bed almost before the door closed.

Elle kept telling herself patience was a virtue. Before she died, everyone always told her she was so patient, but now as a dead woman with all the time in the world, the idea of waiting for Ethan to 'come around' was beyond antagonizing.

She heard the bathroom door squeal. Her head snapped around as the bedroom door opened. The first thing she noticed was his wet hair as it dripped onto the towel draped around the back of his neck. Her eyes followed a large droplet as it ran down his bare chest to the other towel wrapped loosely around his waist. One hand held the towel in place as he shoved the door closed behind him with a foot. He kept his eyes low on the ground as he hurried to the wardrobe.

Elle scrambled off the bed.

"Sorry!" she blurted out without thinking. She didn't know why it hadn't occurred to her that he might be taking a shower, but Ethan usually took a change of clothes into the bathroom when he showered.

He had the wardrobe open now and was busy rummaging through one of the handful of drawers, his back unnaturally stiff. A red flush stained his neck. He still held the towel around his waist, but it was slipping...

Once upon a time, Elle wouldn't have minded, even if Ethan was a little on the skinny side (although he had a few more muscles than she had given him credit for earlier) but now that she knew he was aware of her presence? Well, it was a lot less fun and a whole lot more…creepy.

She turned and hurried away, pausing briefly at the closed door. She never liked to walk through doors. Before she died, the idea of being able to walk straight through a closed door would have seemed like an upside to being a ghost, but in reality, it left her feeling a touch queasy.

She held her breath until she made it through to the hallway, slowly releasing it as she leaned against the wall next to the door. The wall, at least, stayed solid. There was no walking through walls for ghosts. Or at least not for this ghost.

Before she could help herself, her eyes sought out Dean's door on the opposite side of the hallway, and she pouted. She couldn't even watch him anymore without feeling weird, and that was beyond frustrating. Dean wouldn't even care if he knew some girl saw him getting his gear off—it was a pretty common occurrence, after all.

She sighed, head knocking against the wall behind her. Okay, to be fair, it had always seemed a tad creepy, but Dean did have a habit of walking around the house in boxers at any given time of day, even in winter. And wandering around with a towel on was definitely more his style than Ethan's. Elle had never met anyone as comfortable in their own skin as Dean.

In a strange way, she found herself missing him. She'd become so caught up in what Ethan was doing every second he was home that the easy camaraderie she'd found with Dean (one-sided as it was) gained a nostalgic glow in retrospect.

Her fuse had never been so short before Ethan moved in either. Too much time to think was a bad idea for a ghost. Being left alone over the years while her housemates were out and busy living had been boring enough, but she'd always been able to fade out whenever it became too much.

But now? If she tried, her mind started to stew on everything, and it wasn't just about Ethan and whether he would ever talk to her—if he could ignore her, then she could ignore him right back! Hell, plenty of people would be excited to discover they lived in a haunted house, but she had to end up with one who spooked easily.

No, the question of 'why am I still here?' ran on replay in her head. Almost like some ghostly presence was whispering it in her own ear. Most of what she'd gathered about ghosts from her dubious taste in horror movies while she was still alive, made the whole thing seem both a lot more interesting and a hell of a lot more tragic.

What kind of unfinished business did she have, after all? Well, apart from the whole 'living the rest of her life' thing. She felt like she was being punished for being clumsy. And maybe a little tipsy.

Was it possible for a ghost to get a headache? If Elle became any more frustrated, she thought she might even be able to blow another light globe, and why the hell not? They were stocked with plenty of spares now!

If only she could work out how; she'd blow every damn bulb in the house and see how well Ethan did at ignoring her then.

***

In the end, it was Dean who ended the stalemate.

"I don't remember her name, but she was a nurse or something at the hospital. You know Amelia?"

"Huh?" Ethan replied, blindsided by Dean's revelation that some girl had taken a fatal tumble down the flight of stairs right behind the couch they were currently sitting on.

"Amelia Jameson?" Dean continued. "She used to be a nurse too, but she quit and went back to study for her medical degree. Bit ambitious, that one. Never liked having to suck up to the doctors. Said they were all arrogant and on a power trip, but now she's going to become one, so I guess she's just another control freak!" Dean laughed at his own joke, broad shoulders shaking as he shook his head.

Ethan had a feeling ambition wasn't something Dean understood.

"No offense, course," Dean added when Ethan just continued to stare at him blankly, "I'm sure you'll be a great doctor!"

Ethan blinked. "None taken." He'd already gotten used to Dean's propensity for putting his foot in his mouth. He was just surprised that Dean noticed this time.

Ethan felt his blood pump faster through his veins despite himself. This must be the spirit and if she'd died relatively recently, and still young at that, it might explain why she was so strong.

If he found out more about her, he could...well...he didn't really know *what* he could do, to be honest. His knowledge of spirits was pretty woeful beyond the fact that they existed. He didn't have a name for whatever the hell he was either. He'd always been too afraid to try to work it out. All he knew was that he was aware of things others weren't.

He didn't remember when it started. It's not like he fell off the monkey bars and hit his head as a kid and suddenly started seeing ghosts. He had only ever *seen* the one ghost, but he'd made the big mistake of talking about it and ended up on antipsychotic drugs for three years.

He went off the meds when he turned sixteen, but a tiny corner of his mind remained where he worried that they were right. His mother, the psychiatrists. Even Julie at times.

Sure the drugs never made much difference. He'd still sensed them, still heard them sometimes too, but he'd been a lot more careful about what he told his mother afterward. What if they'd decided to hospitalize him next or put him on something worse than the antipsychotics? That was the main reason he became interested in medicine. How many people like him slipped through the cracks, drugged up to their eyeballs?

"I think I remember an Amelia from my Neurology class…"

"I thought you might. She used to live here too, but she freaked out after it happened. And she had to pay a heap of extra rent when she left because the lease was in her name, and the landlord couldn't find anyone else to take the place for ages."

"Can't really blame them, I guess," Ethan mumbled.

"Yeah, I thought it was weird when I moved in, but the guys that were living here back then had no idea about it! I mean, it seems like the sort of thing a guy should know, right?"

Ethan blinked again, and his mouth tightened. "You didn't tell me when I moved in," Ethan said, trying unsuccessfully to keep the accusatory tone out of his voice.

"Well...yeah, but it wasn't really up to me, was it? I don't own the place." Dean sucked on his lips for a few seconds, then conceded with a shrug. "I told a couple of girls who looked at the house once, but the landlord got pissed off and threatened to up my rent since they didn't want to move in after, so you know..." Dean gave his 'what's a guy supposed to do?' shrug and downed the rest of his beer.

Their landlord was a jerk. It didn't take Ethan long to work that much out, even without the list of complaints Dean was quick to impart to him. Still, shouldn't there be some kind of legal requirement to tell people someone died in a house before they moved in?

He gave Dean a sidelong look, but he was clearly about as sensitive as his overly large shoes.

"So you didn't know the girl who died here, but you knew this Amelia?" Ethan asked.

Dean lifted his bottle to his lips again and looked surprised when he found it empty. "Yeah, I used to work with her at the hospital," he said as he got up and headed to the kitchen.

Ethan couldn't help shooting a glance around the room before immediately cursing himself for giving in to the impulse. He got up and followed Dean.

"I didn't know her when it happened, but Amelia told me about a spare room here when I got kicked out of my last place. I still see her around sometimes. Her boyfriend's a resident doctor now, and trust me, he definitely qualifies as an arrogant control freak."

"I thought she didn't like the doctors?" Ethan said, distracted, his mind still on overdrive at the prospect of uncovering the spirit's identity.

"Well, he wasn't one when she worked there. She went back to study the same year he started at the hospital as an intern. I suppose she doesn't see how much of a jerk he is yet!" Dean laughed.

Ethan's mind raced. What did the spirit think of all this? Was she listening?

He hadn't felt a direct presence for days, but he knew she was still there. He was being watched constantly to the point he could barely stand being home unless Dean distracted him. It helped keep her at bay as if Dean created a buffer between them. His hope that she would stop if he ignored her only left him more on edge than ever, constantly waiting for the other shoe to drop.

Ethan mentally kicked himself as he realized he'd already slipped into referring to the spirit as 'her'. For god's sake, it might not even be this dead girl! The energy he sensed was feminine, though. A kind of dismissive derision that Ethan, who looked nothing like the Deans of the world, had felt from many women before, and it came through loud and clear.

***

Elle sat on the bottom step. On her step, the one her head landed on while the rest of her body lay lifeless on the floor. It was a fractured skull that did her in. She'd shattered her shoulder too and broken her left wrist.

It was hard listening to her death being described like an amusing anecdote. Especially from Dean. It seemed she'd been right to feel embarrassed—it was a stupid way to die.

"So this Amelia," Elle heard from the kitchen, "did she tell you anything else about what happened? Do you know how the girl fell?"

"Nah, mostly she bitched about the landlord."

The sounds of the fridge opening and bottles clanking drifted to her as she stared blankly at the floor.

"I don't think they were that close. But she was drunk apparently," Dean added as they returned from the kitchen, fresh beers in hand.

Ethan faltered as they passed the staircase. Elle only noticed because her eyes were on their feet.

"Amelia found her the next morning. Creepy, huh?" Dean continued.

Amelia… Elle's death not meaning anything to Dean shouldn't be a surprise. But she'd never let herself think about it before, and now it struck her somewhere deep inside that she didn't realize she still had. But Amelia not caring? If a ghost could have trouble breathing, she'd be on the verge of hyperventilating.

***

"I can't believe you moved in here knowing that!" Ethan repressed a shiver. He looked over his shoulder. A faint draft blew down the staircase carrying a slight metallic tang.

He rubbed his forehead in an attempt to diffuse the pressure building between his eyes. He took a swig of his beer to dislodge the lump that seemed to be forming in his throat.

He should probably make this his last one. He'd learned quickly that trying to keep up with Dean only left him feeling shitty the next day while his housemate was rarely any worse for wear.

"Why not?" Dean asked, "It's why the rent's so cheap, and it's not like I believe in ghosts. There's not even a blood stain. It's like nothing ever happened."

Was it his imagination, or had that metallic tang grown stronger? Ethan swallowed hard.

***

That was it. That was going to do her in. The edges of her vision blurred, she was slipping away again.

There had been blood. Lots of blood. Head wounds were messy. She'd already known that from working at the hospital, especially her time in emergency, but seeing all that blood pouring out of her own head...it had been too much. No wonder she could never recall it clearly. She didn't want to remember now either.

Her vision was closing in. It wasn't going to be long now. At least she wouldn't have to think about it anymore, wouldn't have to listen to Dean and know that he didn't *care*.

She'd never been so aware of fading out before. This time felt different, and that scared her. What if this was it? What if she became nothing for real now?

She was almost gone, she knew it, but at the last second, she looked up and saw him. Ethan.

He stood in front of the couch, beer still clutched in one hand, but he was looking straight at her, she was sure of it. Their eyes locked for a split second before his widened dramatically, and…she was gone.

Natalie Pearce

Chapter 5

It took dozens of searches before Ethan finally hit on something relevant. You'd think it would be easier, but a dead girl wasn't big news unless she was murdered or died in a public place.

It was the police report section of the local paper from—he scrolled to the top of the screen to double-check the date—just over four years ago. It covered only the bare facts. A twenty-four-year-old nurse had died from head injuries sustained in a fall down the stairs.

Ethan reread it three times, trying to derive more meaning. 'Injuries sustained in a fall.' Did that mean she didn't die right away? If Amelia had found her the next morning…how long did she lie there injured? Dying?

A chill ran down his spine. It didn't bear thinking about. But that wasn't all he was looking for. He had a date now, so he kept slogging through search results until finally, there she was, in pixelated black and white—Elle. He had found a copy of her death notice.

"Who's that?"

With a guilty start, Ethan slammed the lid of his laptop shut before Levi's fingers could reach out and touch her face on the screen.

"She's pretty."

Sweat broke out on Ethan's forehead. The photo was small and blurred when he zoomed in, but she was pretty. He couldn't really tell last night. The brief glimpse of her face before she disappeared had been terrified.

"She's no one," Ethan replied, a little too late. "Just some girl I thought I saw."

Levi stared at him with wide eyes that really didn't blink often enough. With a shrug, he sat back down at the other end of the kitchen table at what was currently his drawing station, complete with the new set of colored pencils and half a ream of office paper Ethan had presented him with today, hoping to keep him occupied.

Ethan had spent a lot of time at his sister's place lately, looking after his nephew after Julie's regular babysitter took off on an impromptu holiday with her new boyfriend, leaving Julie in the lurch for the second half of the school holidays.

As a single mother, she didn't have much leeway when it came to childcare and when Ethan hinted he was looking for an out from his new share house, Julie had been quick to jump in with an alternative.

He'd even stayed the night a couple of times, telling Julie she deserved a night out when in reality, he couldn't face going back to the house. Not that Elle...seemed more active at night. Was that even a real thing or another horror movie trope?

Regardless, everything was spookier in the dark. Especially when said spirit made it darker by blowing a damn light globe. Now that's something Ethan would have thought was just some dumb horror movie cliché, but her anger had been palpable.

He'd almost had a panic attack when Dean volunteered to go out and get another light globe. He'd never suffered one before, but if something was going to trigger one, being left alone in that house right then would have done the trick.

He barely managed to convince himself to go back at all that night. His first instinct had been to head straight to Julie's. Thankfully the second-guessing kicked in before he drove more than a couple of blocks. His abrupt u-turn had left him idling in front of a convenience store, which just happened to be next door to a pizza place. He took that as a sign.

In the end, it had turned out to be a decent night. Once he finally made it home, the spirit had quieted. Ethan, still on edge about the light globe, even let himself forget that he didn't like Dean and, as it turned out, his new housemate was actually good company.

But last night had been very different. The spirit had been a calm presence right up until Dean managed to not only get her attention but also put his foot in his mouth big time. Maybe Ethan shouldn't have questioned Dean like he did. If he'd changed the subject, things might have remained quiet. But the prospect of discovering more about the spirit had been too tempting.

Ethan opened his laptop. Staring at her picture, it occurred to him that he hadn't thought of the spirit as a person. Never truly considered that it was conscious and not just some possibly malevolent shadow. But now she had a name and a face. And not just the little black and white photo in her death notice.

Ethan leaned back and ran both hands over his face, rubbing at eyes dry from staring at his laptop screen for far too long. He would never forget the sight of her faded but terrified face, sitting at the bottom of the stairs in a bright red dress of all things, in the very place she had died.

He'd barely choked back a cry when she vanished. The tightness in his throat had disappeared immediately, but he'd felt so lightheaded that he collapsed back onto the couch as though his legs had been cut out from under him. Dean had laughed, calling him a lightweight as Ethan shoved his beer bottle at Dean and mumbled that he needed to go to bed.

Ethan had hesitated so long at the bottom of the stairs while his new housemate finished off the rest of his beer for him that Dean started to get a furrow between his eyes. Suddenly his orderly side showed itself, and Ethan found himself being gently led up the stairs by his concerned housemate. Luckily he managed to stop Dean at the door of his bedroom, or he might have been tucked in for the night!

On further reflection, perhaps being tucked in would have helped because sleep had eluded him for hours. The brief but indelible image of the spirit on the stairs playing on repeat in his mind.

Armed with more information now, Ethan returned to the search engine and punched in her name. The first result was definitely not her, and the second linked to some South

African woman, as did the fourth and fifth, but the third one looked promising.

Yes! He'd found another photo, color this time. It was a short article, an old sporting section profile from a local paper. It seems she was quite the netball star in her student days.

He scanned through the rest of the search results until they petered out. There were a couple more netball photos, but that was all. He flicked back to reread the profile piece. She had just won her second best and fairest trophy. The questions were pretty basic, but he picked up a few personal details. He reached over and grabbed a blank sheet off the ream in front of Levi and the first pencil that came to hand and started to jot down her answers.

"Is she dead?" Levi asked without looking up, busily drawing away. Ethan's hand froze. He stared at his nephew. His mouth fell open, but he couldn't find it in himself to respond.

What the hell?

He clenched the pencil in his fist to stop his fingers from trembling. His eyes flicked back to his laptop, and he hit the back button until it displayed the death notice again, but the type was so small, and nothing obvious showed what it was. He swallowed hard as he turned his attention back to his nephew, who was now carefully examining two different blue pencils.

"What makes you say that?" he finally asked, unsure if he managed to keep the strain out of his voice.

His nephew didn't look up. Deciding on the exact shade of blue required for his drawing was far more important to the eight-year-old. He shrugged. "You seemed sad when you were looking at her picture."

Ethan blinked. That was all? What kind of eight-year-old went straight from 'sad' to 'dead' that quickly?

"Ah…what are you drawing over there, anyway?"

"Just a girl." Ethan nodded slowly.

He wasn't much good with kids, although he was pretty sure after spending most of the school holidays with Levi that his young nephew wasn't exactly a typical third-grader. He felt a brief flash of shame that the only reason he'd agreed to help Julie out this week was his own desperation to get away from the house. She was right. He needed to get to know his nephew better.

"She's sad too," Levi said.

"Oh…why is the girl sad?" Ethan asked.

Levi looked up at him this time with a funny little crooked smile, his head tilted to the side as well as he watched his uncle.

"Because she's dead, of course."

Ethan's hand hurt. Ever so slowly, he drew his eyes away from Levi's.

Huh.

He hadn't even noticed the pencil he'd been writing with was red. He carefully placed the two broken halves on the table and closed his laptop. An angry red smudge marred his palm.

"You're silly!" Levi exclaimed, looking at the remains of his new red pencil. "But it's okay. She doesn't like red, anyway."

***

"I'm sorry about what happened to you…" Ethan's hushed voice trailed off as he closed the front door behind him.

The house was dark. Dean must be at work or otherwise busy with his extracurricular activities. He switched on the light and hesitated as he approached the bottom of the staircase. He took a deep breath and held it while he listened, both on the spiritual and the physical plane.

Some kind of energy still lingered in the house. He could feel that much, but at the same time, he could tell she wasn't actively there. It was the same low level of energy he'd felt when he first checked out the house after he spotted the vacancy listed on the student accommodation website. He just hadn't known what it meant then. Not that he fully understood its meaning now.

Ethan was used to picking up all kinds of strange vibes he wanted nothing to do with, so he'd become adept over the years at ignoring them all. His mind spun at the thought of just how much he'd been missing out on by feigning ignorance. Maybe what he could do really *was* a gift.

Ethan's plan to stay at Julie's for dinner again as 'payment' for babysitting had derailed after Levi's offhand bombshell. The prospect of sitting across from his sister and pretending nothing was wrong proved more than he could face.

Julie mustn't know what was going on with Levi for sure, or she would have said something. But if she suspected her son had more in common with his uncle than brown hair and blue eyes, that shone a new light on her enthusiasm for Ethan to take over babysitting duties.

She claimed it would be good for Levi to have his uncle around more, but a large age gap meant that he and Julie had never been close, and Ethan hadn't found himself on her shortlist of babysitters before. Except in an emergency.

Admittedly, it was a lot easier to watch a quiet eight-year-old as opposed to a screaming baby.

Ethan sighed. Levi clearly didn't understand that he'd said anything unusual. There was no way he hadn't said something strange in front of his mother.

Ethan remembered all too well what that was like. Not understanding that other people didn't see the world around them the way you did. Levi didn't seem too confused about it yet, but he would be. Ethan had been ten before he'd understood that other people, mostly adults, found him strange. That he needed to be careful about what he said. A ten-year-old shouldn't have imaginary friends anymore. It certainly didn't help when he told them they were real.

If only he'd learned to keep quiet a little earlier, perhaps he wouldn't have spent so much time during his teenage years in a psychiatrist's office.

Ethan stared at the bottom step where he'd seen Elle. He was living in a haunted house. He shook his head. That wasn't what was happening with Levi, though. His sister and her son lived in a poky but nearly brand-new duplex. Julie called it cozy, and the only vibes Ethan picked up at their place were the good vibrations from her 70s record collection.

The girl Levi had seen couldn't have been at their house. He needed to talk to his nephew, but he'd been too thrown earlier to question him, and the kid had gone straight back to examining his pencils with such complete focus that Ethan started to feel like an intruder.

He ran his hands through his hair and nodded. He needed to get his own head straight first. What would he tell Levi, anyway? The only lesson he'd learned about his extra sense since he was Levi's age was not to tell anyone.

He needed to come to grips with his own 'gift' before he could guide an impressionable kid.

Still, Levi's revelation left Ethan feeling vindicated for the first time in his life. Seeing Elle's face last night was part of it too—a big part—but today, for the first time, Ethan wholeheartedly believed that what he'd sensed all his life was *real*. The little voice in the corner of his mind whispering 'crazy' was silent, and even the fleeting thought that mental illness ran in families wasn't enough to bring it back.

Pressure mounted on his shoulders, but it was very different now. Suddenly, he felt responsible for more than his own choices. Levi might not understand what he was doing yet, but once he did, and more crucially, if anyone else did, he would need his uncle.

This was too important to mess it up. This was one of the reasons he wanted to be a doctor, after all. How many other kids, or adults, for that matter, ended up medicated or even institutionalized, not because they were sick, but because they were different? The kind of different that other people didn't understand or believe in. And that was the crux of it. Ethan had never understood either, but his nephew didn't have to live with the same doubts he grew up with.

He still stood in front of the staircase. The house silent around him. He bit his lip and shifted awkwardly from one foot to the other. He needed to find out more about what he could do, what it meant, and not just for Levi's sake. He wanted to help *her* too.

He had no idea how, but she'd been trying to communicate with him almost from the moment he stepped foot in the house. Ignoring her hadn't helped. Running away hadn't either. It just made everything worse. She'd been gaining strength from him somehow, but that's about all he understood, and now she seemed to have...retreated.

Ethan sighed. Apparently, he wasn't just bad with living girls. It was strange but seeing her face last night, seeing how scared she looked as she disappeared before his eyes, made everything else in his life seem meaningless. This, here, was what he was meant to be doing.

He'd been a fool for jumping at every sound in the house. A broken light globe wouldn't hurt him, and his mother couldn't send him to the loony bin now—he was an adult for crying out loud! His eight-year-old nephew was braver than he was.

In the end, Elle was the one who was scared, and he was the idiot who didn't want to see what was right in front of him.

Chapter 6

Ethan closed his laptop with a sigh. He stretched, lifting his arms high over his head, fingers laced, before leaning back in his chair to flex stiff shoulders.

He hadn't achieved much in the last two hours of study. All he seemed capable of doing effectively was procrastinating. His decision to join a new study group hadn't helped. In fact, it proved more of a distraction than anything else, probably because his goal in joining the group wasn't actually to study.

The idea first came to him while he was busy looking for excuses to avoid the house—and Elle. But it was only after Dean spilled the beans about her death that Ethan remembered where he'd heard the name Amelia Lawson before. They only shared one class since she was a year ahead of him, but she ran the pediatrics study group. That seemed too good an opportunity to pass up, and Ethan was quick to join—it was even an area he was interested in specializing in.

So far, the study group was proving more useful than just getting closer to Amelia, and his pediatrics grade reflected his newfound dedication. Unfortunately, the rest of his classes were falling behind. But he didn't want to miss any of the group sessions even though he had no idea how to ask Amelia about Elle.

How did he subtly bring up that he was living in the house where her friend died? What if she got angry? Most people would consider it morbid curiosity to ask someone about the dead body they found.

He sighed, cracking his neck as he continued to stretch. So far, it was a moot point. Amelia hadn't been too interested in talking to a third-year med student who was just starting to consider his specialization. And for his part, Ethan's impression of Amelia to date fell in line with Dean's—stuck up.

Mostly the group met at the library, but they took turns hosting informal sessions, with snacks, and it was his turn to host the study group here next week.

Elle's presence had been little more than spiritual background noise since the night nearly three weeks ago when she'd appeared and disappeared so abruptly.

Ethan kept trying to speak to her even though it simultaneously left him feeling stupid and like his heart was in his throat. He probably deserved it after ignoring her for weeks. He could almost believe she had moved on or...something...except for a faint feeling like a breeze stirring. An imaginary breeze. Some part of her was listening. Something very like the small corner of his mind that used to worry he was crazy.

No matter how hard he racked his brain trying to come up with ways to make contact with Elle again, he kept coming back to Dean bringing up Amelia. Her name definitely got a reaction. It hadn't only been the talk of Elle's death that agitated her, and he couldn't help wondering if Amelia returning to the house would be an even bigger trigger. He needed to get Elle's attention.

The problem was, how on earth would he convince Amelia to come over to the house at all? Head of the study group or not, she might cancel as soon as she found out his address. Even if she and Elle weren't close, it must have been a hell of a shock discovering her housemate's dead body.

With a sigh, Ethan opened his laptop again. He closed a particularly uninformative page on the spirit medium relationship and instead opened the university's online hub. He had a paper due tomorrow. He should be grateful for the quiet house and take the opportunity to focus on his studies rather than trying to contact spirits. But no matter what he tried to tell himself, he was being haunted. Not by Elle's ghost, but by the fleeting glimpse of her face as it faded away.

***

"So, what made you interested in pediatrics?" Ethan asked Amelia as he drove them from the university to his place.

By a stroke of luck, Amelia's car battery had gone flat. She was ready to reschedule the study group, but Ethan was quick to jump in and offer her a lift. Not only did it give him the chance to talk to her away from the group, but also avoided the need to give her his address—her old address.

In retrospect, he might have come across as a little too excited at the prospect. She started talking about her boyfriend—the doctor—as soon as they exited the car park. Ethan had unsuccessfully tried to change the subject ever since. He might not have met the guy, but judging from Amelia's spiel, Dean's arrogant assessment was right on the money.

Did she think Ethan was trying to pull a fast one, that they'd turn up at his place only to find the rest of the group had the wrong date?

He'd be offended if he wasn't actually trying to trick her into going home with him. Just not to get in her pants. Not that they weren't very nice pants, but she was definitely not his type. That much was clear, even if he hardly knew what his type was—he might need to actually date a few more girls to work that kind of thing out. Maybe he should ask Dean for some advice...

Amelia shot him a slanted look, as if he had an ulterior motive in asking even such an innocuous question. "I find children are often easier to deal with than adults."

"I don't know. You still need to deal with the parents, and they can be worse than adult patients," Ethan replied, thinking of his own mother.

That got a reluctant laugh from Amelia. "Then why do you want to go into the field?"

Ethan flicked on the indicator to turn down his street, silently thanking whoever might be listening that he lived so close to the university. Even if it was in a haunted house.

"Sometimes children have trouble finding their own voice," he replied, shooting a quick glance at Amelia. She was watching him now, not the street. Good. "Especially when their parents think they know better. Sometimes they need someone who will just listen to them and not go straight for the prescription pad."

It wasn't only his childhood self on his mind now. There was Levi too. The school holidays were over, and guilt crept in as he realized he'd barely seen his sister and nephew for the last two weeks.

He shot another glance at Amelia as they approached the house. It wasn't anything to look at from the outside. Nor the inside, for that matter. The paint was peeling, and the railing on the balcony looked at risk of ending up in the garden at the slightest touch.

But Amelia hadn't seen the house yet. She was still watching him, her expression more thoughtful than sour for the first time since she'd reluctantly accepted the ride.

She nodded after several more seconds and opened her mouth in reply just as Ethan made a sharp turn into the driveway. Her head moved so fast, he could almost hear her neck snap forwards. Her narrowed gaze took in the dead lawn and bare rosebushes before shifting up to the precarious balcony. She frowned as he turned off the engine.

"You live here?"

"Yeah, it's a bit run down, I know, but the rent's all I can afford at the moment." She didn't respond. "My housemate's an orderly at the hospital," he added awkwardly.

That got Amelia's attention. "But he's out now. That's what you said." It sounded accusatory.

"Yeah, he's working," Ethan replied with a determined effort to keep his voice smooth.

"Good," Amelia said with a firm nod. She eyed him for a few more seconds before adding, "I mean, we wouldn't want him to interrupt the study group."

"Of course not…" Ethan struggled to break away from Amelia's gaze. Seeing her flustered was a distinct contrast to her usually cool facade.

"You really should get that balcony fixed," she said, with a tilt of her chin upwards as she opened the car door. "It looks like it could kill someone."

The facade was back, Ethan thought, a chill running down his back at her choice of words.

"Well, the landlord's kind of an asshole…" he replied as he joined her on the path to the front door.

Amelia gave a startled laugh before jumping as a car horn surprised them both. Ethan took her arm to guide her towards the entrance as another car edged into the driveway behind his. But her eyebrows shot up so fast he dropped her arm like it had burned him and started digging through his pockets instead as he backed towards the door.

He held up his keys and gave them a little wave in triumph as Amelia visibly dismissed him and turned instead to greet the two other members of their study group as they stepped out of the second car.

"I'll just get the door then, shall I?" Ethan mumbled, cheeks warming as he watched her long brown hair blow in the breeze as she walked away. Apparently, Amelia didn't want to risk being alone with him for even a few more minutes.

When she finally entered the house, her eyes locked straight onto the bottom step.

Ethan's breath caught as he watched from his station next to the couch. His senses strained, trying to detect the slightest hint of Elle, but all he could hear were Sara and Justin's voices as they attempted to follow Amelia through the door. Her eyes were wide, and she couldn't pull them away from the stairs as she did an awkward little shuffle to make way for the others. Sara's annoyed huff was completely lost on her.

Amelia took a deep breath and shook her head to break the spell. After a cursory glance around the rest of the room and a frown in Ethan's direction, she turned on her heel and headed straight into the kitchen.

Ethan let out the breath he'd been unconsciously holding. He wasn't sure what he'd been hoping for. The house was quiet. Dean was, as expected, at work, and Elle was...not listening.

The impatient thump of textbooks hitting the kitchen table shook him from his reverie. Sara hopped to it, following Amelia into the kitchen, but Justin shot Ethan a considering look. Between the ride here and Amelia knowing her way around the house, Justin appeared to be drawing some unhappy conclusions of his own. Ethan gave him a weak smile and a non-committal shrug before following the girls.

"Kitchen's this way," he murmured.

Amelia might not be Ethan's type, but he could see the appeal for Justin. Not that Ethan fancied his chances of getting past the doctor boyfriend.

Sara, on the other hand, might actually be Ethan's type. Someone more like the girl next door. Unfortunately, she took her lead from their fearless leader and seemed only slightly more impressed with him than Amelia, so Ethan wouldn't hold his breath.

***

The rest of the study group showed up as Amelia launched into full swing on her revision and note-taking speech. The girls approved of the cheese and crackers on offer, and even Justin ceased giving him the cold shoulder once he discovered the fridge was full of beer, despite Amelia's disapproval.

There were no strange happenings or blown light globes, nor so much as a rude aside from Elle or any other presence that might be lurking in the house.

Ethan was painfully aware of how out of his depth he was. Trying to understand the spiritual plane was beyond exhausting, and he struggled to tell if the slight tension in the air was Elle's awareness or merely his own nervous energy.

As the clock ticked closer to the end of their session, Amelia excused herself. Ethan opened his mouth to direct her to the bathroom, but she didn't so much as glance at him before leaving the kitchen.

Well, of course, she would know that the only bathroom was upstairs. Ethan smothered the impulse to follow her. The look Justin gave him was bad enough as it was. He tried to refocus on the page in front of him, but the longer it took Amelia to return, the more on edge Ethan grew.

He tried to tell himself how famous women were for taking their time in the bathroom. That perhaps she'd decided to sticky beak around upstairs for old time's sake, but it wasn't long before his tension developed into a sharp pain between his eyes, and he could feel his throat tightening by the second.

He reached out and took a swig of beer. It helped for a few moments until he realized he'd grabbed Justin's beer, and now he was the focus of everyone's attention.

"Sorry," he mumbled, face reddening.

He quickly stood and fetched another beer from the fridge. The cool air blowing out of the open door was more than welcome. He resisted the impulse to rest his head against the edge of the door.

Where was Amelia? He took a deep breath as the sound of the toilet flushing upstairs reached his straining ears, followed by the bathroom door opening and closing. But the sounds were far too loud. He shouldn't be able to hear the hinges creak from down here.

He closed the fridge, beer clutched in one hand. He tried to focus on the coldness seeping into him from the glass as he walked over to the counter to find the bottle opener.

He could hear footsteps now and…breathing? He almost expected the steps to falter as they grew louder. Somehow, he could tell they were on the staircase. In his head, he could hear the echo of a scream and a thump. No, not just a thump, a series of thumps and then a final loud but very dull crack.

Ethan shook his head hard, and suddenly all that met his ears was the murmured conversation from the table. His tight throat eased as he retrieved the bottle opener and somehow managed to open his bottle without spilling beer everywhere.

He downed half the contents before Amelia reappeared in the doorway. Ethan exhaled roughly. Not at the bottom of the stairs. No, he shook his head again. That hadn't been Amelia.

He took another long swallow as she sat back down at the table without so much as a disapproving glance at his beer. Ethan tried to read her face as he made his own way back to the table, ignoring the raised eyebrow Justin sent his way as he pointedly finished his own beer and looked at the bottle like he was surprised it was empty.

Ethan barely repressed a snort. It wasn't even his beer, and this was a study session, for god's sake! Justin didn't have a chance with Amelia, boyfriend or not.

For her part, Amelia went straight back to her textbook. Ethan tried to catch her eye, but it was no good. Even Sara's casual attempt to trade notes with her received the cold shoulder.

Ethan almost felt guilty. What had he expected to trigger by having Amelia in the house? Failing anything supernatural, he had hoped she might open up a little, if only because she was off balance, but this had been more than he was bargaining for.

He frowned. Amelia hadn't been keen on stepping foot in the house in the first place, but once she did, she'd seemed genuinely unaffected. But now…he couldn't tell. She was harder to read than anyone Ethan had encountered before, and the hope of her volunteering any information about Elle or the house had well and truly gone out the window.

From what he'd seen of her so far, cool and collected with a splash of disdain (for Ethan anyway) was her default manner. But could she really be oblivious to so much pain?

At least he knew one thing for sure. The spirit haunting this house was Elle, and she definitely died falling down that staircase.

Elle was here now. He could feel her. Her presence was subdued, shaken, but she was listening. And Amelia had no idea.

***

The house was quiet once more. Dean still wasn't home, and Ethan had retreated to his room after dinner. To her room. No, she shook her head—her *old* room.

She didn't have anywhere that was hers anymore. That was the most painful part of being a ghost. She was stuck in place while everyone else kept moving around her. Nothing belonged to her now except maybe this step. She didn't think anyone else would want to claim that.

She felt drained, more so than she could recall being since Amelia moved out. That had been hard. In some ways, it had seemed worse than dying. Being left behind. She remembered the anger. At Amelia. And Adam. They were supposed to be sad, they were supposed to be missing her, but instead they'd found each other. Repeatedly.

And then Amelia left, which meant Adam was gone too, and somehow that had been worse. The anger kept her feeling real and stopped her from fading away.

She shook her head at the memories, but there was still so much she couldn't remember. At least not clearly. In truth, she'd put the both of them out of her mind when Dean moved in. Neither of them had any other attachment to the house, leaving Elle with no reason to believe she would ever see them again.

She wasn't free to haunt whoever she wanted, although even if she could, she wouldn't choose either of them. Especially if they were still together. It would just feel wrong. But she wished she could see her mother and little brother again. Seth would be nearly grown by now. He might even be planning to attend the same university she and Amelia had, only a few blocks away.

But now there was Ethan, and what was he up to bringing Amelia here? Did he know who Amelia was? Did he know who *she* was?

Elle thought she'd heard his voice calling her name more than once. But she'd been too far away, and it had been too faint, whispering at the edge of her consciousness.

Then a corner of her mind that always kept tabs on the house saw her—Amelia. Now she couldn't stop running over the encounter in her head again and again.

Elle had hidden in her room. Ethan's room. Never mind that she was a ghost, retreating to a safe place was pure instinct. She still hadn't been truly conscious until Amelia came into the room. It only took two steps beyond the doorway for Elle to snap back into full awareness, reclining in her usual spot on the bed as if at the whim of some arbitrary creator.

Amelia's eyes lingered on the bed. The cast iron bedhead was distinctive. She'd helped Elle pick it out. The moment of recognition was clear when her eyebrows shot up and her mouth opened in a small 'o' of surprise, although no sound emerged.

Elle's throat constricted, convinced at that moment that her old friend would see her lying there, vibrating with ghostly energy if she only looked a little harder.

Amelia's fingers brushed lightly across the surface of the small desk by the door next, free from Ethan's books and laptop for once.

Elle sat up straight as a rod on the bed. "I'm here..." The words slipping out before she knew what she was saying.

Amelia drew her hand back sharply, as if she'd received a shock from the wooden desk.

Elle stood, feeling more whole by the second. What if Amelia was like Ethan? Surely they would have worked that out years ago, but perhaps with Ethan here now, Elle was strong enough to reach out to someone else.

She stared at the other woman, but Amelia stepped back into the hall before she could make her move. With one last dispassionate look around the room, she appeared to dismiss the signs of Ethan's occupation and quietly drew the door shut. Elle listened to her footsteps as they moved away down the hall.

Elle followed, so distracted she didn't even care that she walked straight through a closed door.

She heard the toilet flush in the neighboring bathroom and braced herself. She'd spent so long in this house surrounded by strangers. So long feeling confused. Abandoned.

When the bathroom door opened, she stood ready. She'd tried so many times after her death to reach out, but Amelia had been distraught back then, and Elle could never tell if she broke through. There had been a couple of moments when Elle thought her friend felt *something*. Very brief moments. But watching Amelia hurt, even before Adam started coming back to the house.

Now everything had changed. Amelia's eyes weren't red from crying, and Elle...well, Elle had never been so strong.

She felt more energized by the second as Amelia walked towards her. Elle took a deep breath, determined to stand her ground as Amelia continued on straight through her.

Elle only let that happen in the very beginning, when she barely knew what she was doing. Someone walking through her always sent her reeling off balance, but right now, it was all she could think of to pierce the barrier between them.

Her mind buzzed, and numbness ran through her whole 'body' as she spun around to watch. Amelia paused at the staircase landing. Her step hadn't faltered as she walked through Elle, but at the top of the stairs, her hesitation showed as she gingerly placed her hand on the banister.

Elle had walked down those stairs so many times, as had Amelia. They both knew the feel of each step, which ones creaked, where the banister was loose. Elle remembered grabbing that banister…as she'd fallen.

"Amelia!" she choked out as her friend began her descent. Amelia's face shone vividly in her mind, not as it was now, but then—younger and scared.

But Elle couldn't make it fit, and her vision blurred. The Amelia in front of her walked down the stairs calmly, head down, maybe a touch sad as she ran her hand along the banister the whole way. Elle could barely keep her figure in focus.

When Amelia hit the second step from the bottom, it creaked. The sound resounded in Elle's mind as Amelia paused before taking a little leap to skip over the last step. The one Elle's head landed on. But she miscalculated. A sharp gasp escaped her as she stumbled for several tense moments before regaining her footing at the base of the staircase. One hand shot straight to her throat, winded, as she whirled around to stare at the last step.

She looked different then. Elle felt as if she could see both Amelias at the same time, as though one were superimposed over the other.

The changes four years brought were suddenly obvious. The clothes Amelia wore were much more expensive. Her hair was perfectly highlighted, her makeup carefully applied, and her earrings sparkled like real diamonds. And another diamond to match caught the light on her left ring finger.

She was far more self-possessed than Elle remembered, but it was all for show. Elle saw those eyes at the bottom of the stairs, and they hadn't changed. They were still afraid.

Natalie Pearce

Chapter 7

Elle ran her hand over the surface of the desk, following the path of Amelia's from earlier in the day. It was late now, or early as the case may be. Ethan went to bed just after midnight.

Dean came home a little while later, disturbing her from her spot on the stairs. A sense of numbness had come over Elle as she watched him with a blonde she recognized from last weekend. They weren't even drunk. Maybe he was making progress.

In some ways, Dean had always seemed as stuck in place as her. Perhaps that was why she felt so drawn to him. He'd been her near constant for the last two years. Hailey had been a nice enough girl, just a little highly strung and completely wrong for him. That he still tried should have told her something. She knew it wouldn't be long before she lost Dean too. Not that he'd ever been hers. It was the worst case of unrequited love a girl could imagine. He literally didn't know she existed.

Elle leaned against the desk, taking comfort in its reassuring solidity. Not only had she used the small desk while she was alive, but it'd been here longer than her. Elle always intended to replace it with something more practical, but it saw her through her student days well enough and afterwards there seemed little point despite Adam's complaints when he stayed over. He'd studied constantly, much like the students downstairs this afternoon. And now Amelia was one of them.

Elle's grip on the edge of the desk tightened. Her friend had always been ambitious, but it was Elle who once toyed with the idea of returning to university to study medicine. But after working at the hospital for a couple of years, the idea of going back to studying and the poor student life had been beyond her.

Not that her lifestyle changed much after finishing her degree. She and Amelia used to be full of big plans to move somewhere flash after graduating, but not long after she had met Adam. Even when their relationship was still fairly new, he'd been keen for Amelia to move out so he could move in with Elle while he finished his degree, and then he'd find somewhere flash for the both of them. He'd been even more ambitious than Amelia.

It used to make Elle nervous when he talked like that. Like he had everything planned out. But Adam was her first proper relationship, and while she thought she loved him, he was always trying to tie her down, and he had a way of making her feel guilty when she rained on his parade. So she kept her doubts to herself and asked Amelia not to move out.

For her part, Amelia complained that Adam was overbearing. At least she thought so back then. Adam hadn't been too fond of her, either. He was polite enough to her face, but the constant barbs and jibes at Amelia's expense behind her back became a point of contention between them.

Now Elle couldn't help picturing that diamond ring in her mind's eye. It could be from anyone. It had been years, and there was no reason to think she and Adam were still together.

Elle wasn't sure they'd even been a couple back when Amelia left, even though it was Adam who encouraged her to move out so quickly. He'd been in her ear constantly, telling her what to do and how she should be feeling. Elle remembered what that felt- like. What he was like, how persistent, and somehow she knew the ring came from him, that he never let Amelia go. She heard Amelia saying her boyfriend was a resident at the university hospital after she went back downstairs and the timing was right.

It confused Elle. In some way, it was like Adam never let *her* go. Amelia would always be a link to Elle. Those were his actual words after they 'slipped up' that first time. He wanted to be close to Elle again, he missed her, they just got carried away. And Amelia had been a mess.

Maybe someone else would have been glad they'd been there for each other, that Amelia had needed him. Adam even said that, Elle remembered. 'She would want me to help you through this.' So earnest, unshed tears in his eyes as he held Amelia's hand. 'It was a horrible accident, and it will never be right, but we're still here…'

Unfortunately, Elle had still been there too. Left behind, bypassed by the non-existent white light, and stuck watching their mutual dislike change into something very different. Like an invisible third wheel.

But it had been wrong. She tried telling herself it was just jealousy. No one wanted to feel replaced. Or that she felt betrayed by Amelia, who spent so long telling her she could do better than Adam, that he was too controlling, that he smothered her. But the more she watched them, the clearer it became that it was more than that.

She never saw her and Adam from the outside, never saw what Amelia had been able to see. He could be so charming, so focused on her. Sometimes she told him he was too intense, but he would just tell her she was afraid of commitment. He always knew better. He was older, smarter. Everything he said made sense, even though sometimes that in itself left her uneasy. Not everything in life was about getting it right on paper. Sometimes you just needed to *feel* it.

The things he started saying to Amelia after Elle died made sense too, but none of them had felt right to Elle.

A thump from the bed drew her from her thoughts. A brief flash of light illuminated Ethan's face as he checked the time on his phone. Elle had no idea what time it was, but minutes and hours were hardly important to a ghost when days and weeks and even months had lost their meaning.

He flopped back down on the bed with a groan. Elle sympathized. She'd spent many nights tossing and turning in that bed, staring up at that stucco ceiling, even before she died.

Not that the bed was uncomfortable, but sometimes it felt like the entire weight of the world was poised to crush you when you were alive. Being dead was simpler. She was either here, or she wasn't. She was either lucid, or she wasn't. Mostly, she was just bored. Although, as it turned out, Ethan was a hell of a lot less boring than she took him for during those first few weeks of constant studying.

Elle leaned forward, but she couldn't make out his face in the darkness. Did Amelia say anything to him about her? She'd spent so long trying to talk to him, and now that she seemed to have his attention, she wasn't sure what to do. Had he really been reaching out to her?

"I know you're there."

Elle straightened up against the desk. She heard more rustling of the covers, and a brighter light shone as he switched on the bedside lamp. He sat up, and his gaze went to the doorway next to her before shifting to the desk.

Elle froze like a deer in headlights. Her hand gripped the desk behind her so hard that it would have left an imprint on her skin if she was still alive. She could feel energy rushing into her, but at the same time, her mind went blank. His gaze moved to the wardrobe before he shifted on the bed to look at the window.

Elle's equilibrium recovered as she realized he couldn't see her. But that was ridiculous. She shouldn't be relieved that he couldn't see her! More than anything, she longed to be *seen* again.

He got out of bed and wandered to the window. He wore a black pair of boxers and a faded Futurama t-shirt. She much preferred Dean's sleepwear, which was to say nothing. Although it didn't feel right to think of Ethan like that, and it wasn't only because he didn't spend hour after hour at the gym every week.

She wondered what he would think of her if he could see her. She never paid much attention to her ghostly attire these days, but she was the epitome of all dressed up with nowhere to go. The dress was such a deep red that sometimes she wondered if the color hid the blood. There had been a lot of blood. Her bare feet were out of place, but at least they never got cold these days.

Elle pried her hands off the desk one at a time and inched her way towards the window where Ethan now stood gazing out at the stars.

Most of the time, she avoided the window up here. This was the smallest bedroom, but she chose it all those years ago because of the view. That's probably why Ethan chose it too. You could see all the way to the ocean during the day, and at night she had always found the lights of the city comforting. The thought of all those people out there going about their own lives somehow took the pressure off her. She didn't have to make a perfect decision every time, and there was a whole world of possibilities out there. For everyone.

Or rather, there had been. Now, most of the time when she looked out a window, anything more than an arm's reach away became obscured by some kind of fog. Some days she could see a little further, but she knew what was out there wasn't meant to be a part of her world anymore. It couldn't be.

She stood behind Ethan now, her gaze fixed on the back of his head. Had he tensed up? Could he really sense her?

She resisted the crazy impulse to whisper 'boo' in his ear again, she knew she was just delaying looking out of the window. Ethan made her feel real, but she was still stuck in this house. If nothing else was left for her in this world, did it matter if she felt more real or not?

He lifted his hand and placed his palm on the window pane. He wasn't looking at the sky anymore. Instead, he gazed down at the lights. She could tell from the tilt of his head. He wasn't much taller than her, so she angled herself until she could see his profile and, ever so carefully, followed his line of sight.

She couldn't see the ocean, but it was nighttime. The last time she looked out this window, there had been no lights in the gray, but now pinpricks of light glowed. She gasped as they brightened and reached out to grab hold of the window sill.

She stood right next to Ethan now. A circle of fog appeared on the window in front of her, which she stared at blankly for several seconds before registering it as condensation from his breath, despite the mild night.

Was the cold because of her? How did that even work?

She gazed out at the city lights in awe. Dim as they remained, they'd never been more beautiful to her. If she wasn't dead, she was pretty sure she'd have tears in her eyes.

"Thank you," she whispered so quietly it was barely there.

Ethan's hand slid down the window pane as he swallowed hard. Elle followed its path until it came to a rest against the glass, just above her own.

"I don't know how this...works," Ethan said.

Elle could see his face reflected in the window pane. He was biting his lip. She lifted her hand and placed it next to his. She imagined she could feel the coolness seeping through the glass, and when she moved her hand away, a few beads of condensation were left behind. Ethan shivered.

Elle watched his reflection. It was faint, barely more than a shadow, with only the lamp lighting the room behind them. She herself cast no reflection, but as he held his breath, she wondered if he was searching for one now.

"I want to help you," he continued as he removed his hand from the glass. "I just don't know how."

"I don't know either," Elle replied, voice still hushed but no longer whispering.

She looked at her hand and then back at the handprint left behind on the glass by Ethan's warm, living hand. As she watched, it slowly turned into beads of condensation. The few beads from her own handprint were almost gone. She felt a thrill run through her entire form.

"But I know you can."

***

Ethan woke not long after dawn the following morning feeling strangely refreshed, despite his broken sleep. For once, his focus was clear, and the feeling of peace within himself was stronger than he could remember since he was a little boy.

He immediately knew Elle wasn't there, not in his room, anyway. Part of him was relieved. The idea of someone watching you whenever they wanted was enough to put anyone on edge. It was a big reason why so many people didn't like to believe in ghosts.

Or so his grandfather told him when his mother sent him to the first child psychiatrist. Some people can't believe.

They lack the imagination for it, or their 'sixth sense' is too dull for them to ever contemplate the supernatural. Others don't want to believe, and they're the most stubborn, the most disdainful.

Ethan suspected Dean fell into the first category. Without any indisputable evidence in front of his face, he couldn't accept what Ethan instinctively knew. His mother had been the latter. Something close to panic came across her face when he talked about grandpa's latest visit.

As he grew older, he assumed it was because she saw it as a sign of schizophrenia, but now he finally understood what grandpa meant. His mental health might have scared her, but the prospect that nothing was wrong with his mind terrified her.

Ethan had been too young to understand his grandfather's advice back then, but it had stuck in his mind over the years, and now, after Levi's revelations, all those conversations were coming back. Both before and after his grandfather died.

Ethan sighed as he got out of bed. Grandpa only came to him at night, usually once his mother and sister were in bed. When he stopped, Ethan thought it was because of the pills, and if the pills prevented him from 'seeing things' or 'hallucinating' that meant something really was wrong with his head. If his grandfather had stayed, Ethan might have learned to understand himself better. Then again, he could have just ended up in the loony bin.

Almost a year passed before he sensed another spirit—a young man at a friend's house. But he never actually saw him, nor any of the spirits he'd sensed since. None had been as strong as his grandfather. He'd made the mistake of telling his psychiatrist about the young man's spirit, but he only prescribed more pills. They left Ethan feeling like a zombie most days. The higher dosage didn't stop him from sensing them, but it made him not care anymore.

Now he wondered whether his grandfather had moved on, and if so—how? Was that what Elle was supposed to do?

He wished he could ask her why she was still here, but he had a strong suspicion she didn't know, and he couldn't imagine how he would go about asking, let alone getting an answer.

Her presence last night had been stronger than ever, but he couldn't get a clear grasp on how to communicate with her. Her intentions came through but without actual words attached to them, apart from the ones his own mind interpreted.

He'd heard voices before from spirits, besides his grandfather, but they were vague, broken sentences or random thoughts that made little sense, like the stilted images that sometimes came into his mind as he fell asleep.

Elle's communication, her intent, was much stronger, despite the lack of clarity. She wasn't trying to hurt him, he knew that now, but she was drawing energy from him, and he had no idea whether it was intentional. She might not even know how she was doing it.

He shook his head. The feeling of peace he'd awoken with was fading away in lieu of the headache he was developing as he tried to wrap his mind around all this.

For all he knew, he went around offering up energy to ghosts like a salesperson handing out free samples.

He barely knew anything about Elle, and the only way he could think of to find out more was Amelia. He cringed at the thought. Maybe he could use the connection with

Dean to work out some way to not sound like a delusional ghost hunter. But that wasn't the only reason he needed to be careful.

Because what he'd felt when Dean mentioned Amelia the night of the blown light globe—and again when Amelia was here—apart from the overwhelming pain and confusion, was betrayal. The turmoil that came from Elle left him with the sinking feeling that if she had fallen down the staircase by accident, she wouldn't still be here.

Quite frankly, he already found Amelia intimidating enough without wondering if she was capable of murder.

Natalie Pearce

Chapter 8

"I...want to apologize. That is for the other day. I didn't realize—" Ethan made a face. Amelia's pursed lips gave off the distinct impression she wasn't pleased.

"I don't know what you're talking about, but I'm going to be late for my next class."

Ethan knew she was lying. He'd been all but stalking Amelia for the last week and deliberately approached her before the one and only class they shared. It wasn't exactly on the other side of campus, and they had at least 15 minutes to get there. Not that he was surprised. Women giving him the brush-off for all kinds of reasons was nothing new, even when he was being far more eloquent.

He ran the back of his hand over his mouth and continued as Amelia turned away and headed down the hall.

"It's just that my housemate, Dean? I was telling him about the study group, and he...ah...recognized your name."

Amelia stopped short. Ethan stumbled and narrowly avoided running into her in his hurry to keep up. He reached out instinctively to grab her arm to steady himself. Thankfully, he quickly regained his balance and was able to keep his hands to himself. She was unimpressed enough without him grabbing her or knocking her over.

His face flushed with both exertion and embarrassment. He turned to Amelia expectantly, but she just looked at him.

"He said you told him about the house when he needed a place to stay, and he told me about...Elle." He paused as Amelia frowned and continued to stare. "Well, I guess it sort of freaked me out," he finished lamely.

Amelia looked away from him now. Her gaze drifted past him and fixed on the wall behind his head. Apart from the unfocused look in her eyes, the only sign that his words had bothered her was the way she tightened her grip on her bag.

"I'm just a bit..." He waved his hands around at a loss, unsure if she was listening anymore. "Not that I believe in ghosts or anything," he hastened to add.

He cleared his throat and tried another tack. "I guess I was hoping you could tell me about her? I...um...looked her up online to make sure Dean wasn't trying to prank me, but there wasn't much to go on."

Her fingers on her bag strap were white now as she continued to avoid his gaze.

"I'm not sure that I like the idea of living in a house where someone died," he finished awkwardly, fiddling with the strap of his own backpack.

"It was just an accident." Amelia looked at him now, her eyes intent on his own.

Ethan nodded, desperately trying to keep his expression neutral. He didn't think he managed well, judging from the way Amelia's lips pursed.

Was he blinking too much? It felt like he was blinking too much. He tried to still his hands.

"She fell down the stairs. It was late, and she'd been drinking. There's not much more to it."

She stepped closer to Ethan as two guys walked past, one whacking Ethan on the shoulder with his backpack in the process. Amelia huffed, shooting a glare at the passing man's back.

"You have Neurology next, don't you? Come on." She turned her back on him and strode off after the other students.

Ethan blinked several times before hitching his backpack higher on his shoulder and hurrying to catch up.

"You were friends?" he asked.

"She was my best friend." Her words were hushed, but little emotion came through, just a simple statement of fact.

"I'm sorry," Ethan replied awkwardly.

Amelia sighed. "After it happened, it seemed to be all anyone wanted to talk about. I couldn't stand it." She shot a look at Ethan as he began making apologetic noises. "Don't, it's fine." She held out a placating hand. "I haven't talked about her in so long. Adam won't even say her name anymore."

"Adam?"

"My fiancé." Ethan's eyebrows shot up as his eyes darted to her hand. The diamond was huge. How the hell had he missed that?

"Oh! You were talking about your boyfriend in the car. I didn't realize you were engaged."

Amelia's step faltered, and she paused, looking at Ethan with surprise. "It's new. He only proposed last month. I guess I'm not used to saying 'finance' yet." She made a face. "It sounds so weird."

"You mean you're having cold feet already?" Ethan quipped, trying to lighten the tone.

"No, it's not that. We've been together a long time, it's just…" she shrugged, "I can't really explain," she finished quietly.

"I guess you must have known him for a long time, if he knew Elle."

Amelia shot him a sideways glance that he couldn't interpret and quickened her pace. Her guard was back up, and the more relaxed atmosphere between them dissolved.

"Ah… Dean didn't seem to know much, but he said you found her…um…after?"

"Well, I hardly could have found her before!" Amelia snapped. She stopped and turned fully towards Ethan. "Look, what's this actually about? I get that it's weird, but I'm not interested in satisfying your morbid curiosity just for the sake of it."

Stern Amelia was back, and she was a little scary. Ethan took an unconscious step backward, straight into the path of a girl who looked like she wasn't even old enough to finish high school. By the time Ethan straightened himself out and apologized—three times—Amelia had nearly reached the end of the hall.

"Shit," he cursed to himself. With all the therapy he endured as a teenager, he should be better at talking to people by now. Living ones, that is.

"Sorry," he gasped as he caught up with Amelia. "It's not morbid curiosity, I swear." He reached out to get her attention, touching her forearm lightly. She stopped and took a deep breath, as if mentally asking the lord for patience.

"Two minutes." She nodded her head towards a doorway a couple of meters down the hall—their classroom.

Ethan let out a relieved sigh. At least she was still willing to listen. He rubbed a hand over his face, debating how much to tell her. He didn't know why, considering she clearly had little patience for him, but something about Amelia made him want to take the risk.

"Honestly, I wasn't really surprised when Dean told me a girl died in the house. It made sense. Something didn't feel right, I..." Ethan's eyes widened as he stared into Amelia's. He could barely believe that he was going to say this out loud to another person. "I could feel her presence."

Amelia didn't reply, but her eyes grew wide as well, and she didn't blink as Ethan felt the panic setting in. "Not that I knew it was Elle, or even a *her*, only that there was something...*someone* who died there."

Amelia wasn't staring anymore. She had shut her eyes by the time he finished babbling. She gave her head a little shake. God, Ethan wished he knew what she was thinking—so much for not sounding insane.

"I'm not crazy," he blurted into the strained silence before immediately cursing himself for doing so—that's exactly what a crazy person would say...

It got Amelia's attention, though. The poker face was back, and her narrowed eyes watched him closely. "So you see ghosts?" It wasn't so much a question as a statement. Perhaps a challenge.

Ethan desperately tried not to squirm in place, although he couldn't stop his fingers from twitching. He had never liked the term 'ghost.' It sounded too unreal, too horror movie. He bit his lip before replying. "Not usually. It's subtler than that."

"So you're what? A medium?" The impatience was coming through loud and clear now, accompanied by a distinct unfriendly light in her eyes. "I suppose you have a message or something from Elle, then?"

"No, no, no…it's not like that. I just want to help her. She's…stuck, I think."

Amelia's nostrils flared as she hitched her shoulder strap higher. Her eyes drifted towards the classroom door.

"Look," she started, "I don't know what this is about. I get that you're freaked out living in a house where something like that happened, but it has nothing to do with me. Elle was my friend, but she's dead, and we've all moved on." The last was said with a quiet force that she obviously didn't want overheard.

Ethan felt about two inches tall, but he also noticed that she couldn't look him in the eye until she'd finished speaking, and then it was a defiant kind of look, as if daring him to continue.

Before he could open his mouth again, not that he knew how to respond, she turned on her heel and marched into the classroom, which was quickly filling up with their fellow students.

Two girls turned in unison to glare at him as they entered the room, causing Ethan's rising blush to turn bright red. It wasn't only from embarrassment, however. Amelia was lying. She hadn't moved on, and neither had Elle.

Now Ethan needed to work out why.

***

How on earth he made it through an hour and a half of class after that, Ethan had no idea.

Amelia sat rigidly on the other side of the room and stared at him whenever he wasn't looking in her direction. His attempts to catch her eye failed repeatedly. She would simply raise her chin and turn her attention back to the tutor as if he was beneath her notice. It wasn't just uncomfortable. It was confusing. Her anger appeared to have dissipated, but what replaced it, remained unclear.

Did he actually get through to her? Or maybe it wasn't him. Perhaps Elle made more of an impression on her old friend than she let on. Had Amelia sensed something during the study session? Or after Elle died, before she ever moved out of the house? She might be more sensitive than he gave her credit for.

It wasn't until the last half hour that Amelia finally managed to keep her focus on the lecturer. Ethan spent the rest of the class going back and forth in his mind about whether to try and talk to her again after it finished. He hadn't come to a conclusion by the time Amelia decided for him, rushing to pack up and leave the room before he got any further than closing his laptop.

Ethan bit his lip as he watched his best avenue of information rush out the door. His shoulders slumped as he stared at his laptop bag for several seconds before gathering the rest of his things and making his way to the library.

He'd spent half of the morning before class searching the internet for information on mediums. Unfortunately, what he found amounted to a whole lot of ghost stories, frauds and a confusing mess of articles and advice, which he did not have the patience to wade through after a day of classes.

Most of what he read sounded nothing like what he could do, anyway. Of course, that might have something to do with the fact that he'd been suppressing his abilities for years.

So Ethan decided to go old school and logged into the library catalog. The number of books listed when he typed in 'ghosts' was startling. He quickly filtered to non-fiction, but that didn't help as much as he expected. He noted the classification number and made his way to the Philosophy and Psychology section. It didn't take long to find the right shelf.

He ran a finger along the colorful spines of a few books before pulling them off the shelf. He barely repressed a snort. As it turned out, even non-fiction ghost books had some pretty out-there covers. Who knew, if nothing else, Elle might get a kick out of them.

***

"This one says I should meditate. What do you think?" Ethan asked out loud.

It didn't surprise him when he received no response, but it was probably the best piece of advice on how to communicate with the dead he'd come across so far. The same book also said the best times to make contact were on the verge of sleep or on waking, which fit in with his experiences so far.

He felt Elle's presence so strongly last night. He didn't know if she'd been there when he went to bed, but when he woke in the middle of the night, he immediately knew someone else was in the room. At first, he'd thought it was an actual living person, the feeling had been that strong.

The other times he'd felt her so intently, she'd been upset or angry, but last night she felt like a calm and peaceful presence. Elle wasn't some poltergeist who went around blowing up light globes and messing with the wiring. She was lost, and she was sad. And she was fast becoming more real to him than any other girl in his life ever had been. Which was also pretty sad if he thought about it too much.

He placed the book beside him on the bed. He'd been flicking through several of his finds from the library for the last hour. One book turned out to be a complete waste of time. The blurb sounded promising, but it ended up being little more than a collection of 'real life' ghost stories from so-called mediums. There was little consistency between the stories, with one medium talking about shadow people and another being badgered by spirits on every corner.

When he saw Elle she certainly hadn't looked like a shadow, a tad insubstantial granted (especially as she disappeared) but still in full color.

At some point, he had become aware she was in the room. He'd resisted his first instinct, which was to hide the books under his pillow. For some reason he felt embarrassed that he didn't have a clue what he was doing. He'd been aware of spirits around him almost his entire life, after all. How had he ignored them for so long? Maybe he wasn't only supposed to help Elle, maybe they could help each other.

He read another story out loud, hoping to get her attention. It felt a bit ridiculous lying in bed and reading a story about an encounter with a succubus to a girl, even if he couldn't see her. It seemed to do the trick, though. By the time he'd finished the story, his face shone bright red and the mood in the room had lightened considerably. He was pretty sure that he not only had Elle's attention, but he'd just made a dead girl laugh. It was a good feeling. He just needed to work on his sense of humor with the living ones now.

He reached for the third book and flicked through a few pages, but his eyes glazed over at the small type. Putting the book aside, he got up and opened his laptop. He sat down at the desk and quickly typed Elle's name into the search bar again while he knew he held her attention. He was looking for the death notice and after accidentally clicking through to the South African Elle, he found it.

He hit full screen and leaned back in his chair. There she was again. It was a pretty good photo but grainy at this size. He couldn't help feeling that if he stared at it for long enough, he'd be able to see her again for real.

He held his breath as he waited for some kind of response from the spirit. He thought he sensed a stirring next to him, over his right shoulder, but that could just be him imagining her leaning over to read the screen. What would it be like reading your own obituary? He looked in that direction anyway.

"It doesn't say much about you, but I wanted to find a photo. It's not the first time I saw you, though. I saw you on the stairs…" he trailed off uncertainly. She wasn't next to him anymore, if she ever had been.

He looked around the room.

"I'm sorry about ignoring you. I know you were…angry."

His eyes settled on the bed. It was beyond frustrating not knowing where she was. Like being in a dark room at night. You had some sense of where things were, but you still needed to reach your hands out in front of you to stop yourself from running into anything. He was blindly stumbling around now, but it felt like she was listening. He could only hope he wasn't wrong about her, that she wasn't still angry. Or at least not angry with him.

"It's been hard for me…" He stopped. That got a reaction. He wasn't sure what exactly, but she was definitely not impressed.

"Not that its been easy for you. I didn't mean that," he rushed to add. "It's just…I've never been able to talk to anyone about any of this before, not without them thinking I was crazy, except for my grandpa and that was mostly *after* he died." Ethan took a deep breath before he added in a whisper. "And then they really thought I was crazy."

He took a shaky breath, but he couldn't continue for a few minutes. He was listening for Elle every way he knew how, but he wasn't sure if he was getting a response or not. Talking to Amelia earlier had been almost liberating, despite how mortifying it had been. He had no idea if she believed him or not, but this should be easier—Elle already knew he wasn't crazy.

"I don't know what I am. I don't even know what I can do, but I think he was like me, my grandfather. He never told me while he was alive, but I don't think he ever told anyone."

Ethan sighed. It felt good to talk about it. He hadn't realized how much he'd been holding this in over the years.

"I wish he had," he continued. "Maybe if he'd talked about it, mom wouldn't have freaked out so much when I started to see him."

He shook his head. He could feel a pressure, but he didn't know what it was. It wasn't like the times before when Elle was angry. He could still breathe, but it was insistent.

"I don't know what you're saying…what you want…I'm sorry, I'm not very good at this." He thought she was questioning him, there was frustration too, although that could have easily been his irritation at himself. If he could only make it past this block, he knew he'd be able to hear her.

He walked over to the bed and sat, putting his head in his hands. He started to lie down but a sharp pain in his back brought him up short. He shifted over and sighed as he spotted *Insights from a Medium* with its tacky (and quite pointy) cover. Retrieving the book, he propped an extra pillow behind his head and got more comfortable.

He should be going over his notes for his classes tomorrow, and he had an assignment he'd barely started due in two days, but he knew there was no way he could focus on anything else with Elle in the room.

He flicked to the chapter list at the front of the book.

"Here we go—'Getting to Know Someone in Spirit'—what do you think, worth a read?"

He only got through a couple of paragraphs before he groaned and tossed the book aside again.

"Maybe I should just meditate," he mumbled as he stifled a yawn.

He pulled the second pillow out from under his head and put it back in its spot beside him. Rubbing his face, he yawned once more before he lay back and found himself blinking up at the ceiling.

The stucco effect really was a dust catcher. His mother had ceilings like this too, although not in the bedrooms, thankfully. What was it she called them? Popcorn ceilings, that was it. He remembered how much she'd complained about cobwebs growing up. Her fear of spiders hadn't helped.

"I have no idea how many times I've stared at that ceiling exactly like that. It's easy to get lost in it, all those little bumps and cracks."

Ethan froze.

"There are even two dead spiders stuck right in there over near the window. No one ever cleans it. They've been here longer than you have."

Ethan let out the breath he was holding. It sounded shaky.

"I never noticed."

***

Elle turned towards Ethan. Surely he wasn't talking to her? He must still be talking to himself.

She bit her lip as she continued. "I tried to clean it once, when I was still alive, but little bits fell off and got all over the bed. It was gross." She ran her hand over the covers as she spoke. She was lying on the other side of the bed, leaving at least a foot in between them.

Ethan's gaze left the ceiling, his face turned towards her, his eyes fixing on the pillow. The rest of him stayed stock still. She could see his Adam's apple bob as he swallowed hard.

"Sometimes there's some grit on the sheets. I never really thought about it, just wiped it away."

His gaze was a bit off, focused on the pillow. It was a strange disconnect for Elle. Pillows were no good for her, of course, she sank right through them. When he'd put the pillow back, she'd quickly scooted further down the bed before she got smothered.

She'd been talking to him nearly non-stop for the last half hour, but seeing her obituary right there up on the screen had been jarring. She'd needed a break and had retreated to the bed. She turned away. His gaze was too much.

"I come up here sometimes when I'm so bored I just can't stand it anymore. If I stare up at the ceiling for long enough, I can…slip away for a while." She turned back to him with a small lopsided smile. "I suppose its kind of…meditative."

Ethan let out a surprised laugh before slapping his hand over his mouth, eyes wide. Elle's heart jumped into her throat, metaphorically speaking.

He half sat up, elbows propping himself up as his eyes shot around the room, before quickly returned to the pillow by his side. Elle didn't move, too worried she would break the spell. His mouth hung half open, and he closed it periodically as if he just couldn't find the right words.

Elle understood. She couldn't think of the right words for the life of her, pun not intended. She still wasn't certain he was truly hearing her words, though. He had responded before without actually *hearing* her, especially when he'd been drinking.

"You look like you're worried I'm going to jump you or something. Is it because I'm a ghost, or are you that unused to having a girl in your bed?"

Ethan's eyes looked in danger of falling out of his head as he ran his gaze over the length of the bed. A small startled sound slipped out of Elle, but as his eyes returned to the pillow, she knew he couldn't see her.

"Or maybe it's both," she said. "You did seem to like that succubus story after all."

"Oh, my god!" Ethan exclaimed, "I didn't mean it like that!"

Elle couldn't help the grin that spread wide across her face. It was kind of adorable how awkward he was, and there was no mistaking now that he heard every word she was saying.

"Well, thank god for that!" she exclaimed, flopping back down on the bed.

She turned to Ethan again and couldn't help bursting into laughter when she caught sight of his expression. He looked like he didn't know if he should be relieved or offended.

"Oh my god, your face!" she burst out with another laugh. "I didn't mean it like that either, but…you can hear me now, can't you? I mean properly?"

Ethan's eyebrows lowered back into their original positions as he huffed out an embarrassed laugh. "Yes, yes I can," he replied, as he flopped down next to her. "Thanks to meditative ceilings, I guess."

"Hmm…" Elle bit her lip to repress the wild laughter that threatened to break out. Her heart felt halfway to her throat and if she wasn't careful, the laughter might tip over to hysterical.

"Yeah… I can't see you though," Ethan continued, turning towards the pillow once more. "You're, ah…on the bed, right?"

"Yes," Elle responded. She raised her arm up above her head and let it fall through the pillow. "Could you move the pillow, though? I can't actually use them."

Ethan blinked, "Oh, okay, no problem." He sat up and grabbed the pillow. He looked at it in confusion for a few moments before propping it back up behind himself again.

Elle shifted up on the bed, turning and leaning her head on her hand so she could look him in the face. Ethan seemed to be looking anywhere but at the spot where the pillow had been.

"How old were you when your grandfather died? I tried to ask before, but you couldn't hear me."

"I was ten," he replied, gaze fixed on the ceiling once more.

"And you've been able to see ghosts ever since?"

"I don't usually see them. Most of the time it's just an impression." He sighed. "Sometimes I'm not even sure if there's actually a spirit or just some type of residual energy."

Elle edged closer. Now that Ethan could hear her, she found it fascinating to watch his face as he spoke. The fact that he couldn't see her made it easier. It seemed so intimate. She had never watched someone this closely before, but he was still facing away from her.

"Is that what you thought when you first came here, that I was...residual energy?"

He shook his head, but not in denial. "I'm not sure what I thought. I was still trying to ignore everything. The last place I lived always had a strange energy, but not like here, not like you."

Elle wasn't sure if she should feel flattered by that or not. Still, hers must have been a better energy, since he moved into the house.

"I was worried you were going to move out..." she trailed off, unsure where to go with that thought.

She shouldn't have said anything—what if he decided to move out now? She scanned his face anxiously for any hint of his thoughts as she waited for his response.

He was still staring resolutely at the ceiling. "I thought about it honestly, but I've been running from this for so long and...I don't want to end up like him."

Elle's brow drew down in confusion. "You mean your grandfather?"

Ethan nodded. "He was never happy, that much I can remember, not before at least. After, it was like he was a different person." Her heart leapt as he finally turned to look in her direction, only to blink aimlessly and roll back over onto his back. "And I don't mean because he was dead," he continued with a frown a shake of his head. "It was more like that was the first time I ever saw him truly relaxed."

He looked toward her again, but his frown only grew when his eyes couldn't connect with anything. He closed them.

The crease in Elle's forehead deepened. "I don't think ghosts end up stuck on earth because they're relaxed."

"Why do you think they do, then? Why are you still here?"

"I don't know, but you're the one with all the books. Perhaps you can tell me."

He sighed and rubbed his temple with a knuckle, eyes still closed.

"I think he might have stayed to talk to me, to tell me it was all right, because he finally knew that what he'd felt his whole life was real."

"What do you mean? What was real?"

"The spirit world." He opened his eyes. The sun had begun to set and the glare from the orange tinted light filtering through the window made it harder to read his expression.

"He spent his whole life afraid to tell anyone, afraid he was crazy." He took a deep breath and rolled over to face Elle's direction. "Afraid I was like him, I guess. But when he died, he realized all that fear had been for nothing. At least I think that's what he wanted to tell me. I just couldn't understand it then. I was ten and only just starting to appreciate that other people didn't feel what I felt."

He took a deep breath, eyes staring through her but looking at nothing as he continued, lost in the past. "When he was still alive, I'd tell him things, something strange from school, or a random voice at a friend's house. He'd always listen with this stern frown on his face, but then he'd brush it off. About the only thing he ever told me that was any good was not to tell my mother."

"But you told her? In the end, I mean?"

Ethan nodded. "Grandpa stopped coming to see me after that. I don't know if he moved on, or if he was just trying to make it easier for me. At the time mom said it was because of the medication." He scrubbed another hand over his face, eyes tight.

"I'm sorry. I guess…" Elle trailed off, not knowing how to ask about such an obviously painful subject.

Ethan swallowed and gnawed on his lip for several moments before replying. "I thought if the medication worked, then that meant they were right, and it was all in my head. So I kept taking the pills, for years."

"But they didn't work, did they?"

He shook his head. "They made me feel duller. I don't know whether that blocked anything or not, but if they ever did work, they definitely stopped by the time I was fifteen. The doctor was always upping my dosage and my mother just went along with it, but then I developed this twitch in my left hand." He clasped his hands together and looked down at them. "It's one of the side effects of anti psychotics…"

Elle looked at his hands too, recalling all the times she had seen him fidgeting, or when he had knocked something over. She had thought he was just clumsy.

"That must have been so hard. What does she think now, your mother?"

"Who knows? She's too afraid to ask, but I think she knows it never really stopped." Ethan shrugged. "We're not close."

"What about your dad?"

"Never knew him. Well, that's not quite right, I don't remember him. He died when I was three and no, before you ask, I never…" He waved a hand vaguely in her direction.

Elle nodded, not that he could see. "I didn't know my dad either. He didn't die though, just left after he found out my mother was pregnant with my little brother. I can't imagine things being like that with my mother though, she was always my rock."

She couldn't help but choke up the last. She missed her mother so much that it hurt to think about her at all. Her dad could be dead like her for all she knew. He could have died years ago, and she would have never known. All she ever got from her mother was his name and a few old photos, the only ones she hadn't torn up when he left. She wondered if her brother had them now.

They were quiet for a couple of minutes, both lost in their pasts, before Elle turned to Ethan, startled to find him staring right back…nearly, he was slightly off.

"Is that why you're still here?" he asked in a hushed tone that seemed to match the quickly fading light. He rubbed his arms as if he felt a chill. "Because of your family?"

"I don't think so," Elle replied just as quietly. She stood and wandered over to the bedroom window. "It wouldn't make much sense, would it? Being stuck here in this share house with a bunch of strangers while they're busy living their lives on the other side of the city."

She didn't know why she went to the window. The view didn't even face the right direction. She placed her palm flat on the glass. It had grown darker outside, but the gray fog was rolling in.

She leaned her forehead against the window pane hoping to see more, but all the colors were draining away. Soon there would just be grayness.

***

Ethan rose from the bed. He was freezing and a dull throbbing had started in his head. He didn't know if that was due to Elle or his own insomnia lately. He couldn't stop a yawn as he opened the wardrobe and rummaged around for something warmer to wear. Elle was talking about her family, but she sounded distant, and sad.

"I suppose I could try to give them a message for you…" he offered somewhat reluctantly. Just because Elle and her mother were close didn't mean she wouldn't think he was crazy or a fraud, or if he was really lucky—both.

The memory of Amelia's face flashed in his mind, bringing him up short.

"Or I could write them a letter?" he continued. That seemed like a safer option.

When Elle didn't respond, he turned around. The bed was empty, of course, but more so than before. With a sinking feeling, he looked around the room.

"Elle?"

Something drew him to the window. He reached out to pull the curtains closed before he noticed it, a slight fog on the glass. It was a little below his own head height, but he wasn't exactly a tall guy. He reached out to touch it and a shiver ran through his body.

At least the headache was gone.

Natalie Pearce

Chapter 9

Ethan spent the next morning walking on eggshells. He couldn't feel Elle's presence, but he was on alert for the slightest sound, hoping it might be her.

"Good morning!"

Ethan's heart tried to jump into his throat at the overly cheerful greeting. Still half expecting Elle, he looked over his shoulder and got an entirely different kind of shock.

For one thing, he actually recognized the tall blond woman wearing one of Dean's shirts and little else. Dean's latest hookup was also his last hookup. It was the first time Ethan had seen his housemate with the same girl more than once. The blonde was also the first to stick around for breakfast.

The white shirt was very thin, her legs were very long, and he was pretty sure he could see her nipples. When she crossed her arms in front of her chest, the hem of the shirt rucked up a little more, as did his eyebrows, although the movement helped him to regain his focus despite his blazing face.

For the first time that morning, he was grateful Elle hadn't made an appearance. He'd already played the fool around her too many times, with Jenny though (if he remembered correctly) he was just beginning. To make a fool of himself, that was. He really needed to ask Dean for some advice about women.

The man in question followed her down the stairs after several excruciating minutes in which Ethan somehow managed to pour her a cup of black coffee without spilling a single drop. Two sugars. When Dean finally entered the kitchen, his wide grin had almost as much to do, in Ethan's opinion, with the way he was trying to edge around the kitchen table and out of the room, as it did with seeing Jenny in his shirt. Nevertheless, he gave her an enthusiastic greeting.

Ethan was briefly tempted to linger and try to pick up a tip or two, but when Dean's hand disappeared up the back of the shirt, it was pretty clear he'd been forgotten. He made a beeline for the stairs before he saw more skin than any of them bargained for.

He called Elle's name tentatively once he closed the bedroom door behind him, but to no avail. Still, if he was a ghost, he would probably have stayed downstairs watching Dean and Jenny.

Ethan gave his head a self-deprecating shake. That was one upside to the fact that he got no action—at least Elle hadn't gotten an eyeful of him with another girl.

***

His day dragged slower than most. He took the ghost book with him and read chapters at every opportunity in between lectures. All the while keeping a careful eye out for Amelia.

He had no idea what he would say if he saw her, but until he got the chance to ask Elle about her, Amelia was a no-go zone as far as Ethan was concerned. He spent every second in the halls ready to dart around the next turn or make a quick exit through an open doorway.

By the end of the day, he not only felt like an idiot, he was thoroughly exhausted. Instead of making his way home, however, he headed back to the library, this time to actually study.

The ghost book was making more and more sense the further he read, but Elle would have to wait. He might be eager to talk to her again, but there was no way he would get any work done at home if he was wondering whether every sound or slight draft in the house was her.

***

Over the next week, Elle's continued failure to make an appearance weighed on Ethan.

He had more than enough time to finish his essay, read the rest of the book, and catch up on the neglected reading for all his classes. All the while, not so much as a sarcastic comment came his way. A vague feeling of her presence lingered around the house, but never anything that…coalesced.

Staring at the ceiling before bed hadn't even worked. The prospect of enrolling in a meditation class became a serious consideration. He'd checked online and found the university gym ran sessions a couple of days a week. It didn't seem like the most relaxing setting, but he figured it was the only way he'd ever set foot in the gym.

As the weekend came around, Ethan's concern only grew. He had made a genuine connection with Elle, so why wouldn't she want to talk to him again?

It was Friday night and Ethan lay on his bed with his laptop propped open on his chest. He stifled a yawn. Surfing the net for paranormal sites felt a bit like being sucked into a black hole.

He'd been at it for hours. But the more he read about spiritual energy, the closer he came to an understanding. Coming through to him like Elle had the other night took a lot of energy. Most of that came from Ethan himself and probably even from Dean, despite the fact that he was about as spiritually sensitive as a doorknob. Even so, Elle was probably depleted now, kind of like a supernatural battery.

He clicked on another link, rubbing his eyes as he attempted to focus. Negative emotions tended to be stronger than positive ones, meaning he'd essentially been feeding her ever since he moved into the house. His freak-outs at her ghostly antics had only strengthened her.

He found his gaze drifting to the spiders in the corner of the ceiling. When Amelia came to the house, she'd been stressed, not to mention the fact that Ethan had been on tenterhooks waiting for something to happen. Add in the rest of the study group downstairs, and that was a lot of energy.

He sighed. Now that Ethan actually wanted to talk to Elle, things were apparently more complicated. He didn't know how to recharge her, but he certainly wasn't afraid of her anymore. He kept running through their conversation in his mind. He had learned little about Elle except for the rather important fact that she meant him no harm. She didn't know why she was still here, but she'd been surprisingly lucid in general.

Talking to her about his grandfather was eye-opening. He'd never really considered how things must have been for him, either before or after he died. Now with Elle's disappearing act, he couldn't help but wonder if part of why Ethan stopped seeing his grandfather was because he was no longer grieving.

According to *mediumsrus.net*, grief was one of the strongest negative emotions and a key reasons why relatives could see or sense departed loved ones who 'lingered' in the days after their death. But as time passed, inevitably, the rawness of the emotion dulled. Especially if the visitation gave the grieving person comfort.

Ethan's sigh turned into a wide yawn. He didn't see how that helped him with Elle. She'd been dead for over four years, and he hadn't even known her when she was alive. Amelia might still be grieving her. At the very least, there were negative emotions there, and likely strong ones. But he couldn't see how to convince her to come back to the house.

It wasn't only a matter of whether she believed him either. No, Ethan had a strong suspicion that if Amelia truly believed Elle's ghost was still here, he would have even less chance of convincing her to return.

The talk about his grandfather also brought up another awkward issue for him. Levi. If he blamed his grandfather for not helping him with what he went through as a child, then he couldn't ignore what he now suspected about his nephew.

Julie wouldn't be as gung-ho as their mother about getting 'help' for her son, but Ethan had never really recovered from the treatments he received when he was younger. And the odd twitch that he couldn't control, thanks to the anti-psychotic regime, was far from the limit of that damage.

Another yawn caused his eyes to water. He closed his laptop and shoved it out of the way on his bedside table.

He hadn't seen either his sister or Levi for a few weeks now and had been dodging Julie's phone calls ever since he'd connected with Elle.

He shook his head and reached for his phone. He needed to stop worrying about what Julie would think and concentrate on his nephew. After all the time he'd spent with Levi during the school holidays, he actually missed the little guy.

***

"You really should change the voicemail message on your phone, you know."

"I already told you, I had a big assignment due. I couldn't afford distractions."

"Maybe to something like…if you're over twenty-five and/or related to me…please take a number," Julie continued.

Ethan huffed out a laugh, more in exasperation than actual amusement.

"That's not even funny!" he complained. "Anyway, it's not like I'm getting many calls from anyone under twenty-five, and certainly not any girls."

"Oh?" Julie feigned surprise. "Is there something you want to tell me, then?" she asked in an overly innocent tone.

Ethan narrowed his eyes suspiciously for a few seconds before it hit him. "What! No, I don't mean like that. God, why does everyone think I'm gay?" Ethan pouted. "I want calls from girls, or texts or whatever, they just don't want to talk to me..." He finished the last on a surprisingly bitter note.

God, he was pathetic. He was so hard up for it, he might actually be developing a crush on a dead girl.

He avoided his sister's eyes. She was far too amused at his expense already, not that there was anything new about that. He ran a hand over his face, reddening further as he felt how warm his cheeks had grown.

"Oh my god, I don't think I've made you blush for years!" Julie exclaimed with a grin. "I think there might be something you need to tell me after all—who's the special girl?"

Ethan lowered his head to the kitchen table. At least the smooth wood was cool against his cheek. It was bad enough that he'd just admitted to himself that he might have inappropriate feelings for a ghost, and now his sister wanted to know about them? No. No way. There was only so much embarrassment a guy could deal with in one day, even if it was only in front of his sister.

Julie's laughter died out slowly. "Okay, when you're ready. It would be nice to see you with someone, though. I know mom worries too. That you're lonely."

He grunted. Ethan had been avoiding his mother since he moved into the house. Their relationship had always been difficult, but with the supernatural drama invading his life lately, he couldn't bear the thought of seeing her or even talking on the phone. He didn't think he would be able to keep the resentment out of his voice.

"I thought you said Levi was supposed to be home by now," he complained, changing the subject. "I need to remind him how lucky he is to be an only child."

"Oh, really?" Julie murmured unimpressed as she headed towards the oven.

She paused behind him to put a hand on the back of his neck and push his face back down to the table just as he tried to straighten up. Ethan's smirk quickly disappeared, and he shot a scowl at his sister's back.

"He's a bit late, but his friend's mother should be dropping him off any minute."

Ethan fought the impulse to tell her off, but she was going to be annoyed enough with him if she didn't want to listen to what he had to say about his nephew.

"How's Levi been doing lately?"

"Good..." Julie responded absently as she checked on the roast potatoes. If nothing else, he could always count on his sister to make a mean roast dinner. "He's been asking about you, actually." She shot a quick look his way, which he failed to interpret. "I didn't realize you two had bonded so much during the school holidays."

"I don't know about bonding," Ethan said. "I think maybe he's a little lonely."

Julie snorted, "What happened to how lucky he was to be an only child, then?"

"Fine," Ethan conceded with a reluctant smile, "I suppose there were some advantages to having a big sister growing up."

"I'm glad to hear it," Julie replied as she put the roast back in the oven and adjusted the timer. "You didn't exactly make it easy, you know."

Ethan felt a flash of irritation. "That wasn't my fault. I was a kid." He took a deep breath and forced himself to calm down at Julie's quelling look. "Mum's the one that made it so hard." He looked away.

"She was trying to do what was best for you," Julie said quietly. "She was afraid…"

There was something in her voice that made Ethan's head snap up. His eyes caught his sister's and held them as she tried to turn her head away.

"Were you afraid?" he asked heavily.

"I don't know what I felt. I was just a kid too," she said, still quiet.

"That's bullshit." Ethan shook his head, frowning.

"You were always saying strange things when you were little…" She trailed off, making vague gestures with her hands as if trying to gather the right words to her and Ethan had a feeling he knew why.

"Like Levi?"

The question hung in the air between them as Julie's eyes widened. Ethan could hear the breath catch in her throat as her mouth opened. Her nostrils flared. It wasn't a good look. His fingers gripped the table in front of him, bracing himself for her response.

She closed her mouth, eyes narrowing as she visibly took a hold of herself and turned away to open the pantry door.

"You spend a couple of weeks babysitting and you think you know him better than me?" she asked.

Several responses ran through Ethan's mind while her back was turned. He bit his lip as he dismissed them all. Finally, he settled on one, and he waited anxiously for Julie to turn around so he could say it to her face. What was she doing in there, reorganizing all the dry goods?

The sudden sound of the doorbell made them both jump as it chimed an abbreviated version of *Greensleeves*.

Julie cursed as a bottle hit the ground. Red pasta sauce and glass spread out around her. Ethan was on his feet before he knew what had happened.

"Can you…" she gestured vaguely towards the door, already gathering a handful of paper towels to swipe at the red mess.

Ethan hovered for a few moments staring at the mess, but the doorbell rang again and his sister's impatient huff had him on the move to the front door.

He opened it only to come face to face with a woman a little older than his sister, mouth pursed and fist raised. He fought the impulse to duck when he realized, despite the expression on her face, that she was only raising her fist to knock on the door again.

The dour expression was quickly replaced by a confused one. Levi hovered behind her, looking chastened.

"Uh…hi?" Ethan managed to get out, hoping he didn't look as much like a deer in the headlights as he felt.

The woman blinked rapidly at him before flushing and abruptly lowering her hand. "Who are you? Where's Julie? I need to speak to her."

"That's just Uncle Ethan," Levi supplied, slipping past the woman. Her hand opened and closed as he did, as if she wanted to grab him and pull him back to her side. Levi was pretty small for his age though, and dodged past her hands before taking refuge behind his uncle.

Ethan looked at him in confusion and then back at the woman, who was now trying to act as though she hadn't just tried to grab hold of someone else's child.

He frowned and called over his shoulder, "Julie! You better come to the door!"

Julie shouted back from the kitchen. The words were indistinguishable, but clearly annoyed.

"Is there a problem?" Ethan asked the woman, stepping up to play the protective uncle.

The woman, who still hadn't identified herself but presumably was Levi's little friend's mother, pursed her lips, crossed her arms, and shook her head.

"Just tell Julie it would be best if Levi doesn't come around for a while." With that, she unfolded her arms, shot a quick look past Ethan's shoulder to see if Julie was on her way to the door and then nodded her head as if dismissing Ethan.

Before he knew it, she'd turned and was halfway to her car parked behind his in the driveway.

Confused, Ethan turned to his nephew who still hovered behind him.

"Do I want to know what that was about?" he asked as he shut the door.

"She doesn't like me," Levi responded simply. Now that the woman was gone, he didn't seem to be terribly concerned about that fact. "Are you here for dinner?"

"Yeah, your mother's in the kitchen."

"Okay!" With that Levi, pushed his backpack into Ethan's hands and trotted into the kitchen. Ethan followed, the surprisingly heavy backpack hanging limply from one hand.

Julie was washing her hands. Red pasta sauce swirled from them and down the sink. A vein throbbed in Ethan's forehead as he watched. He knew he had missed something important at the door, but Levi was either completely unconcerned by whatever his friend's mother thought of him, or he was a budding expert at deflection. He was already busy chatting to his mother about his school day. No mention of his after school activities.

Ethan held the backpack up. "Ah…" he began, trying to get Julie's attention.

"Levi, go put your backpack in your room and wash up. Dinner will be ready in ten minutes!"

Ethan wasn't sure what the look Levi gave him as he collected his backpack meant, but he felt increasingly uncomfortable that his suspicions about Levi were right. It seemed clear that whatever had happened at his friend's place was off limits as far as his mother was concerned.

Ethan felt torn as he watched his nephew disappear through the hall doorway. He needed to tell Julie about Levi not being welcome at his friend's house anymore, but he didn't think she was ready to understand why.

He took a deep breath, steadying himself. If he got this part out of the way now, he could always skip out on dinner before Levi came back into the room.

"So who is Levi's friend?" Ethan asked cautiously.

"Just a boy from school. They've been virtually inseparable since their first day," Julie replied, preoccupied with the final preparations for dinner.

"So he's over at this boy's house a lot, then?"

Julie paused as she stirred the gravy. "Well, I usually try to have them here, but it's been hard lately with the extra shifts."

Ethan nodded slowly. Perhaps that's all it was. Julie did have a tendency to take advantage of people, and as he knew very well, that included free babysitting.

He realized his sister had stopped stirring and was now looking at him cautiously. "Why? Was that Beth at the door? Did she say something?"

"Um…yes, I guess? Just that it might be better if Levi didn't come around for a while." Ethan looked away as he spoke. "She wanted to talk to you, but she seemed to be in a hurry."

Julie went silent. The gravy sizzled in the pan. "That was all?"

Ethan shrugged. "Levi said she doesn't like him."

She turned the stove top off. 'Why didn't you get me?' she asked impatiently before turning towards the hall. "Levi!"

"Sorry, like I said, she didn't want to wait."

Julie faced him with both hands on her hips, and Ethan felt his mind regressing. He didn't envy Levi.

"She seemed stressed," he added with a slightly desperate air.

Julie's tone softened in response to that. "Yes, well, it must still be hard for her," she conceded, whatever that meant.

"I can go if you need to talk to Levi..." Ethan offered, seizing on the opportunity to get out of the firing line.

Julie huffed. "There's no need for that. Here, make yourself useful." She handed the spoon she had been stirring the gravy with to Ethan. "Finish this up, will you?" She headed down the hall toward Levi's bedroom.

When mother and son returned to the kitchen ten minutes later, Levi had an innocent look plastered on his face for his mother but slightly shifty eyes that darted occasionally in his uncle's direction. Ethan found it hard not to squirm throughout the entire meal.

Julie played big sister well, asking him about his studies, and he, in turn, complimented her on her cooking. He avoided looking at his nephew, who ate quietly as usual. It wasn't only because of the looks Levi had started shooting him before they even sat down. It was the way his sister's eyes tightened around the edges when she noticed.

Ethan dutifully offered to help clean up when dinner was finally finished but when Julie waved him off, he was quick to make his apologies and take his leave. He sat in his car for a few long minutes, staring back at the front door.

Julie wasn't stupid, she knew something was up and Ethan was pretty sure she also knew what. She just wasn't ready to admit it yet.

Levi was like him.

Chapter 10

"Elle?" Ethan called in a hushed voice as he opened the bedroom door.

It was late. He'd spent another long night at the library after a particularly awkward pediatrics study group. At one point, in the hope of sparking a reaction from Elle, he'd offered to host another session, but Amelia had stared him down so intensely it had been difficult to finish getting all the words out. She'd left him hanging for several moments before stiffly pointing out that they had a roster, and it was her turn next.

Sara looked a bit uncomfortable, and dare he say disappointed, but that could have just been due to his taste in cheese. Tristan, on the other hand, didn't even try to hide his smug grin and proceeded to suck up to Amelia for the rest of the hour.

As he stepped into the room, Ethan found his gaze drawn straight to the window. Something felt different. The air wasn't quite as still. It had been almost a week since he'd spoken to Elle.

He dumped his backpack on the small desk next to the door and took several slow steps towards the bed.

"Elle?" he called again, voice pitched a touch higher.

It was still silent, but with a shiver, he suddenly registered how much colder the room was compared to the rest of the house. He'd been exhausted when he got home, barely able to keep his eyes open on the short drive. He'd nearly driven past his own driveway, his thoughts focused primarily on his bed. But Elle's presence (or rather lack of it) must have been playing on his mind more than he was willing to admit. Or maybe it was the cold, because suddenly bed was the last place he wanted to be.

A woman's cry startled him. Wide-eyed, he surveyed the room before spinning around to face the door, which led out onto the small landing before the staircase. His heart beat so hard it felt like it was jumping around in his chest as another cry, a shriek this time, carried up the staircase.

The sharp clip of a heel on a stair nearly did him in before a thump and a distinctly feminine giggle had his hand going to his throat. But the giggle was quickly followed by a much deeper muffled laugh and the type of loud whispering common to drunken people who had no idea how loud they were being.

Ethan slumped onto the bed. His face felt so hot it must be blazing red, but now that he knew his housemate was just getting lucky (again!), he realized the room wasn't just a bit chilly anymore, the temperature had plummeted. The breath he'd been holding in fear of ghostly reenactments on the stairs, now visible as he exhaled deeply. His hands felt like ice blocks against his burning face.

There was still no sign of Elle, but Ethan founds his eyes drawn inexplicably towards the window once more. It had fogged over, and beads of condensation gradually appeared as he watched.

Dean and Jenny, or whoever else he'd picked up after his shift, were still in the hallway, or he would be dashing down the stairs. Not only was the chilling temperature oppressive, but as much as he tried to tell himself it was only Elle, something in a small corner of his mind beat against the inside of his skull in terror. Elle had never had this kind of effect on the room before.

He heard the door opposite slam shut, followed by a muffled sorry and more laughter. Clearly, whatever was happening in his bedroom hadn't affected the rest of the house. Ethan bit his nails as he stood in front of the door, torn between the perceived safety of the hallway and something he desperately wanted to understand.

He couldn't hear Dean and his companion anymore, but that could have been due to the ringing in his ears. The fog of breath in front of his face was more distinct now, and he found himself almost struggling for breath. He put a hand to his head. His face certainly wasn't warm anymore. Vertigo blurred his vision.

Every instinct screamed at him to get out of the room, but he fought them off desperately. He wasn't afraid of Elle anymore. She was trying to communicate with him, he was sure of it.

Still, something felt wrong, something was stopping her. It was like she was just around the corner. He couldn't see her, but he knew she was near. Did that even make sense?

It was becoming harder to think clearly.

He stumbled back towards the bed. The room spun around him as he held his head in pain. The urge to throw up was strong, even though all his stomach contained after his night in the library was a packet of chips from the vending machine. He sat on the edge of the bed and his gaze fixed on the window again, like it had been pulled there.

So much condensation had built up that he almost missed the handprint. He blinked rapidly, trying to focus his eyes, but he could feel his fragile grip on his mind slipping away.

He put his head between his legs. As a kid, he used to have fainting spells, but this helped him get back his equilibrium. He tried to take deeper breaths and his head cleared slightly, but the air was too cold, and he couldn't seem to get enough into his lungs.

"Elle!" he called weakly as he felt his grasp on his surroundings disappearing.

"What...oh god—" Ethan cut off abruptly as the chips decided to come up after all.

Somehow, he managed to avoid getting any on his shoes, although that was his last coherent thought as he slipped off the edge of the bed and into unconsciousness.

***

"That's pretty gross," Elle commented as she looked down at Ethan's prone form.

"I mean, I'm a ghost, so I don't actually have a sense of smell anymore, but if smelling salts can bring someone around after they've fainted, then I think spew should do that too."

Elle perched on the edge of the bed, feet carefully placed to avoid the remnants of Ethan's study snacks splattered over the worn floorboards. It's not like it mattered, of course, she was hardly going to 'step' in it, but it was the principle of the thing.

She'd been talking to Ethan for a while now, but he hadn't stirred at all.

At first she'd been worried, but Ethan was breathing normally and, if it wasn't for his cheek resting in the largest pile of said throw up, he would have looked like he was sleeping. Why he would sleep at the end of his bed on the bare floorboards, rather than on the bed and under the covers, was a whole other question.

Elle glanced at the window again, but the hand print was long gone. She'd barely been able to pull her eyes away from it after everything had…cleared…earlier. Even the sight of Ethan's crumpled form hadn't drawn her attention as much, despite how hard she had pushed to make it through to him.

A force had been stopping her. It had nearly felt like she was being pulled in the opposite direction. She sensed it as soon as Ethan entered the bedroom. She'd been sure she was finally strong enough to talk to him again before everything went horribly wrong.

She didn't know how long it lasted for. It had felt like she had struggled for hours. But she prevailed and made it through stronger than ever. If only there hadn't been a price to pay for that.

Ethan's glasses had fallen off his face. Luckily, the lenses were still intact. Her fingers itched to retrieve them and place them on the bedside table for him, as she'd watched him do each night before he went to sleep.

She'd been trying to bring him back around for hours, and it was now close to dawn. The gray light filtering through the window wasn't the usual ghostly fog that seemed to hold everything, including her sight, in the house. It was the light of false dawn.

A sense of calm came over her at some point during the night, leaving her more focused than she could remember feeling since before Amelia moved out. Talking with Ethan had made her feel realer than she had in years, but this feeling was something else. Something more.

If Ethan woke up now, he would be able to see her, almost as solid as a living person in the room, she was sure. Her conviction was so strong that after failing to revive Ethan, she'd popped over the hall to Dean's room. Elle had gotten more than an eyeful of Dean and his mystery girl (not Jenny, she was quick to note), but he remained, as ever, oblivious to her presence.

It had frustrated her but Dean didn't so much as entertain the possibility of ghosts. The idea that he'd suddenly be able to see her just because she felt more solid, was simply wishful thinking.

Dean's companion also had no clue a ghost was in the room, although she may have been too distracted to notice Elle standing at the end of the bed even if she'd still been a real life solid living person. Elle couldn't say she blamed the woman for that. Dean had a lot of practice, after all, and he certainly knew how to focus a woman's attention on himself, or rather on what he was doing. To her.

The disappointment was still sharp, even as she sat watching Ethan's slack face for any sign of consciousness.

Dean was the one she'd been hopelessly pining after for years. Getting his attention usually didn't take much more than a pretty face, long blonde hair, and you know, *being alive*. Elle didn't meet the criteria on at least two of those points. She had no chance under the sun. Clearly.

She shook her head, letting out a slow breath as she chided herself. Dean wasn't even her type. It just never mattered whether he could hold an intelligent conversation when there was no possibility of anything more than a one-sided monologue on her part. Not to mention Jenny hadn't stuck around long, much like all the others. Getting Dean's attention wasn't the hard part—keeping it was.

Ethan was proving a far more intriguing prospect. Not that she found him particularly attractive at the moment—there was drool as well as throw up now—but that was still a moot point. She was dead and somewhere along the way, a girl had to face facts. But when you got right down to it, Ethan was closer to her type. Maybe even more so than Adam had been.

Elle leaned forward to examine his face close up. His lips were twitching. Perhaps the drool was a positive sign that he was finally coming around. His eyelids fluttered for a few moments, but remained closed.

With a sigh she leaned back. There was only so much staring at an unconscious man a ghost could do, even with her limited entertainment options.

Elle's gaze drifted aimlessly around the room before coming to a rest on the window. There was some pink in the sky now. She wanted to take a closer look but a part of her was still reluctant. The handprint might be long gone, along with whatever had made it, but the image remained imprinted in her mind.

It hadn't been much larger than her own handprint, but somehow she knew it wasn't a woman's. What she wasn't sure of was whether Ethan saw it before he passed out.

She spread her own hands out in her lap, turning them over again and again as she examined them. They seemed smoother than they had when she was alive. She didn't know which line was her lifeline, and which was the heart line, but both were faint. She supposed neither mattered now. She laughed as she wondered whether her face was the same. Perhaps her pores were less visible now.

Suddenly, she found herself standing directly in front of the window. Her fingers reached out to the frame even as she turned to look over her shoulder at the bed where she'd been sitting only moments ago. Disorientated, she couldn't tell whether she'd walked towards the window lost in thought, or had faded in and out again.

Her non-existent stomach clenched. How could she feel more real than ever on the one hand and...she shook her head. Her fingers drifted over the glass where the handprint had appeared.

If Ethan had seen it, did he think it was hers? He probably thought the whole thing was her. But strong as she felt now, she still wasn't up to drawing so much energy out of a person that they passed out for hours. So far she'd managed a blown light globe and maybe making Ethan's morning toast pop up early. She didn't quite have her horror movie credentials down yet.

It wasn't the first time she'd felt some other presence, although not anything as strong as earlier. While there had never been any light or doorway, sometimes, when she was just on the edge of things, she sensed there was something just out of reach. Or out of her line of sight. Could that something be on the other side?

She shivered. Unknown things waiting for her in the shadows made her want to hold on even tighter to her life here, or rather, what remained of her life.

The sun was rising in all its glory now. Orange and deep yellow streaked the sky. The view reached all the way to the ocean on the horizon. How many times had she watched the sun rising over the water? Between all-nighters studying and then nursing shift work...surely she had lost count.

"Elle?"

She spun around at the shaky voice. Ethan was sitting up, head tilted back against the end of the bed. He raised one arm in front of his face, hair hanging in his eyes as he looked towards the window, towards her.

She froze. Was he looking at the window, or at *her*?

The room was lighting fast, the sun shining in the sky behind her. Ethan wiped his mouth and raised himself up to perch on the edge of the bed.

"Is that you?"

Elle took a hesitant step forward, trying to determine if his eyes tracked her movement. She would be little more than a silhouette in front of the window if she were visible. His eyes squinted.

"What happened?" he asked, wiping his mouth again, this time with the bottom of his t-shirt.

His gaze shifted from Elle's figure to the mess on the floor. A faint grimace crossed his face.

"Sorry about that, I'm not sure what's wrong with me..."

Elle slowly moved away from the window and approached the bed. Ethan's eyes followed her the whole way. They were ringed by dark circles now, but that was hardly surprising considering he'd spent half the night passed out on the cold floorboards.

It wasn't a big room, but it suddenly seemed huge as Elle paused in front of the bed, keeping her feet clear of the remnants of Ethan's late night snacks. Her eyes never left his face.

"I'd get you a glass of water and some painkillers, but..." She held her hands out in front of her, making a fist with one as she watched his eyes drop to them. They seemed perfectly solid to her, but she couldn't so much as move aside the curtains, let alone fetch and carry.

Ethan made a fist with his own hand in his lap as he gasped. His eyes shot back up to her own. Wide now and fully awake.

"What does this mean?" he asked, blinking rapidly as if she might disappear again, or maybe she wasn't that clear in the first place.

Elle huffed, unsure if he meant her being visible or the forces that caused him to pass out last night.

"I have no idea," she responded. "I'm just a dead girl, stuck here. You're the one who can see ghosts. Why don't you tell me?"

Ethan folded in on himself a little and Elle immediately regretted her tone. She'd been waiting for years for something like this to happen, and it wasn't Ethan's fault she was stuck here. She felt a hysterical laugh bubbling up and forced it down.

"I'm sorry," he began hesitantly. "I'd say I'm new to all this, but that isn't exactly true." He took a deep breath. "But I've always pushed it away before."

He sighed, brow furrowed and eyes locked on his closed fists, held tightly on his knees.

"But that hasn't exactly been working out for me and I want to help you, Elle." He looked up as he said her name, eyes squinting as if she was too bright.

Elle held his gaze until she could see him start to relax inch by inch.

"I really do want to help you," he finished, the last almost a whisper but so sincere that it made Elle's ghostly heart clench.

She nodded and sat down on the bed next to him. She instinctively drew her feet up beside her as she did to avoid the mess still on the ground.

"I don't know what happened," she began, pulling her lip between her teeth for a moment. "Last night...that wasn't me."

She gazed over at him. His eyes were uncertain. It felt strangely intimate to look into them this close, so she looked at his hands instead, now folded around each other in his lap.

"The window..." Ethan started, headed turning towards it as he trailed off. Elle watched the hands in his lap grip each other tighter. She shook her head and spread her own hands out over her lap in a helpless gesture.

"It wasn't me," she said simply.

The urge to hold his hand was overwhelming, but it wasn't just to comfort him. She didn't know what to make of the events of last night, but some reassurance for herself would be welcome about now.

Ethan nodded, still looking at the window. "The cold...that wasn't you either, was it?"

"I don't think so," Elle replied.

"But you don't know what it was." Ethan shifted to lie on the bed. "Do you?"

She couldn't respond, she just shook her head.

Ethan stared at the ceiling, breathing shallowly. He wouldn't look at Elle now. "I think I need to borrow some more books from the library."

Elle laughed, but it was weak. "As long as they're not about succubi..."

That startled a laugh from Ethan, followed by a low groan and a smothered yawn.

"I'm never going to live that down, am I?"

Elle smirked, on the verge of making a crack about saving that for their second date, but when she looked over again, Ethan's eyes were closed and his breathing had evened out.

She wouldn't describe him as peaceful, but hopefully he would lose the bags under his eyes if he got a couple more hours of sleep.

She looked to the window again. It was going to be a beautiful clear day. The bright sunshine made the shadows from last night seem far away, but Elle knew that whatever had sucked all the energy out of the room, it wasn't done with either of them yet.

Something had tried to use the connection developing between her and Ethan. Elle no longer doubted whether another side existed. She knew. And she had felt it last night.

Chapter 11

"How does it feel?" Ethan asked, hand moving in a vague gesture up and down her body.

"What do you mean?" Elle shifted in Amelia's old armchair. She tapped her fingers in an uneven rhythm against the fraying armrest.

"Well," Ethan began, pulling his bottom lip between his teeth before releasing it with a pop, "You look so real, solid, but..."

"What?" Elle asked, head tilting slightly to the left as her hands stilled.

"Just not quite...there. Like if I saw you out of the corner of my eye, it would take a few seconds to focus on you." Ethan answered. He tilted his head from one side to the other, as if to examine her better. His brow lowered. "It's almost like if I wasn't looking at you straight on, you might disappear."

Elle held both of her hands up in front of her face. She flipped them around, examining them from all angles. What was that old saying about knowing something as well as the back of your hand?

They looked solid enough to her eyes. They certainly felt solid when she clasped them together. But everything else? Even if she touched something that seemed solid to her, it never felt quite right. It might be hard or soft, smooth or rough, but it was never warm or cold. She couldn't pick anything up. Couldn't open or close a door, even though she didn't need to worry about doors.

"It's like—" she began, but stopped, still needing to gather her thoughts.

This was the latest in a series of questions about 'ghost world' as Ethan had dubbed it, since he found her waiting for him at the door when he came home. It was the first chance she'd ever had (and quite possibly the last) to explain any of it to another person. It felt important for both of them and even though she didn't have all the answers, talking to Ethan helped her understand her state of being more with each new question.

"Everything I do, or feel, is based on a memory. How I remember it feeling, just less...vivid."

She released a slow steady breath and paused for several seconds before drawing in the next, just as slowly. She focused on the sensation of air filling her nonexistent lungs, faint as it was.

"It's like most of the time I breathe in and out, just as I did every day of my life without thinking twice, but every now and then, I realize I'm not breathing." She paused as she raised her head to meet Ethan's eyes. "Because I don't need to breathe anymore."

Ethan made a small sound she couldn't identify, somewhere between a squeak and a grunt. She closed her eyes for several seconds, steeling herself, afraid to see fear, or worse—pity. When she gathered the courage to look again, his mouth hung open slightly, wide eyes completely transfixed on her face.

She chewed on her bottom lip for a moment before releasing it with a little huff of a laugh, unnerved by the fascination directed her way despite the small thrill of exhilaration that ran through her.

"Does that make sense?" she asked

"I think that makes perfect sense," he replied, eyes still fixed on her face.

She nodded, a strange sense of relief flowed through her. She might not understand herself anymore, but that only made the prospect of someone else understanding her, or trying to, more enticing.

"What about..." He made the gesture again, taking in her appearance from head to toe. "Your dress? I mean, it's very nice," he hastened to add when she raised a single eyebrow. "But is that what you were wearing when you...?" he trailed off awkwardly, hand still waving in front of him as if trying to make up for the fact that he couldn't finish asking his question.

She nodded, a slight flush suffusing her. Would Ethan be able to see a blush tinting her face red or was the warmth running through her just another ghostly imagining? She resisted the urge to tug at the hem of her dress. It wasn't even that short.

He nodded, a thoughtful twist to his mouth despite the pink in his own cheeks. Elle didn't think Ethan was used to talking about women's clothing.

"And..." The gesture just took in her feet this time.

Elle looked down and couldn't help wriggling her toes as she kicked her feet up a little before crossing them at the ankles.

"I don't remember." She turned her head away, a crease forming on her forehead. "I wore high heels that night but...I guess I took them off before I went upstairs. I remember my feet hurting..."

She took a deep breath and tucked the feet in question further under the chair. The truth was, she never understood why she wasn't still wearing the heels when everything else from that night had stayed the same, right down to her freshly manicured red toenails. Taking them off when she came home made sense, but she remembered Adam saying...

She shook her head, needing to clear her vision. She inhaled deeply and let out a slow shaky breath.

"Are you all right?" Ethan asked.

The battered leather of his armchair made an undignified sound as he leaned forward, hand reaching out to her before he abruptly snatched it back. Either because he remembered he couldn't touch her, or maybe because he just didn't want to. She hadn't forgotten how freaked out he was those first few weeks at the thought of living in a haunted house.

He leaned back in his chair with a ragged breath. He raised his hand to rub at his temple, eyes tightening.

What was it that Adam said? Or had it been Amelia? She had broken an ankle. She remembered hearing that, one of her many injuries. Was that from the heels, or the fall, or both?

"Elle? What's wrong?" Ethan asked. "What's happening?"

Elle closed her eyes. She fought against that feeling—the fuzziness. She shut her eyes tighter, trying to squeeze out all the light as if that would make the world make sense again.

Ethan was still talking, louder now, a new urgency in his tone, but she couldn't make out the words anymore.

And then she was gone.

***

"Did you know an Adam?" Ethan asked carefully as he picked at the bedspread the next day.

Following Elle's last disappearing act, he'd put two and two together and came to the conclusion that certain topics were off limits for Elle, but he wasn't sure if this was one of them. Not because she didn't want to talk about them. At least he didn't think that was the problem. No, it was more like she couldn't, and that gave *him* a headache.

Elle sat up, all lethargy gone. She'd been drifting off when Ethan came home. The blush that set fire to his face when he found her lying in bed as if waiting for him, must have been something to behold because Elle couldn't stop giggling for what felt like an age, which only made it ten times worse.

"What…how do you know that name?"

"I take it that's a 'yes'?" Ethan's tone was dry. The sudden interest in Elle's voice was unmistakable. "Amelia mentioned an Adam."

Elle's gaze drifted across the bed towards the window.

"He was my boyfriend."

"Oh...never mind then." Ethan cursed himself. Why hadn't he thought of that? He'd just assumed since they were together now, that Amelia and Adam had also been a couple when Elle had known them.

"What do you mean? What did Amelia say about him?" Elle insisted, eyes fixed on him now.

Ethan tried not to squirm too obviously. He didn't think Elle would want to know that her old boyfriend had moved on with her best friend. Talk about rubbing salt in the wound.

"Are they still..." Her jaw clenched as she trailed off.

"Still?" Ethan asked, eyebrows rising along with the pitch of his voice, which had turned a touch squeaky.

"Apparently, they were lonely," Elle replied with a twist of her mouth. "After."

"Oh, wow..." Ethan blinked down at the bedspread. "That's..." He shook his head and changed tack. "I didn't think Amelia was like that."

"Like what?" Elle asked, one eyebrow quirking up as if in challenge.

Ethan frowned at her. He knew he was behind the eight-ball when it came to understanding women, but surely Elle wasn't going to defend her friend for hooking up with Elle's boyfriend right after she died?

"It wasn't her fault, not really," Elle said, visibly deflating. "She didn't even like Adam because she thought he was too manipulative. I never saw him like that back then, but it turns out she was right."

Ethan blinked, struggling to hide his confusion. "So he what, seduced her?"

"When she was crying," Elle's voice was dull. "Then he wanted to move in,, so she wasn't alone. And to help with the rent."

"They lived here? Together?" Ethan asked, voice rising again although not quite reaching the squeaky note from before.

"No, he started moving some of his stuff in, but Amelia couldn't cope with living in the house where I died. She spent so long trying to get the blood stain out from the floorboards at the bottom of the stairs. They hadn't been varnished for years, so it kind of soaked in. I guess that's what happens when it's left overnight," Elle said absently.

"Shit," Ethan murmured, his eyes drawn to the closed door as if he could see the bottom of the stairs from the bedroom. He swallowed hard, his stomach unsettled.

"Is there still—" he began, but had to swallow harder as he tasted bile rising in the back of his throat. He remembered Dean telling him there was no bloodstain, but he hadn't given it any more thought.

"I don't know," Elle answered. "Adam's solution was to buy that ugly hall rug." Her shoulders rose as she brushed a stray tress of hair away from her eyes. "I can't exactly check under it, can I?"

Ethan's mind pictured the floorboards in the kitchen. He'd suffered a nasty splinter in his big toe on his second day in the house because he'd gone down to breakfast barefooted. Ever since he'd made a point of at least wearing socks. He'd barely noticed the rug in the entryway since moving in, but he knew he would not be able to ignore it again.

"Are you sure they weren't together...before?" he asked, careful emphasis on the last word.

"No." She shook her head, face set. She seemed sure, but the possibility made Ethan more nauseous.

"Amelia felt guilty about it," Elle continued. "But Adam told her I'd be happy for them if I knew."

"What!" Ethan exclaimed.

Elle let out a laugh that sounded suspiciously like a snort. "I know—happy they had each other!"

She shook her head. "You know what the most messed up part was?"

Her expectant eyes caught and held Ethan's own. He forced himself not to blink. It was pretty messed up as it was, especially considering his growing suspicion that the reason Elle remained stuck in this house was because there was more to her trip down the stairs than a simple accident.

He shook his head.

"I actually believed him for a while." She glanced down when she caught sight of the incredulous expression on Ethan's face. "I know," she said. "But it was like I thought I *should* be happy for them. Like, if I was a good person, I would be happy."

She sighed, gaze drifting to the window again, and that distant tone crept into her voice. "I tried to convince myself I was only upset because I was stuck here watching it happen. That I was just jealous."

Ethan shifted uneasily on the bed. Her eyes returned to his, intent now, as if trying to imprint her meaning with them.

"But I wasn't jealous, not at all. And I wasn't happy for them. It's like the scales had fallen from my eyes. Everything Amelia ever said about Adam kept playing on repeat in my head. I don't know why I couldn't see it while I was still alive—while I was in the relationship." She exhaled heavily and shook her head. Ethan almost expected to see tears of frustration welling in her eyes. "I guess I loved him."

"But if Amelia thought he was such a bad person, why would she—"

"Fall for it, too?" Elle asked with a huff. "Yeah, I know. I always thought she was smarter than me. But it turns out love really is blind."

She deflated after that, leaving Ethan wondering whether he should put his arm around her. He started to reach out but checked himself just in time. The idea of comforting a girl left him so off balance he'd actually forgotten he couldn't touch her. It was hard to believe, seeing her on his bed like this, appearing so solid, so present. So much more real to him, more important, than anyone else in his life at the moment.

"I can't believe she's actually going to marry him!"

The indignant declaration shocked Ethan out of his stupor. He still held one arm half raised as if to reach out to her, and he wrung it in, capturing it with his other arm as if he was going to hug himself instead.

"How do you even know that?"

Elle gave him that look, the one he'd received from so many women over the course of his life. Most recently (and frequently) his sister.

"She was here, wasn't she?"

Ethan blinked, still lost for several moments, until it hit him like the huge rock it was. He didn't understand how he'd missed the over-the-top engagement ring himself when he first joined Amelia's study group.

Elle must have seen the revelation on his face because she huffed before hiding her own face in her hands.

Shit, it must be bad enough for your ex to marry someone else, let alone your best friend. Even if you were dead. How much worse must it be when one of them might have had a hand in that death?

Not that Elle seemed to believe either of them were involved. But if that was the case, why on earth was she still...well, on earth? What better 'unfinished business' could there be than seeking justice from beyond the grave?

Elle's shoulders shuddered, and she turned her face away. Ethan froze, eyes widening as he contemplated with considerable horror how one actually *could* comfort a crying ghost. If he tried to put his arm around her, and it went straight through her instead, would that be worse than doing nothing at all?

Elle saved him from his internal dilemma when another huff, followed by a snort, quickly transformed into laughter. Possibly hysterical laughter, but at least it wasn't tears.

Yet, Ethan amended, when he caught sight of Elle's face as the laughter wound down.

"You know what's even more messed up?" she asked as she wiped at her face and her shoulders finally stilled.

Ethan opened his mouth but didn't get the chance to respond before she carried on.

"Adam didn't like her either." She shook her head as she ran both hands through her hair. "He thought she was a stuck up bitch. And—get this—a bad influence on me!"

Ethan made an indignant noise on Elle's behalf. Adam sounded like a bigger ahole than he'd already imagined. Granted, he could relate to the stuck up part. Amelia didn't exactly come across as warm and friendly. Still, if she'd been Elle's best friend, there must be more to her than he'd seen so far.

Maybe she just didn't let people in easily. Ethan had done his fair share of keeping other people at arm's length for most of his life. It wasn't just ghosts that scared him.

He eyed Elle now as she continued to shake her head, seemingly lost in the past. But she hadn't disappeared, leading him to believe that despite her bitter feelings on the subject, Adam and Amelia's relationship wasn't a factor in her untimely fall down the stairs. If either of them had been involved in her death, there must be more to the story.

"I can't imagine you being a bad influence on anybody," Ethan stated with a quiet force that brought Elle up short. The building anger in her face drained and was replaced by a wry smile.

"Oh? You know me so well now, do you?" she teased.

Ethan's smile in response was a tad crooked. "Actually, I think I know you better than anyone else in the entire world."

Elle's smile widened but turned a shade sadder with a sense of melancholy that could also be heard in her voice. "Ah..." She nodded. "Well, that wouldn't be too hard these days."

Ethan's heart sank. "I'm sorry," he said in a rush. "I didn't mean it like that. I'm sure there are plenty of people you would rather talk to than some geeky medium like me."

He turned to her, apology written all over his face, desperate to make up for his insensitive choice of words, but his eyes only widened as he searched from one side of the room to the other.

Elle had disappeared. Again.

Natalie Pearce

Chapter 12

"What does it matter if Dean thinks you're asking because you have a crush on her?"

Ethan fought off the blush that threatened to turn his cheeks dark crimson, but he didn't respond. Ever since he'd asked Elle about her old boyfriend, she'd been after him to lure Amelia back to the house.

The problem was, Ethan didn't know how. The study group angle had already proved a dud, and he was out of other ideas. Elle, however, was full of them. Her latest involved their housemate.

"I had no idea he even knew Amelia," Elle continued, her gaze drifting away as she spoke. "And all this time, she's the one who told him about this place."

"It's a small world, I guess. Do you think he worked at the hospital when you were a nurse there?" he asked, mostly in an attempt to distract the persistent ghost.

"I don't know." Elle tapped a finger against her lips. "I think I would have noticed him."

Ethan rolled his eyes as he turned away, stirring his freshly made coffee. Elle, perched on the kitchen bench by the refrigerator, swung her long legs as they spoke. She looked strangely solid sitting there, if a little incongruous in her red cocktail dress, but that only made the way her bare feet sometimes disappeared into the cabinet door beneath her all the more disconcerting.

"What's wrong with you anyway?" Elle asked after several seconds of silence.

Ethan started, hot coffee sloshing over the rim of his mug and stinging the back of his hand. Elle was standing directly behind him now, peering over his right shoulder. He hadn't heard her jump down from the bench. Was that because of her bare feet, or because she was a ghost? Or maybe she hadn't actually gotten down from the bench—could ghosts teleport?

Elle giggled at his startled expression but continued to lean down, focused on his steaming cup of coffee.

"Oh god, you have no idea how much I wish I still had a sense of smell!" she exclaimed. "I can't even remember not starting my day with a cup of coffee while I was alive. I think the aroma woke me up more than the actual caffeine," she finished on a wistful note.

Ethan couldn't remember the last time he'd been so close to a woman. Certainly not one he wasn't dating. Not that he'd dated many women. It seemed ghosts lost their sense of personal space along with their physical bodies.

He stepped to the side, taking his mug with him. He blew on it carefully as he avoided Elle's eyes. Not that she was looking at him, she was still fixated on the mug. He took a cautious sip. Now she was staring at his lips.

It proved too much for Ethan, and he nearly stumbled over his own feet in his rush to retreat to the kitchen table. He placed the coffee down in front of himself, just out of easy reach. He might desperately need his morning caffeine hit, but the nerves swirling in his gut as Elle watched him drink it so avidly were causing all kinds of inappropriate thoughts to run riot through his head.

That was bad enough considering Elle had given him no sign she suffered from any of the same thoughts (unless they were about his coffee) but it was also impossible. Elle's red lips might look perfectly kissable, but they were far from.

"You know, Dean wouldn't make fun of you if you had a crush on Amelia."

Ethan blinked. He opened his mouth but closed it again before any response came to the fore. Apparently, it wasn't as easy to distract a ghost as it was for this ghost, at least, to distract him.

"Amelia seems like she's good at keeping people at arm's length," Ethan replied carefully.

"She never used to be that way." Elle shook her head. "She was the fun one. At least between the two of us," she added the last with a self-deprecating note.

Ethan snorted. "That's hard to imagine." When Elle only narrowed her eyes at him in response, he conceded. "I suppose it must have been pretty hard for her, though, finding you like that."

Elle's brow furrowed. Ethan watched her face carefully as her gaze drifted across the room. Something in her eyes seemed to dim. A dull throb began beating at his temple.

"I don't remember—"

Ethan cleared his throat roughly. The last thing he needed was for Elle to disappear again. Anything touching too close to her death, either before or after, proved a risky subject. It was becoming clear the only way he would find out more about how Elle died was from the people who were around her back then.

"How do you know she'll listen to Dean, anyway? He didn't say they were friends. They just worked in the same place."

Elle gave her head a shake, her eyes were slightly unfocused, and a small frown marred her face as her gaze drifted down to her feet. They looked like they should be cold on the bare floorboards.

Ethan laughed. It sounded a touch forced even to his own ears. "I suppose every woman at the hospital notices Dean, though, huh?"

Elle's eyes lifted to his, and her frown smoothed out. "Jealous?" she teased. "He'd be more than happy to help you out with Amelia, you know. I bet he could give you all kinds of tips." Elle smirked.

Ethan found himself both irritated and relieved. Her eyebrows wriggled suggestively.

"But I don't have a crush on Amelia!" he spluttered, landing on irritated.

Elle waved a hand, brushing away his objections as if they were a nuisance fly. "You don't have to date her. You just need to get her *here* again."

He shook his head. "Trust me, she's less likely to come back if she thinks I have feelings for her. She doesn't even like me..."

"Nonsense," Elle said. "Why wouldn't she like you? You're perfectly likable."

Ethan just continued to stare at her.

"Plus, you're totally her type! More than Adam, anyway. She always liked the smart ones." Elle nodded as she spoke, smiling encouragingly all the while.

Ethan blinked rapidly. Were they even talking about the same woman? "But isn't Adam one of the smart ones? He made it through medical school, after all."

"Barely!" Elle huffed. "All he ever did was study."

Ethan gave an incredulous laugh. "All I ever do is study!" he declared indignantly before a frown took over his face. "At least I used to," he amended as he narrowed his eyes at Elle.

"Yeah, well, he certainly didn't have any time to research succubi, or help a ghost out."

Ethan groaned. That succubi story was not going away. He almost groaned again at the thought of the Chem assignment he'd been neglecting for the last several days. Maybe Adam needed to work harder for his grades, but Ethan wasn't sure he had as much time to be helping a ghost out as Elle seemed to think. At this point, if he wasn't careful, he'd be taking Chem again next year.

He reached for his now cooled coffee mug and downed the remaining liquid in a few deep gulps. He wiped his mouth and gathered his laptop, which sat untouched on the kitchen table. If he was going to get any work done before classes started this morning, it would be at the library.

Elle sighed, and her eyes lifted to the ceiling before returning to his own.

"Well, I suppose that's my cue to leave," she said and disappeared with a wink.

Ethan jumped a little, only just managing to save his laptop from crashing to the floor as he fumbled to put it in his backpack.

Well, that was new. Usually Elle's departures were less planned, but this felt different. Ethan found his gaze drawn to the ceiling as well.

Was Dean up yet? Is that where Elle had gone?

The flash of jealousy at the thought was ridiculous, and he fought himself to push it down. Elle might be the type of girl he could imagine falling for, but in all honesty, he would have more luck trying to date Amelia.

At least she was alive, even if she was engaged.

***

Elle joining Ethan for his morning coffee was fast becoming a reliable routine. That is, if you can call three days in a row a routine.

Elle would just appear from the stairway after he started making coffee. Apparently, regardless of her lack of a sense of smell, the very idea of coffee still 'woke' her up in the mornings.

While Ethan appreciated the company (especially Elle's company) he was relieved this morning to see the covetousness in Elle's eyes ratchet down a few notches as he sipped the hot coffee.

Even so, a small wistful smile lingered on her lips as she watched him put down his mug down to pop a couple of slices of white bread into the toaster. A scattering of stale crumbs spread over the counter as he shifted the ancient toaster closer.

As Elle watched him push the lever, that strange little smile became more intent. He paused, lever halfway down, as a question came to mind that had been bugging him since the morning he fled to Julie's house.

"Ah..." he began, unsure how to word the suspicion that had been growing in his mind since Elle blew the light globe in the lounge room, something she assured him she'd never done before and had no idea how to repeat.

Elle's eyes crinkled at the edges as she raised them to his face.

"Don't you want breakfast?" she asked, waving a hand towards his, still paused on the toaster, bread peaking out the top instead of happily toasting away.

He glanced down at his hand, only for his finger to slip from the lever and send the two slices of bread springing back up. Goddamn tremors again.

Elle's laugh was light, but the way Ethan's heart rate doubled only reminded him again of the morning when he first admitted to himself, and then to his sister, that he'd moved into a haunted house.

"Was that you?" he asked. Even to his own ears, his voice came out more strained than he intended.

Elle's laugh cut off, and her eyes narrowed in confusion, head tilting to the side in a manner he was coming to recognize.

He cleared his throat, focusing on his breathing as he struggled to find the words.

"The morning after..." he started uncertainly. He needed to clear his throat again. "When the toast popped up."

Elle's eyebrows rose. "You mean when you freaked out when the toast popped up?"

Ethan squirmed. He turned back to the toaster and pushed the lever down with considerably more force than required.

"I don't think so..." Elle began, but trailed off as Ethan literally jumped. She stood right behind him again. For god's sake, she needed those heels! At least if she was still wearing them, she couldn't keep sneaking up on him like this.

Wait, would ghost heels still make noise when she walked? A deep crease formed on his forehead as he contemplated Elle's dress. Did it make a swishing noise when it moved? He had never noticed, but it looked like the type of material that would swish.

Elle retreated a couple of steps, blinking as she flipped her wavy hair back over her shoulders. She watched him carefully as if afraid he was going to freak out and flee the house again.

Ethan felt a flush of shame as he recalled his panic on the morning in question. How long ago had that been? It felt like forever rather than only weeks ago.

Elle's eyes drifted to the toaster. They narrowed as one corner of her mouth tilted up, and she pursed her lips in concentration.

Ethan held his breath. Elle continued to stare with a single-minded fixation for several long moments until his stomach rumbled loudly. Elle leaned back, a short laugh escaped her lips, and then another louder one as the toast sprang up.

Ethan's eyes shot to Elle's before he dived forward to examine his breakfast. The bread was lightly toasted.

"So?" he asked as he frowned and turned each piece over again and again.

Elle just shrugged. Ethan nodded slowly before looking back at the slice in his hand as he remembered how spooked he had felt that morning. It was probably just his imagination that the toast popped up too early.

He put the slices back into the toaster. "I like it more medium," he said defensively as Elle giggled behind him.

"Hey, Ethan!" Without knowing, Dean cut Elle's laughter off, his greeting preceded only by the creak of the second last stair.

Ethan froze, eyes comically wide as he spun around and tried not to stare at Elle.

Dean paused under the archway that divided the kitchen and dining area from the entryway before taking a hesitant step forward. He craned his neck around, taking in the empty kitchen. His eyes returned to Ethan on his lonesome at the bench.

Ethan gave him a strained smile, all the while trying to ignore the expression on Elle's face, which looked like she was desperately trying not to break out in laughter.

"Is...there someone else here?" Dean asked, drawing each word out.

"Uh...no?" Ethan flushed again.

"Right." Dean nodded, then kept on nodding, clearly at a loss for words, much like Ethan seemed to be now that he and Elle weren't alone in the kitchen.

Dean's eyes brightened as he spotted Ethan's mug. "Hey, is there any more coffee?"

Elle, who had perched herself on the bench again near the coffee maker, gave a low groan.

Ethan shot her a quelling look before returning his attention to Dean's hopeful and still slightly confused face. "Yeah, sure, you want some?"

He left the toaster and reached up to pull another mug from the cupboard just next to Elle's head. He proffered it to Dean with both hands.

"You might want to pour some actual coffee in there first," Elle piped up.

Dean ran his hand through his sleep-ruffled hair. "That would be great," he replied, venturing further into the room.

Ethan turned away to pour the still-hot coffee, hiding his heated face in the process. Elle giggled again.

"So you...ah...talk to yourself a lot?"

"Huh?" Ethan spun around with the now full mug in hand. The liquid sloshed with his movement spilling over and onto a socked foot.

Ethan glanced down at his fluffy green feet before shoving the mug at Dean, who had come to a stop directly in front of him. At a loss for what to do with his now empty hands, he folded his arms across his chest, surreptitiously drying the back of his hand on his t-shirt in the process. Luckily, the coffee wasn't boiling hot anymore.

"I was living on my own in my last place. I guess it's a bad habit."

Part of him wanted to turn away again, but then he would have to face Elle and from the continued snickering behind him, he could tell she was struggling not to burst out in laughter.

Perhaps it had been better when he couldn't actually talk to her. At least then, he'd only felt vaguely judged.

Dean nodded as he took a sip, but his eyebrows were still slightly raised. Suddenly, Ethan remembered his own coffee abandoned by the toaster. He had to restrain himself from diving for it as an out to the awkward conversation.

"Smooth Ethan," Elle chimed in as he lifted the mug to his mouth in victory.

Well, perhaps he had hurried a little.

"So you didn't like living on your own?" Dean asked.

"It was fine for a while, I guess." Ethan shrugged. "Got too expensive, though."

"You don't need to tell me about that. It was kind of nice not having the girls here for a few weeks until it started eating into my spending money." Dean winked.

Ethan nodded uncertainly. "Ah...are you still looking for someone to take the third bedroom?" he asked.

Dean took a big swallow of his coffee and shrugged as he propped his hip against the bench right next to Elle, who was watching him expectantly.

"You said you could afford half the rent, so as long as that's still the case..." One eyebrow raised in question as he brought his mug to his lips again.

Ethan nodded with considerable enthusiasm. Technically, he already had two housemates—he definitely didn't need a third.

"Cool," Dean continued, nodding. "Three can get a bit crowded in here. It's not exactly a big place."

"No kidding!" Elle interjected.

Ethan jumped as his attention shifted to Elle. She was swinging her legs again. It made him a little queasy.

"What?" she asked. "You try being stuck in this house all day, every day!" As Ethan watched, she spread one arm out to her right towards the living room, the other fanned out to encompass the kitchen, then she brought them both together over her head, palms facing upwards. Ethan looked up at the ceiling.

"There isn't much to it!" Elle concluded with a huff, arms collapsing into her lap.

Dean wiped his mouth after finishing the last of his coffee. He turned away, leaving the empty mug in the sink. Ethan took another quick sip from his own mug and made a face. It was lukewarm at best.

Dean drummed his fingertips on the edge of the sink. Shit, Ethan was acting weird again, wasn't he? But Dean would think Ethan was even weirder, or you know crazier, if he told him about the extra housemate he'd had for the last two years without ever knowing it.

He frowned at Elle, who was busy leaning back to get a better look at Dean's face.

"The third room is kind of poky, anyway. It barely fits a double bed." He shot Ethan a quick look before turning around and leaning against the kitchen bench. He crossed his arms over his chest and avoided Ethan's gaze as he continued. "I was thinking it might make a better study. Or something."

He shrugged as he raised his eyes to Ethan's level again. One side of his mouth quirked up in a self-deprecating smile.

"That sounds great!" Ethan said encouragingly, even as he struggled to hide his confusion.

As far as he knew, Dean had never enrolled at the university, despite the close proximity. It was his job at the hospital that kept him close by.

"I was thinking of studying occupational therapy. I've been working in the rehabilitation wing lately, and it's not so different from being an orderly in some ways. Just more specialized, you know?"

Ethan blinked. "Wow, that's great!" he exclaimed, mind grasping for something more to add, but it seemed enough for Dean, whose grin stretched wide across his handsome face.

"Jenny suggested it," he continued in a strangely bashful tone, a slight blush tinting his otherwise tanned skin. "I mean, I've thought about it before, but I just didn't think I could do it—the study, you know? But she's a nurse so she said she'd help me."

"I can help you, too." Ethan was quick to offer before the rest of the sentence sunk in. Huh—Jenny? Well, good for Dean.

"So, you two are together, then?" he asked awkwardly.

Dean's smile widened. "Yeah, she's pretty great."

Ethan cut his eyes across to Elle, whose mouth hung open as she stared at Dean. He couldn't help the laugh that bubbled up in his throat. But it was a good-natured sound, and Dean let out a self-deprecating laugh of his own, the red in his face darkening.

"Oh my god, I didn't know Dean *could* blush!" Elle piped up, hands coming together in front of her face. "I guess you're not going to get too much sleep from now on, considering how loud those two were the other night."

Ethan scowled. He'd only thought Elle was relentless before. Now that he actually knew her, he realized she was utterly ruthless. It hadn't taken him long to work out that the pettiness and hostility he'd sensed from her when he first moved in was her slightly twisted sense of humor, regularly seasoned with a whole lot of boredom.

Dean cleared his throat as he checked his watch. "Anyway, I've got a shift starting in an hour, so I'd better get on with it."

As he pushed himself away from the bench, Elle jumped off the counter. "Wait!"

She turned to Ethan at Dean's unsurprising lack of response.

"You haven't asked him about Amelia yet!" she hissed in an urgent undertone.

Ethan blinked. "Ah..." he started, unsure whether that was in response to Elle or an attempt to stop Dean from leaving. And why was she whispering? She certainly hadn't bothered trying to be discreet before.

He got Dean's attention, though, and he turned back at the archway. Ethan was still staring at Elle, so when he saw the expectant expression on Dean's face, he was even more wrong-footed. As if this wasn't embarrassing enough!

"Do you remember how we were talking about Amelia the other week?"

"Amelia? You mean Amelia Lawson?" Dean asked, brows drawing together in confusion as though a conversation about someone dying in the house wasn't that memorable.

Ethan nodded and took a deep breath to steady his nerves. Elle's strained smile and imploring eyes urged him onwards.

"She's in one of my classes, and we got to talking the other day, and I kind of put my foot in it when I mentioned Elle."

"Elle? Is that the dead girl? Why would you mention her?" Dean asked.

"Well, we're in a study group together. We had our last meeting here, but Amelia was, um...a bit distracted? I realized why after you told me about..." He waved a hand vaguely towards the staircase behind Dean. "So I just wanted to, I don't know, clear the air..." Ethan trailed off, unsure if Dean was following his meaning. He was nodding along, but his eyebrows nearly met over his perfectly straight nose.

"Oh, for god's sake!" Elle exclaimed. "Just tell him you've got a crush on her already." Ethan sent a distressed look her way, but it only generated another huff from the ghost. "Trust me. *That*, he will understand."

Ethan took a deep breath and bit the bullet. "It's just...she's been avoiding me ever since, and I thought maybe we were becoming friends...or something," he finished lamely.

Dean still looked unsure, although the deepening red rapidly spreading over Ethan's face and down his throat probably helped clue him in.

"Oh!" Dean exclaimed. "Well, good for you, although I wouldn't have thought Amelia was your...type?"

Ethan laughed weakly as he tried not to glare in Elle's direction.

"I guess opposites attract, right?" Dean continued.

"That's what they say," Ethan mumbled. Elle giggled.

"But you know she's engaged, right? Of course, he is a jerk, so you never know. Maybe you've got a shot!" Dean finished on an enthusiastic note.

Elle was laughing outright now. "Such a jerk." She nodded in Dean's direction. "You have no idea."

Ethan sighed. Amelia certainly wasn't his type. In some ways, she scared him more than the thought of a haunted house had. Of course, Elle hadn't turned out so scary in the end, even if she was trying his last nerve at the moment.

He sighed again. At least Dean didn't think he was creepy for having a crush on Amelia.

"So you, what? Want me to put in a good word with her?" Dean asked. He tapped a finger against his chin. "I don't see her much these days, though, since she's not a nurse anymore."

"Oh, of course not. Sorry, don't worry about it," Ethan said, shooting another quick glare at Elle, who was pouting. Apparently, ghosts forgot that the world moved on.

"Still, she comes into the bar on campus sometimes. Only for lunch, though. She's not much of a drinker. I've got a couple of day shifts coming up later this week." He tilted his head to the side as he gave Ethan a smirk and a wink. "I could tell her about my cool new housemate."

"Cool?" Ethan asked in a slightly strangled tone.

It didn't help when Elle nearly doubled over in laughter. He kept his body carefully turned away from her.

Dean grinned. "You're not so bad, even if you do talk to yourself," he said as he advanced on Ethan and gave him a hearty slap on the shoulder.

Ethan coughed.

Dean turned around and started to make his way up the stairs.

"If I see her, you can count on me!" he called back over his shoulder.

***

Elle finally got her laughter under control as the sound of Dean's footsteps faded.

"That was so unfair!" Ethan hissed as her spluttering died down.

The indignant look on his face was nearly enough to set her off again.

"No," Elle replied. "That was so hilarious, and after all the trouble you gave me, ignoring me for weeks? Well, simply put—you deserved it."

Ethan blinked, mouth opening and closing. He was quite cute when he was flustered.

Elle's commentary on her 'housemates' lives was nothing new. Admittedly, after so many years when no one could hear her, she may have become a tad...sharp.

But it wasn't only for her amusement or to elicit a reaction from Ethan. It made her feel like a part of the conversation rather than the eternal onlooker she thought she was doomed to be until Ethan showed up.

"Plus, it's not like Dean didn't already think you were weird," Elle continued with a slight smirk since she was still a little put out about him leaving her hanging after he moved in.

"What!" Ethan exclaimed before furtively glancing back at the stairs and whispering furiously at Elle, "I'm not—"

She smiled fondly. "Don't worry. It's not the bad kind of weird."

Ethan spluttered for a few moments. "There's a good kind of weird? What..." Ethan began before trailing off, seemingly at a loss.

Elle's smile widened. "Dean is about as insensitive or... un-medium-like as you can get. I'm pretty sure even if he had a sixth sense, he'd be too oblivious to whatever was going on around him to connect it with anything supernatural."

"Yeah, that's great, except for one thing." Ethan held a finger up to illustrate. Elle raised an eyebrow, the corner of her mouth quirking up again.

"Oh?" she asked.

Ethan put his hand down and crossed his arms in a protective manner. "I might have, kind of, told Amelia I...." He made a face as he cast his eyes around the room as though that would help him find the words. "I told her I could sense you—your spirit, I mean—here, in the house."

Elle's eyebrows rose, and she leaned forwards involuntarily.

He took a deep breath. "She probably thinks I'm crazy, not just weird." He deflated at the last.

Elle's heart went out to him, but she knew her friend better than Ethan did. Amelia had talked to her back then after she died. While Elle wasn't deluded enough to think Amelia realized she actually was listening, it showed an openness to the idea and a desire to connect with Elle.

If it was something Amelia wished to believe, she might listen to Ethan.

***

"This used to be your bed, didn't it?" Ethan asked.

"What makes you say that?" Elle propped herself up on her elbows to stare at him.

"You seem much clearer here." Ethan rolled onto his side to face her.

"And what does that mean? You could hear me pretty clearly downstairs earlier, couldn't you?"

"It's not just your voice. It's everything." Ethan rolled onto his back again. "I don't know how to explain it..." He sighed. "I'm not very good at this."

"You mean talking to ghosts or talking to girls?" Elle was proud that she managed not to laugh as Ethan's cheeks reddened.

"I guess this is where I spent the most time while I was alive. I still do, I suppose. I always feel more comfortable here." Elle said, still watching Ethan's face close enough to notice his deepening blush. "Not like that!" she snapped. "I don't just lie here watching people sleep all night long!"

"I never said you did," Ethan retorted.

"But that's what you're thinking, isn't it?"

"Oh, come on," Ethan said, rolling onto his back again and, she was pretty sure, rolling his eyes. "You're honestly going to tell me you haven't watched anyone getting busy on this bed?"

Elle huffed. Ethan's chiding tone got under her skin, and part of her couldn't help but feel accused (and guilty).

"Well, I certainly haven't watched you 'get busy' on it."

Ethan's blush, which had nearly dissipated, came back with a vengeance. "Well, perhaps you're too busy hanging out in Dean's room!"

Now Elle felt like blushing or whatever the ghostly equivalent might be. She had actually been avoiding Dean's bedroom since Jenny had been his only female visitor for almost two weeks. He wasn't exactly a different girl every night kind of guy, more like a different girl every weekend with the occasional reappearance for a booty call. At least, that had been Dean's modus operandi for the last couple of years. Minus his brief ill-fated fling with his last housemate.

"Oh, my god, you have!" Ethan accused, eyes widening.

Elle spluttered. The urge to defend herself was strong, but what could she say? It hadn't seemed to matter because she was dead?

Ethan's gaze shifted away from her and drifted across the room.

Elle sat up a little. Was he looking at the bedroom door? It was closed now, although Dean's door was just across the hall.

She couldn't feel any warmth in her cheeks, and she had no idea if they had colored, but she certainly felt like she *should* be blushing. It didn't help when Ethan started laughing. She really wished she could pick the pillow lying next to her up so she could hit him over the head with it.

"It's not that funny, you know!" she exclaimed. "My whole world is this house, and I can't even touch most of the stuff here anymore. It's like a piece of my life disappears every time someone replaces a piece of furniture! Let alone when people come and go, and they never even know..."

Ethan turned back to her. The mirth still showed on his face, but his expression was falling. She took several deep breaths, but she couldn't seem to catch her breath.

"I'm sorry," he began. "It just occurred to me that Dean would probably like it if he knew the cute ghost in the room next door was watching him."

She laughed, but it came out sounding almost like a hiccup. She supposed that's what happens when a dead girl can't cry.

She'd been quite fond of a few of her unknowing housemates over the years, not just Dean, but he's the one who stuck around the longest. To say it was hard never having the chance to say goodbye was an understatement.

"I really am sorry," Ethan said, quieter now. "It's still your house. Still your room." He ran his hand over the pillow he'd moved out of the way for her. "Still your bed."

She nodded, but the empty ache that had started as embarrassment opened up into a deep well of loss. She didn't understand where it came from. Sure, being left behind again and again sucked. At first, when she died, then Amelia and Adam, then all the others, but suddenly it felt like more than that.

She couldn't look at Ethan's face. He could see her now, talk to her, but what did that really mean? He wasn't going to stay here forever, but what if she did?

Her gaze drifted almost unseeingly across the room. She thought Ethan was still talking, but she wasn't sure. She couldn't quite make out the words. His voice sounded strange, further away and...younger?

Her eyes unfocused until her gaze crossed the bedroom window. She stood. It was fogged again to her sight, but beads of condensation were forming before her eyes over a large section of the bottom pane.

Her legs swung off the edge of the bed. She was barely conscious of moving them.

"Elle!"

She stopped. She turned around, unsure for a second if Ethan was calling her, or...

His face was right in front of her, almost leaning over her on the bed. No, wait, he wasn't just leaning over her. His arm was *in* her. She cried out, jumping away. She looked back at the bed and could see his arm now, hand still braced against the mattress where she'd been sitting.

His eyes were wide and dark as she stared into them.

He leaned back slowly, arm returning to his side as his mouth twisted. He rubbed his forearm as if trying to bring back the feeling in it.

"Sorry, I wasn't thinking," he mumbled.

She swallowed and nodded, mind spinning in confusion even as it cleared. She took a deep breath and turned to the window. The fog was gone. It was dark. She could see the city lights reflecting on the glass.

She pulled her gaze away without too much difficulty. She didn't want to see more. She lowered herself back onto the bed, her back to Ethan.

"Are you all right?" he asked.

Elle didn't think so, but she nodded anyway. She wasn't sure if Ethan would want to know what she only now realized.

It hadn't been Ethan calling her name.

Chapter 13

Ethan hesitated at the entrance to the university bar despite the lack of customers. At nearly two o'clock, most of the lunch crowd had cleared out, so it didn't take him long to spot Amelia sitting alone at a small table in the far corner.

As he lingered, Dean spotted him from his place behind the bar and began unsubtly gesturing towards Amelia with the empty beer glass he was cleaning. Ethan took a deep breath, sent a tight smile Dean's way, and headed to Amelia's table.

The remnants of a sandwich lay on a plate pushed to the edge of the table to make way for her book. As he drew closer, Ethan was surprised to see her reading a battered paperback novel rather than the textbook he'd expected. Curiosity got the better of him, and he took advantage of her preoccupation to tilt his head and try to spy the cover.

He couldn't make out the title, but that looked like a six-pack and not the kind he brought home for him and Dean.

He felt his cheeks heat, and he must have made a small sound as Amelia's head came up. She pinned him with a tight frown as she lowered the book, cover face down, but careful to keep a finger in her place. She raised a questioning eyebrow.

Ethan cleared his throat. He'd rehearsed this part on the drive over after Dean called to tell him Amelia had shown up for lunch in the student bar. Dean had even given him some helpful advice, suggesting that he could offer her a drink, or say he didn't want to eat alone.

Unfortunately, it all flew out of his mind as he stood in front of her. Not that he could have pulled any of those lines off as well as his housemate.

"Ah...hi?" The corner of Amelia's mouth quirked up at the questioning note in Ethan's voice before she pursed her lips and narrowed her eyes.

"What are you doing here?" she asked.

"Lunch?" Ethan replied uncertainly.

Amelia's lips twitched.

"Hey Ethan, here you go," Dean interjected, beer in hand, which he smoothly passed to Ethan.

"Hey, thanks, Dean," Ethan said, barely managing not to make that sound like a question as well.

"Sorry about this. I'm supposed to be finishing up, but Daniel's running late, so I have to cover. You don't mind waiting around for that lift, do you?" Dean asked as he made deliberate eye contact with Ethan.

Ethan stared at him blankly for several seconds. "Oh, yeah, of course, no problem!" Ethan replied, finally catching on, although he was a trifle unsure who was supposed to be giving who a lift in this scenario.

Dean nodded for a couple of seconds too long before shifting his attention to Amelia. "Haven't seen you round the hospital for a while. Been busy?"

Amelia looked from Ethan to Dean and back again.

"You know Ethan, right?" Dean continued, cocking his head at his housemate. "You guys are studying together, aren't you?"

Ethan repressed the urge to fidget.

Amelia looked a little like a deer in headlights. "Oh, yes, we have a couple of classes together." She turned to face Ethan and gave him an awkward nod in acknowledgment.

"So, how do you two know each other?" she asked ingenuously.

Ethan blinked, mouth opening slightly as his brow furrowed. Dean looked a little confused too, but Amelia kept her expression even.

"Well, Ethan moved into the house on Gardenia Street at the start of the semester."

"Oh, of course," Amelia said, "I didn't know you were still living there..."

Dean shrugged. "It's a good place, despite the landlord."

Amelia's face clearly showed her disbelief, prompting Dean to add, "Well, it's a good location, at least!"

"Yeah, much closer than my last place," Ethan chimed in. "That's why I moved."

And the main reason he forced himself to ignore the ghostly presence in the house rather than move straight out again. Traveling halfway across the city almost every day for the past couple of years had seriously cut into his study time.

"Yeah, Ethan's a great guy!" Dean enthused. "Since you're hanging around for a while," Dean gestured to her book, "do you mind keeping Ethan company? He's giving me a lift home, but my shift's running over..." He checked his watch before returning his attention to Ethan as he shook his head. "I'll probably be another twenty or so, that cool?"

Ethan felt like curling up in a ball. It took all of his concentration to hold back the flush that threatened to overcome his face. He forced out a smile for Dean and a small nod before taking a large mouthful of beer.

And he had thought Dean was the smooth one. Surely he was laying it on too thick? But when he finally glanced up from his beer, a warm smile lit Amelia's face and even more surprising. It appeared to be directed at him.

"Awesome! I'll send you over a sandwich to go with that beer." Dean nodded to the already half-empty glass in Ethan's hand before shooting a grin Amelia's way and heading back to the bar.

They both watched him for several seconds as he greeted two young women who were impatiently waiting to be served. The sound of their laughter soon drifted over.

Ethan couldn't help but shake his head as he turned back to Amelia, amusement also clear on her face.

"I bet he gets a lot of tips," Amelia commented.

"Trust me, he gets a lot more than tips," Ethan replied in an offhand manner. The slight jealous note in his voice must have shone through, because Amelia started laughing.

She shook her head. "You should ask him for a chicken club sandwich." She gestured to the crumbs remaining on the plate beside her paperback, which she shifted further out of the way. "It's the best thing on the menu."

"That does sound good," Ethan replied. "I'm not that hungry, though, and I might need to get it to go if his workmate turns up soon."

He glanced around the room. It had further emptied out, students heading home or back to their classes.

He took a deep breath to steady himself. "Is it all right if I sit here?" he asked. "It's okay if you just want to read your book, of course," he hastened to add with a nervous air.

"No, it's fine," Amelia replied as she nudged the chair opposite with one of her sensible shoes, pushing it out from the small table in invitation. "I'm waiting for someone, but I have a few minutes to kill."

Ethan pulled the chair the rest of the way out with a grateful smile and swung his backpack under the table as he sat. Apparently, Dean was good at this kind of thing after all.

Amelia watched his movements with a pleasant if somewhat neutral expression, but as he started to relax into the seat opposite, he caught sight of an intense glint in her eyes. His shoulders stiffened in response, and his nerves returned twofold. Amelia picked her book up and dropped it into the open bag at her feet, her focus narrowing in on Ethan.

He swallowed uneasily.

"So, seen any ghosts lately?" she asked with a small smile.

Ethan blanched as he struggled to hold her gaze. Amelia's expression was still pleasant, but the glint shone brighter, fixing him with her eyes like a moth pinned to a specimen board.

"It's not that simple," Ethan hedged. A lot had happened with Elle since they last spoke, but admitting that he *could* now see Elle didn't seem like a safe bet. It didn't feel like Amelia was making fun of him exactly, but he honestly couldn't tell. She certainly didn't come across as a true believer.

She pursed her lips and leaned back. Ethan released a shaky breath he wasn't aware he'd been holding. Amelia's smile faltered as her gaze shifted away from him for a precious couple of seconds. The tension in Ethan's shoulders ebbed slightly.

"So how does it work, then?" Amelia asked, eyes returning to him, but only for a second. She seemed as off balance as Ethan now.

"I don't really know, to be honest," Ethan replied somewhat helplessly. "I'm still working that part out, although Elle—" Amelia's eyes shot straight to his at her friend's name, causing him to falter for a brief second, "—has been helping me."

She blinked rapidly for several seconds. Ethan knew his statement was inadequate, but his mind raced trying to find the right words. He'd rehearsed this part too, but he didn't do well when put on the spot.

"Helping you what?" The words were sharp. "Work out your ghost *thing* or—" she cut herself off, either because she couldn't vocalize the thought or perhaps because of the way Ethan's mouth had dropped open.

Her own mouth sealed shut, lips tightly pursed. Her nostrils flared a little. Ethan didn't think it was from anger, at least he hoped not. That glint in her eye was more of a gleam now, one that threatened to spill over if he didn't step carefully.

"Helping me understand," Ethan replied. "Although I want to help her too." He looked away. Amelia was biting her lip now. He had no idea what he would do if she cried. Tears were the last thing he'd been expecting.

"Do you actually believe me?" he asked, ashamed at how small his voice became as he uttered the plaintive words. It was a struggle to meet her eyes again.

"No."

It was a simple denial. Quiet, accompanied by a slight shake of her head. It should have been discouraging.

"Of course not." Her eyes dropped to her lap.

"I don't believe in ghosts..." As her words trailed away, Amelia's weak statement almost sounded like a question.

Ethan felt his mind clearing as he glimpsed a tempting future opening up where not everyone thought he was crazy when he tried to be honest with them. He gave his head a firm shake. The sudden feeling of acceptance made little sense, given her words.

"I don't think of them as ghosts so much as spirits." Ethan took a breath, steeling himself. "Do you honestly think nothing happens when we die? That we just end?"

Amelia's lips parted slightly. "No..."

"But you're not religious, are you?"

She shook her head. Ethan nodded his, encouraged.

"It was a sudden death," he said, pausing to take a deep breath. It was hard not to feel like a phony trying to explain something he didn't fully understand himself. "It may sound cliché, but the confusion, the sense of things being...unresolved...I think that's why they stay sometimes."

"But it was an accident." Amelia's eyes widened, but the tears were still contained.

"She doesn't remember dying."

A small gasp escaped her, but Amelia quickly shook her head, holding onto denial. She squeezed her eyes shut, and a single tear finally escaped.

Ethan swallowed, mouth dry as he watched it leave a wet track down her left cheek.

She took a deep breath, a little shaky, before opening her eyes. She sat up straighter as she swiped at the tears but had trouble making eye contact with Ethan. Her gaze drifted away several times as he, too, struggled for words.

"So, who is this, then?" Another voice, male, interrupted Ethan's troubled thoughts.

Amelia's gaze shot to the space behind Ethan and her shoulders tensed. "Adam!" she exclaimed. "You're early."

Ethan forced himself not to strain his neck too far as Adam came to a stop in an awkward position to Ethan's left, but a step behind his chair. The guy was taller than Dean.

"Early?" Adam asked, checking his watch. "I thought I was late." His eyes shifted to Ethan, taking him in from head to toe with a hard look. "I guess you were distracted," he finished as he turned back to Amelia.

Her brow pulled down. Angry, or embarrassed at his rudeness? Ethan couldn't tell. He cleared his throat to introduce himself, but Amelia beat him to it. Her words carefully even.

"This is Ethan. From my study group."

"You don't look like you're studying," Adam commented, stepping forward with a pointed look at Amelia's empty plate.

"Oh, hey, Dr Scott," Dean interjected, plate in hand containing Ethan's lunch. All eyes went to the sandwich. Adam's eyebrows rose as he looked at his fiancé.

"Ah...maybe I should get that for the road," Ethan said, eyes seeking Amelia's, which had tightened but relaxed a little at his words.

So much for his chance to find out more about Elle's death. He looked up at Adam, who now exchanged tense but superficial pleasantries with Dean.

Ethan cleared his throat and was startled when all eyes jumped to him. He felt the warmth creeping into his face. Goddam it, would he ever learn not to blush like an awkward teenager?

"Sorry, it's just," he pulled his phone out to check the time. "We should probably get going soon if you've finished your shift?"

"Yeah, no worries. Daniel will be here in a minute. I can get you a take-away container if you're in a hurry." Ethan and Amelia both stared at the plate as Dean gestured to it with a flourish.

Adam's eyes narrowed, shifting from Dean to Ethan and back again. "Home?" he asked with an edge to his voice.

Dean smiled, with his mouth if not his eyes. Ethan imagined it was far from the first time he'd worn such an expression around Dr Scott. "Yeah, Ethan's my housemate."

Adam drew in a sharp breath. He looked down his nose at Ethan before addressing Dean again. "The house on Gardenia Street?"

Dean nodded. He put a hand on Ethan's shoulder and gestured with the plate back to the bar. "Should be ready to leave in a couple of minutes if you want to wait at the bar."

Ethan gave him a grateful look as he rose. He sent a strained smile Amelia's way, but she wasn't watching him, which was a good thing judging from her expression. Her tight eyes and pinched lips were directed solely at Adam.

Despite himself, Ethan followed her gaze instead of following Dean back to the bar. Adam's nostrils were flaring, and he worked his mouth for a few seconds as the two of them tried to stare each other down before Adam spat out, "So this is the guy who's been asking about Elle?"

Ethan stepped back as Adam's gaze swung from Amelia to him. He looked helplessly over his shoulder at Dean's retreating back. Ethan winced as he saw Dean's shoulders stiffen a little. He must have heard Adam, who wasn't exactly using his inside voice.

Ethan took another step away. His mind might be telling him to take the chance to find out more about Elle, but a much more basic part of his brain prickled as it sensed danger.

"I told you to stay away from him!" The words were intense, but at least they were more of a whispered shout this time. Hopefully Dean (and everyone else in the bar) hadn't heard him.

Ethan drew his eyes away from Adam's tense face long enough to check Amelia's reaction. Dean had said he was an arrogant jerk, but this was on another level.

The tightness around her eyes and mouth was still visible, but to her credit, she was sitting up straight in her chair and looking him in the eye.

Ethan tried to draw himself up taller as Amelia gathered her bag and stood. Adam didn't even step back to give her room, so she stepped around him, putting herself, intentionally or not, between the two men.

"He's not doing any harm," Amelia said.

Her eyes darted to Ethan's, but only for a second. She glanced down before meeting Adam's angry eyes again. The gleam in her eyes was not from tears this time.

Ethan felt oddly proud. She was tough, and not just on the surface. Why on earth would she agree to marry a bully like Adam? The guy wasn't *that* good-looking, sure he topped six feet and had Ethan beat in the looks department, but with his skinny legs and weak chin, he was no Dean.

"Not doing any harm?" Adam asked in that hushed but hostile tone. He looked around briefly, shooting a dismissive glare at Ethan in the process, before reaching out and taking Amelia's bag from her. "The last thing we need is some jumped up ghost whisperer wannabe interfering in our lives!"

Ethan felt it like a punch to the stomach. His breath whooshed out, and both Amelia and Adam were suddenly staring at him—Amelia concerned and a little embarrassed. But that was nothing compared to the pure mortification that ran through his entire body. He knew he wasn't blushing now because he could feel the blood draining from his face. He blinked as he grew lightheaded. Being called crazy was bad enough, but 'ghost whisperer wannabe' was a new one for him, and it was way worse.

He took two steps back before it occurred to him that he could still turn around and walk away.

"It's not like that!" Amelia protested in a hushed but intense tone of her own.

"Ethan!" Amelia called as he began to edge away.

"It's all right," he said. "I'm just going to..." He waved his hand vaguely in the direction of the bar. "See Dean."

Adam's derisive laugh as he started to walk away cut, but it also brought him to his senses a little. He turned back to face them both fully. "I'm not crazy."

Adam laughed again. "Yeah, right, you keep telling yourself that. But I can tell you one thing for sure—if you think my fiancé would have anything to do with a guy like you—then you've completely lost it."

Ethan's jaw hurt. He was grinding his teeth. He raised his chin as he glared at Adam, the insulting way he eyed Ethan made it clear he didn't consider ghost whispering Ethan's only shortcoming.

"For god's sake, Adam, he wasn't hitting on me either!" Amelia hissed through clenched teeth. She threw an apologetic look at Ethan before reaching out and grabbing her bag back from Adam.

"You expect me to believe that?" Adam asked her.

"I don't care," Amelia declared. "We're leaving."

"Damn right we are! I already had to cut my shift short to pick you up, thanks to your piece of shit car."

"You know I can't afford to buy a new car," Amelia responded in a frustrated tone that said they'd had this conversation before.

"*You* don't need to buy a new car," Adam replied. "*I* can afford a new car for you, or at least something reliable."

Ethan took the chance to beat his retreat to the bar. Adam probably sneered at his back, but he didn't care anymore. He could still hear them arguing, if not the specific words.

He put both hands on the edge of the bar and leaned forward, focusing on his breathing. The urge to look around the room was hard to resist. He imagined everyone staring at his back, even though the rational part of his brain told him that if anyone actually cared, they would be focused on the still arguing couple as they exited through the beer garden.

"So, do you really need a lift?" Ethan asked.

He tried to avoid visibly cringing from embarrassment as he finally looked over at Dean, who kept a careful distance while he cleaned glasses behind the bar. It was bad enough that Adam took him for such a loser. What must Dean think of him now?

"Nah, it's all right. I have another hour left on my shift." Dean fidgeted with the glass in his hands. Apparently, Ethan wasn't the only embarrassed one. "Sorry, man, I didn't know she was meeting that jerk, or I wouldn't have called."

Ethan tried to shrug away his awkwardness, but the careful way Dean avoided his eyes told him more than he needed to know. Adam was definitely a jerk, but in this case, he was also a loud jerk.

Ethan's mind went to all the times Dean had teased him about talking to himself or given him a strange look when he was distracted by Elle. Ethan wouldn't blame him if he wondered whether he was living with a crazy man.

"Still," Dean said with a lopsided attempt at a grin, "at least you know she would be better off without him."

Ethan gave a weak laugh. "You really think I have a chance with Amelia after that?"

"Well, maybe not," Dean conceded. "But you didn't see the way she glared at his back as they were leaving." He shook his head as he continued. "If she hadn't already worked out how much of a jerk that guy is by now, I think she just got a pretty good idea. Guys like that..." His mouth tightened and he shook his head. "That's not jealousy. That's a red flag flying high."

Ethan frowned, also disturbed by the way Adam spoke to Amelia. If he was jealous of a guy like Ethan, that didn't bode well for their future. He and Amelia barely knew each other!

He took a deep breath as a darker thought stirred. He couldn't imagine Elle with an entitled jerk like Adam. Sure, he was still a student when they were together, but did people really change that much?

And Elle had ended up dead. Amelia still grieved for her friend, but did Adam? Was he trying to scare Ethan off because he was worried about losing Amelia? Or because he was feeling guilty?

Chapter 14

Ethan closed his laptop without bothering to power it off first. His fingers lingered on the edge of the desk as he leaned back in his chair. His head dropped forward, and he found himself staring at the holographic Transformers sticker on the cover of his computer as it caught the last rays of the afternoon light.

He swallowed hard, vision blurring as his mind ran over the extensive list of injuries from Elle's coroners report. Broken ankle...contusions...and, let's not forget, the skull fracture and subdural hematoma.

'Injuries consistent with a fall down the stairs.'

The report was a matter of public record, as he well knew after his years of studying medicine. If he'd thought to look it up online as soon as he discovered Elle's name, he could have spared himself some awkward moments.

He'd skimmed over many of the details, but the finding was simple—

> *'...tripped or lost her balance on the steps and suffered a fall causing fatal head injuries and, unfortunately, her death.'*

Elle had been alone at the time of her death after returning home early from a night out with Amelia and a group of other nurses. The report didn't say why Elle left early, but there was no question that Amelia was still out on the town at the time of Elle's death, and only discovered her body upon returning home in the early hours of the morning.

Not exactly the impression of 'the next morning' he'd received from Amelia, but still technically correct.

He leaned forward and flicked his laptop open again, scrolling through the report to find the exact time. There it was, the call to emergency services at 4:23am. There was no transcript, but the description made it clear that Amelia was both still drunk and in shock.

Ethan repressed a shudder as he recalled the night (also technically morning) he'd come home after finally admitting to himself that he'd moved into a haunted house. He was quite possibly the drunkest he'd ever been, and he could barely recall heading upstairs to bed.

No wonder Amelia was so hesitant to talk about the night Elle died. The combination of alcohol and shock would be enough to confuse anyone's memory. And that thought led him inexorably to Elle's lack of memory. She'd been drinking too, but...

He scrolled through the report. Surely they took her blood alcohol, given the circumstances. Probably a drug screen too. It took him a couple more minutes to find it—.08.

He blinked rapidly at the screen. Not exactly the level of high reading he'd expected. Sure, alcohol affects everyone differently, and she shouldn't be driving a car at that level, but negotiating stairs safely?

He remembered the broken ankle from her list of injuries, and the image of Elle's bare feet flashed across his mind. The shoes were mentioned in the report too, as a contributing factor. Elle had implied as much herself despite her lack of clarity, blaming her fall on drinking and high heels that had given her blisters.

It seemed plausible. Ethan could understand the doctor and coroner coming to such an obvious conclusion. But if the reason for her fall was that simple, what reason did Adam have to be so hostile? Was he that worried about Amelia cheating on him? When would she even have the time? Adam had been a med student too. He should know that much.

He stood to stretch his back out, shoulders stiff not only from hunching over the small desk tonight but all the nights he'd done so since he moved in. He nudged a leg of the offending piece of furniture with his toe—it wobbled on the uneven floorboards.

He mentally reviewed his budget. Surely he could afford a new desk. Nothing fancy. A cheap one would be perfectly serviceable if only it were bigger. He surveyed the sparsely furnished bedroom. There was plenty of room for a decent desk, maybe near the window?

Wait, the window...something strange about the quality of the light streaming in caught his attention. He blinked. Outside, the sky had turned yellowy-orange as the sun began its descent, but that wasn't what had sparked his notice.

He stood and took a few steps towards the window. He felt the chill come over him as he drew close enough to make out condensation beading on the glass.

He stared. It had been a clear, sunny day with warmth lingering in the air when he arrived home only an hour ago.

"Elle?" he called as he turned back to the bed, half expecting to see her reclining on her usual side, arm propping her head up in place of a pillow. But the bed remained empty. He narrowed his eyes and tried tilting his head to the side to no avail. He couldn't see her, but he could feel her close by.

He chewed on a ragged thumbnail as he returned to the window. He reached out to pull the thin curtain closed. It snagged on the curtain rod and wouldn't budge more than an inch. Frustration mounted as he tugged ineffectually. He moved closer, trying to pull it from a different angle.

A cloud of breath puffed out in front of his face and left a noticeable fog on the window pane. He blinked and spun around, checking the bed for Elle again. His stomach churned as pressure mounted in his head. Not painful this time, more like being at a high altitude. The need to pop his ears to relieve the pressure was strong, as if he were on a plane.

"Elle?" he called, louder this time over the ringing that now sounded in his ears.

He released the curtain and moved away from the window. The atmosphere didn't feel as oppressive as the time he'd passed out, but he had no idea if the changes in the room were because of Elle or the *other* presence. He trusted Elle meant him no harm. In fact, he didn't think she could harm him even if she wanted to, but that meant little if *this* wasn't Elle.

He retreated to the bed, rubbing at his arms as he went to create some friction, his thin t-shirt providing little protection from the chill. The pressure in his head lessened as he neared the bed, but that didn't help his breathing as his anxiety ratcheted up several notches.

He eyed the closed bedroom door, contemplating his exit. He'd heard Dean come home a little while ago, and the faint sounds of the TV drifted up the stairs only minutes ago.

He turned back to the window. That proved a mistake as the ringing in his right ear, which had dulled as he approached the bed, now rang loudly in both ears. He swallowed hard, trying to unblock them. He shook his head, rubbing at his ears.

It was difficult to think like this, but despite the charged atmosphere in the room, he could detect no sense of threat. He slowly made his way around the bed to Elle's side. He pulled at his left ear in aggravation as he lowered himself to the edge of the mattress. Elle had always felt the strongest right here, ever since those first few weeks.

The room was still cold, but the ringing in his ears cleared as he shifted himself back onto the bed. He toed his shoes off and pulled the covers aside, and wasted no time drawing his bare feet up and under the covers. He scooted to the head of the bed but didn't lie down. That would have felt a tad too vulnerable under the circumstances. Instead, he rested his back against the wall as he gathered the covers up and tucked them around his shoulders. The warmth was a welcome relief. He leaned his head right back and stared at the ceiling, trying to focus only on Elle, picturing her face in his mind.

"You look cold."

Ethan let out a long, shaky breath. A smile spread across his face even as he lowered his head to see her sitting cross-legged at the end of the bed.

"Hi," he said simply.

"You know you nearly sat on me, right?" Elle asked, head tilted at an imperious angle so that she gazed down her nose at him.

The laugh her words startled out of him was far from graceful, more of a snort than an actual laugh.

Elle's serious expression transformed into a wide grin at the sound, although the good humor faded as they continued to stare at each other. Elle's gaze broke first, troubled eyes drifting towards the window before swinging over to his laptop, which still rested on the small desk by the door.

"I don't understand why you couldn't see me," Elle said, brow crinkling. "I've been here since..." she trailed off as her eyes drifted back to his, but her meaning was clear enough. Ethan wondered if she'd stayed on the bed or had read over his shoulder. What would it be like to read about your own death?

Coroners reports were dispassionate but surprisingly detailed, taking into account the myriad of circumstances surrounding a death, not just the medical facts. The report even mentioned Adam had been here that night before the girls went out for the evening.

"I knew I wasn't *that* drunk!" Elle exclaimed with an air of vindication despite her still troubled eyes.

Ethan nodded. He needed to bite his lip to stop himself from asking what he truly wanted to ask. He knew she didn't remember, and too many questions too fast wouldn't get either of them any answers.

"How much did you read?" he asked instead, excavating an arm from his blanket cocoon to point at his laptop.

Elle's gaze dropped to her lap. "Not much..."

The way she rearranged the folds of her dress over her crossed legs while she gathered her thoughts was distracting.

"I wanted to read more, but..." she shrugged and spread her arms wide, indicating the bed.

Ethan cocked his head, prompting her to continue.

"It got too hard to focus, so I...shifted."

Ethan nodded. He was pretty sure she didn't mean she walked over to the bed. "Can you remember why you came home early that night?"

Elle pulled her lip between her teeth, gaze still focused on her lap. Ethan waited, watching her expression shift subtly until she finally shook her head.

"I guess I just wasn't in the mood to party."

Ethan eyed her doubtfully. The hair, the dress, the nails. It was a lot of effort for someone who hadn't been in the mood. There must be more to it, although did it matter why she came home early? What happened afterward was the key.

"It was an awards dinner?" Ethan asked, recalling the details from the report. "For Amelia?"

Elle nodded, then shook her head.

"Um..." Ethan stumbled.

Elle laughed. "The dinner was an industry award night for nursing. Amelia won Young Nurse of the Year."

Ethan smiled at the thought of ambitious Amelia accepting the award.

"Did you read the part about Adam? That he was here that night?" Ethan asked, carefully watching her face for any sign of disengagement. The last thing he wanted was for her to disappear again.

As soon as Adam's name left his lips, Elle's eyes sharpened.

"No, I didn't see that. I don't..." Her expression seemed to cloud and turn inwards. Ethan tensed until her head snapped up, eyes wide. "Yes, he was here. I..."

She shifted to the side of the bed and popped her legs over the edge. Ethan had the strange impression she was about to jump up and start pacing, but she put her hands on her knees and leaned forward slightly instead, head moving from side to side as if she was trying to catch sight of something. The memory?

"He was angry." She blinked, and her shoulders dropped further. "I..."

Ethan took a steadying breath and released himself from the covers. He slid off the bed and leaned down until he crouched in front of Elle. She didn't look at him. He wasn't sure she even noticed he'd moved so close.

"The report said he was here before you went out, that he was still here when you left." He paused, unsure whether to take the risk, but he pushed on. "Was he here when you got home?"

Elle shook her head, but she still wasn't looking at him, and Ethan couldn't tell if the head shake was a 'no' to his question or the result of her confusion.

"Elle?" he asked, quiet urgency creeping into his tone. Something was wrong. He knew he should have left it. She shook her head again. He fought the impulse to reach out to her. Brown curls hung down, obscuring her face from his view. He wasn't sure her eyes were even open.

"I can't..." Her words were strangely quiet. Ethan wished he could see her face. He couldn't shake the uneasy feeling she hadn't actually trailed off, that she was still speaking. He just couldn't hear her anymore.

"Elle?" It was a shout this time as she raised her head, but she wasn't looking at him. Her eyes were unfocused, but her gaze shot straight past him.

She stood and turned slowly, unnaturally slowly, hair still partly covering her face. Ethan desperately wanted to touch it, to brush it behind her ears so he could see her better.

"I can't hear you..." Her voice was faint, although she looked like she was shouting. A chill ran up Ethan's spine and back down again. It wasn't like someone walking over his grave this time, more like they were jumping up and down on it.

Suddenly she turned, a swift movement that left her hair swinging in the stillness of the room. She skirted the end of the bed and headed towards the window. She wasn't just moving away from the bed, though, and it wasn't only her voice fading.

Ethan watched helplessly, rubbing his arms for warmth, as Elle vanished along with the last rays of the setting sun.

***

"Elle?" Ethan half whispered as he descended the last step and ducked his head around the archway to peer into the lounge room.

Dean was upstairs. He could hear the water running in the bathroom, but he still kept his voice hushed as he called her name again.

The room was empty. He made his way to the kitchen and took in the empty table and chairs, the bench where Elle swung her legs and...the coffee maker. He smiled and smothered a yawn as he started making his morning coffee. Hopefully the aroma would draw her out if she wasn't still upset about last night.

He heard a creak behind him and spun around, her name falling from his lips once more.

"Ah...did you just call me Elle?"

Ethan froze as he came face to face with Dean, who hesitated as he entered the kitchen, eyebrows twitching and mouth twisted just enough to make his discomfort clear.

Ethan's mind stalled in shock at being caught out, leaving him fumbling for an excuse. "Um..."

One of Dean's eyebrows continued to rise. He looked back over his shoulder and up the stairs.

"Have you got a girl up there?" His voice rose distinctly at the end of the question. The hint of incredulity should have been offensive, but Ethan's mind was still on standby.

The expression on Dean's face grew more uncomfortable as Ethan only stared back at him. He ran a hand through his just-washed hair.

"Wait a minute, isn't that the name of the girl who fell..." He craned his head around to look at the staircase again before turning back to Ethan with an expectant air.

Ethan could only shrug in response. He didn't trust his voice to stay even, and he'd never been a good liar.

"I heard Adam say that name at the bar. It is *her* name, isn't it?" He made a vague gesture to the stairs this time, thankfully looking away from Ethan as he did so.

Dean paused and lowered his hand as his gaze came to rest on the ugly rug at the base of the stairs. Ethan found himself staring at it too. He still hadn't gathered the courage to check if Elle's blood had left a mark on the floorboards. The reminder made him swallow hard.

"It is?" Ethan asked, still playing dumb in the feeble hope Dean would let him off the hook for talking to 'himself' again.

"Yeah, I'm pretty sure. I remembered it when I heard Adam saying her name. I mean, you're not...you know..." He made another vague gesture, and Ethan held his breath, waiting for him to start making circles next to his head in the universal sign for crazy.

He was used to people thinking he was strange, and that was fair enough, but people thinking he wasn't right in the head? After growing up with his mother, and all the doctors, it hit far too close to home.

"Not what?" Ethan asked carefully when his housemate failed to continue.

Dean cleared his throat and crossed his arms over his broad chest. "Afraid of ghosts or something?" he eventually got out. He uncrossed his arms and shifted his stance, brow furrowing again as he spoke a little too quickly. "Because the house isn't haunted or anything. I know it's weird that a girl died here, but it was years ago, and nothing else like that has ever happened here."

Ethan wasn't sure if he opened his mouth to respond or if it had just fallen open in shock.

"I mean, I know I should have told you before you moved in, but I needed help with the rent and..." Dean shrugged and changed tack. "You've been acting off since I told you about her dying." He paused for a long breath before finishing with a rush. "You're not thinking of moving out, are you?"

Ethan closed his mouth, strangely touched. Dean didn't think he was crazy. He was worried Ethan wanted to move out! He huffed out a relieved breath, not quite a laugh. Dean certainly didn't need to worry about that now. The thought of leaving Elle here alone made his stomach clench.

"You've never felt anything strange here?" Ethan asked.

"What do you mean?" Dean asked. His arms hung awkwardly at his sides, leaving Ethan with the distinct impression the other man was trying not to fidget.

"A presence, or anything weird like a light globe that blows all the time." His attempt at a playful smile fell a little flat, and he let out a self-conscious laugh.

"I don't believe in ghosts." Dean shook his head. "And I don't think there's anything wrong with this house beyond faulty wiring."

Ethan nodded, not in agreement, but to encourage Dean to continue. Something hesitant in his expression wasn't consistent with his words. Even if Dean never gave it any real thought before, a spirit as strong as Elle must have thrown around plenty of spooky vibes over the years.

Surely Dean picked up on something at some point. He'd been living here for over two years, and while she hadn't admitted it outright, Ethan suspected Elle had spent most of her time hanging around Dean before Ethan moved in and disrupted everything.

Dean crossed his arms again. He shifted as if in discomfort, eyes drifting to the lounge room ceiling and the naked light globe.

"Well, other people have thought there was something strange about the house. And no one ever stays long." His mouth twisted a touch at that, and Ethan couldn't help but feel sorry for him.

Dean was the type of guy who'd been popular his whole life. What must he have thought when people kept moving out? Is this why he was so worried about Ethan leaving? Were they actually friends now? An unfamiliar warmth bloomed in Ethan's chest, and for once, it wasn't the beginning of a blush.

"This one guy said the place had a creepy vibe," Dean continued. He scoffed, but there wasn't any real contempt behind it. "That dude always got the chills—he was even jumpier than you!" Dean shot Ethan a grin before shaking his head. He let out a slow breath.

"But I don't believe in ghosts."

Ethan stared at him for several tense moments, trying to judge how firm that last statement was. He shook his head to clear away the little voice in his head that still whispered 'crazy'. Amelia claimed she didn't believe in ghosts too, and yet she had listened to him, at least until Adam showed up and ruined everything. But Dean was nothing like Adam.

The anxiety he'd let rule his life for so many years still prickled in his mind. Ethan took a deep breath, steeling his nerves.

"I do." He nodded his head for emphasis. In fact, he found he couldn't stop nodding his head as he made an effort that felt heroic beyond all reason to lock onto Dean's confused eyes. "Ever since I was a little kid."

"Okay." Dean's responding nod also went on a few seconds too long as he looked down at the shorter man before lowering his gaze further to the floorboards. Ethan's eyebrows rose as he watched his friend bite his lip in thought, head still bobbing slightly.

"But that doesn't mean she'd be a scary ghost. It's not like she was murdered or something."

Ethan blinked. As surprised by Dean's acceptance as he was by his use of the 'M' word. Not that he hadn't thought it himself. Especially after meeting Adam. Still, he couldn't help but wince at it a little. Luckily, Dean didn't notice.

"I mean, why would someone stick around here as a ghost?" He paused, opening his arms to take in the dated room, faulty wiring, 70s fixtures and bits of plaster falling from the goddam popcorn ceiling. "Unless they'd been wronged or like walled up in the basement."

"I think you've been watching too many horror movies!" Ethan laughed uneasily. Thank god they didn't have a basement. "But yeah, you're right. It doesn't make much sense."

Unless there was more to the story, but Ethan was definitely keeping that thought to himself.

"So you're not going to move out?"

Ethan smiled, touched, and a little startled that Dean still wanted him to stay.

"Of course not," he replied. His laugh this time came a little easier as Dean joined in. "Why would I want to move out? And in the middle of the semester too! We're friends now, aren't we?"

Dean grinned. Those thick arms swung out towards Ethan now as he clapped him on both shoulders. Ethan let out a whoosh of breath at the unexpected force.

"Oh, course, man, even if you do talk to yourself all the time." Dean's eyes shone with good-natured mirth. "Or to Elle," he added with a wink.

Ethan found himself laughing again, this time in relief, even if he was still a little uncomfortable. Of course, that was partly due to Dean squeezing his right shoulder a tad too hard after giving it a final hearty clap.

Ethan may have stopped short of telling his new friend he knew for a fact Elle was haunting the house, but somehow the sense of acceptance he'd just received from Dean went far beyond that of any past friendship.

Now, if only he could work out what really happened to Elle, maybe he could give her that same sense of acceptance. Even if it was something she didn't want to hear.

Natalie Pearce

Chapter 15

Things had actually come to this point. Meditating. Or more accurately, trying to meditate. Ethan really needed to sign up for that class.

He lay flat on his back on the bed, streaming a guided visualization from his laptop but so far, trying to imagine himself lying on the beach, smelling the fresh sea breeze and soaking up some rays, wasn't helping him get in touch with his inner being. Or, more importantly, the spiritual being he actually wanted to contact.

With a low groan, he pushed himself up and rolled to his side to scroll through the other tracks. *Rainy Night* sounded more promising. Ethan clicked it and turned up the volume before flopping onto his back with a ragged exhalation.

Instead of closing his eyes, he found himself staring at the popcorn ceiling again. It really was a dust trap. How on earth did anyone ever think this style was a good idea?

Ethan inhaled sharply, senses pinging as he felt a stirring in the room. He tried to settle his breathing down again, but a loud banging startled him. His eyes shot to the closed bedroom door, but an increasingly loud series of knocks drifted up the stairs—the front door.

Ethan ground his teeth in frustration. Just as he was starting to make some progress. What was it about this ceiling anyway that seemed to draw Elle out? Had she really spent that long staring at it?

The thud of a fist on wood continued as Ethan rolled to the edge of the bed and slipped his shoes on. But he only made it as far as the bedroom door before an insistent buzzing forced him to backtrack and check his phone, which was jumping around on his bedside table.

Julie. Huh, guess that explained all the knocking. His big sister had never been the patient type.

He rejected the call in favor of a more direct method, shouting at the top of his voice as he hurried from the bedroom. "I'm coming!"

The feeling came again as he rushed down the stairs. That movement in the air that had nothing to do with air at all. He paused at the bottom of the staircase. Julie's response drifted through the door. While the sound of her voice was unmistakable, he couldn't make out the words. His gaze instead caught on the hall rug.

Elle's voice rang in his mind about why the faded runner was there. So far, he'd resisted the morbid impulse to move it aside and see if Dean was right about there being no bloodstain. He didn't really want to know. But now, as he found it hard to pull his eyes away from the rug in question, it occurred to him that if Elle still cared, shifting the rug might be the push needed to get her attention.

Another loud thump derailed his train of thought. Julie's voice came through clearer now, and the accompanying yell was definitely his name in a particularly cutting tone only his older sister could manage.

Ethan hopped down the last few stairs, trying to avoid, well he really wasn't quite sure what—despite reading the coroners report, he didn't know exactly where Elle's body had come to rest. Her not so final rest.

"Coming!" he yelled back as he finally reached the offending door. He wrenched it open only to almost get clocked in the nose by Julie's raised fist. The shock sent him reeling back as Julie overbalanced forwards and came stumbling into the house. He kept a hold of the door handle, swinging it wider in an effort to both shield himself behind the door and stop his sister from colliding with it face first.

"Hi, Uncle Ethan!" Levi bounced into the room past her, oblivious to the tension that wafted off his mother and settled between the two siblings.

They stared at each other wide-eyed for a few more seconds before Julie finally put her fist away with a huff.

She swallowed and seemingly took another tack. "Can you look after Levi for a couple of hours?"

Ethan had barely opened his mouth to reply before Julie passed over the backpack that had been dangling from her other hand—the one that wasn't still halfway raised for another knock. Ethan reached out to take it, more out of reflex than anything else.

He shifted around until he could see his nephew. Levi stood in the lounge room, one arm resting on the back of the couch as his head craned around to look up the staircase. Ethan couldn't help but follow his gaze up the stairs too. Was Elle in his room?

"I'm sorry Julie, this isn't really the best time—" Ethan began, backpack still held out awkwardly in front of him.

Julie put her hands up as she backed away. "It's just for a few hours. I had to pick him up from school early—he got into a fight." The last was said with a frown in Levi's direction. He was no longer looking up the stairs and instead had taken a seat on the bottom step.

He glanced up briefly at his mother before turning his head to face Ethan. "It wasn't my fault."

"That's beside the point," Julie snapped, cutting Ethan off before he had a chance to respond beyond raising an eyebrow at his nephew.

"But we will definitely be talking about that later!" Her words were accompanied by a stern motherly finger pointed at her son before she abruptly turned her attention back to Ethan.

"I've missed too much work lately. I need to get back to the office." She had half turned away to head back to the car when she seemed to register from Ethan's sputtering that he hadn't actually agreed.

"Ah..." She looked up sheepishly. "Sorry, but my boss has a deadline on a case, which means *I've* got a deadline."

Ethan took a deep breath, pushing his irritation down. "Okay, Julie, I can do it this time."

He looked over his shoulder at Levi. He still sat on the bottom step, but now his back pressed up against the wall so he could see more easily up the staircase.

Julie reached out and placed her hand over her brother's. The one still awkwardly holding her son's backpack.

"Thank you, Ethan. I owe you." Ethan huffed as she hurried out the door. "And I mean it this time!" she called over her shoulder as she aimed her keys at her car.

Ethan heard the beep, followed by the loud slam of the car door and the engine revving, all within seconds of each other. The driveway was empty before he even shut the front door.

"It's not work that she's so stressed about, you know."

Ethan jumped as he looked down to see Levi standing at his shoulder now. Well, not quite his shoulder. He reached more of a mid-chest height. Ethan had no idea if that meant he was tall for his age or short. He hadn't spent much time around kids since he was one himself. Which was somewhat ironic considering pediatrics was at the top of his shortlist of possible specialities.

"You scared me!" he exclaimed. Levi gave him a strange look and shrugged it off. "Is there someone else here?" he asked, his small brow furrowing.

"No..." Ethan replied, heartbeat quickening, and not from Levi sneaking up on him this time.

He looked at the staircase. A slight breeze caused the lightest hairs on his arms to stand up. He stepped back and closed the front door. He avoided looking at the stairs again, but goosebumps covered his arms now.

His nephew's expression didn't change, but Ethan felt he was being inspected. At least until, in typical ten-year-old fashion, his nephew shrugged it off and focused on more important concerns.

"I'm hungry," he complained.

Ethan huffed out a laugh and ushered Levi into the kitchen. He dumped the backpack unceremoniously onto the table.

"I don't have much," Ethan warned as he rummaged in the fridge. Two guys in a share house didn't exactly keep a stocked fridge. Having located half a block of cheddar, Ethan took to the pantry. He emerged victorious with a half-empty packet of rice crackers.

Levi, busy spreading his books out over the kitchen table, said nothing in response, but he eyed his uncle's sad offering, served up on a chipped side plate, with obvious doubt.

It was nearly two o'clock, but presumably the rumble resulting in Levi's abrupt presence *here* had taken place in the schoolyard during lunchtime.

Levi picked up a cracker between thumb and forefinger and nibbled at a corner. He gave his uncle a flat look. "They're stale."

"Ah…" That shouldn't be a surprise, considering Ethan was pretty sure they were leftovers from his study group.

"Did you have lunch at school?"

Levi shook his head.

"Have you got lunch in your backpack?" Ethan asked hopefully.

He wasn't sure if Julie was a sandwich-making mom or more of the 'here's some lunch money' type, but Ethan suspected the latter.

Levi bit his lip and stared down at the notebook in his hands. That wasn't a good sign.

"How about I order pizza, then?" Ethan suggested in an overly bright voice.

He had only finished off the remains of last night's pizza dinner before starting his meditation attempts, but it was better than nothing.

"Okay," Levi replied.

That wasn't quite the enthusiastic response Ethan had been aiming for, but it was accompanied by a small smile and actual eye contact.

Half an hour later, Ethan had to admit that the pepperoni pizza with extra cheese proved considerably more satisfying than the couple of pieces of cold leftover meatlovers he'd consumed earlier.

Levi had remained subdued while they waited for the delivery, but once the melted mozzarella started to work its magic, his nephew's mood perked up.

"So, what was this fight about?" Ethan asked as he picked up another slice.

Levi paused mid-chew to shoot his uncle an unreadable glance before his attention returned to his own slice. He picked at a loose piece of pepperoni that threatened to slide off the edge.

"It was Charlie's fault."

"Charlie?" Ethan asked, confused for several seconds before he recalled the woman who dropped Levi home while he was at Julie's. The one who didn't want him coming over anymore.

"Is that your friend...ah, Beth's son?"

Levi shot him an impatient glance. "No, that's James. He's my best friend." Levi looked away, picking at another slice of pizza as he continued. "Charlie's his sister."

"Oh, so you had a fight with Charlie?" Ethan asked uneasily. He'd assumed from how Julie had spoken about it that Levi had physically fought with another kid at school.

"No," Levi said, putting his slice of pizza down without taking a bite. "I wouldn't hit a girl!"

It might be old-fashioned, but Ethan couldn't help feeling relieved that his nephew wasn't fighting with girls. Apparently chivalry wasn't dead after all.

"She wanted to play a prank on James."

"Oh, I see, and he blamed you?"

Levi nodded. He put both hands flat on the table and leaned forward towards his uncle. "He didn't believe it was her. I don't think he ever really believed me, but he never got mad before." Levi's eyes were wide and imploring.

"And Charlie, let you take the blame?" Ethan asked.

Levi bit his lip. "She thought it was funny at first, until he pushed me. Then she yelled at him, but he couldn't hear her."

The pizza roiled uneasily in Ethan's gut, and not because of the high grease content. Even so, he vowed to steer away from extra cheese next time. He put his own slice down and rubbed his fingers together, ineffectually trying to rub the greasy crumbs off.

Levi watched him carefully. He had leaned back a little, shoulders still tense. He bit his lip again as Ethan watched him in turn. It started to wobble.

"What happened next?" Ethan asked, holding off on making any assumptions, even though his gut told him exactly what was going on.

"I pushed him back," Levi said, raising his chin with a defiant glint in his eye. Ethan just nodded, prompting him to continue. "I know I shouldn't have, but he said his mother was right, that I was a liar, and he didn't want me to come over to his house anymore, either."

Ethan nodded, careful to keep his expression neutral even though he needed to grab the edge of the table to stop his hands from shaking.

"And then a teacher came?"

Levi nodded slowly. "But before that, Charlie tripped him up. She was mad too because she doesn't have any other friends anymore. She said James was trying to take me away from her."

That brought Ethan up short. "She tripped him?" he questioned before he had a chance to really think about it.

"Yeah," Levi nodded, but his mouth pulled down on one side, leaving him with a strange pout. "Well, he fell over. I don't know if she really did it." He shrugged. "She can't do anything to me. We tried. It's just James. She thinks it's because they were twins." His pout morphed into a full-on frown as he stared down at his hands, which now rested loosely on the table in front of his plate. "I mean, they *are* twins..."

Ethan swallowed as he tried very hard to keep the shock out of his expression. "When did Charlie die?"

Levi shot a quick look at him from under his eyelashes before focusing on his hands again. He'd pushed his plate with the remains of his last slice of pizza away.

"Last year, just before term ended." He shook his head, tone subdued. "But she hadn't been at school for ages. She was too sick."

Ethan nodded, then kept nodding. He hadn't given this part enough thought yet, even though he'd known it would come at some point. That his nephew would need guidance.

"How long have you been seeing her spirit?" he asked, in part to buy time to try to come up with some appropriate advice for an eight-year-old medium.

"Since the first day James came back to school. She's always with him, but I didn't know she was a ghost at first."

Ethan felt out of his depth. He'd caught glimpses while he was out and about as well. Things, people, seen out of the corner of his eye. He'd never tried to focus on them, too worried they'd latch onto him if he showed any interest. He knew not all spirits were bound to a place like Elle, but that only begged the question—why was she bound to this house? Especially when she had her own family she could be trying to connect with.

"Was James with Charlie when she died?"

Levi looked up, wide eyes confused. "I don't know. She died in hospital."

"Is she the first one you've seen?"

"I think so... I mean, no." Levi shook his head as Ethan watched his facial expression go through several changes until he finally settled on one response. "I'm not sure."

Ethan nodded. "It gets easier to tell," he said, then hesitated before adding, "and easier to ignore them if that's what you want to do."

"I don't want to ignore Charlie!" Levi protested, eyebrows shooting up. "She's my friend too!" He frowned. "I don't want her to be alone."

Ethan's smile was sad. He thought of Elle, of Dean's worry that he would move out. There was no way he could do that to her. Not now.

A sudden knock on the door caused Levi to jump out of his chair and spin around like he just got caught with his hand in the cookie jar.

"Mom never lets me talk about it," Levi stated, turning away from the door and back to his uncle. "She's not like you."

"Most people aren't," Ethan said as he stood. He hadn't expected Julie to finished work so early. He reached into his pocket to check his phone for the time but came up empty. His head turned in the direction of the stairs. He must have left his phone upstairs on the bedside table when Julie tried to beat his door down earlier.

As another knock sounded, he pulled his gaze away from the stairs. Just a normal knock this time, a little quiet, if anything. He probably wouldn't have heard it from upstairs.

Ethan opened the door, surprised to see a nervous Amelia instead of his older sister. Her weak attempt at a smile slipped off her face as he stared at her in surprise.

"Ethan, sorry for dropping by like this. I tried calling, but it rang out, then I noticed your car in the drive just now on my way to class, and I just wanted to say sorry for the other day in the bar. And for Adam."

Ethan blinked as the long-winded explanation wound down. Thank god, he almost felt like *he* needed to take a breath. Amelia's nerves were clear enough, but something more was going on. She was anxious, and he couldn't help noticing how her mouth turned down as she said her finance's name.

"Sorry, my phone must still be on silent," Ethan replied as he realized he'd never switched it back after Julie interrupted his failed meditation session.

"Do you want to come in? I can make you a cup of tea or coffee? I have some cheese..." Ethan added the last and immediately regretted it as he recalled Levi wrinkling his nose up at the stale crackers.

"Oh, that's okay. I can't stay long," Amelia replied, eyebrows rising as she gazed over Ethan's shoulder.

For a second, his stomach lurched, wondering if Elle was behind him. A slight cool breeze brushed the back of his neck as it drifted down the stairs, but when he turned, he saw only Levi leaning against the archway to the kitchen.

"Hi." Levi gave Amelia a small wave.

Amelia visibly relaxed as she smiled and waved back to Levi with her own 'hi'.

"Ah, Levi, why don't you finish the pizza and start on your homework or something, Amelia and I just need a few minutes."

Levi shrugged in typical kid fashion, although Ethan didn't miss the quick glance he shot up the stairs before heading back to the kitchen table.

Had he felt the breeze, too? Or something more?

Amelia turned back to Ethan, her smile still warm. He blushed. "My nephew," he said simply in explanation as he waved his hand behind him.

"Shouldn't he be at school?" she asked.

Ethan huffed out a laugh, shaking his head. "Long story," he explained when he caught the disapproving frown on Amelia's face.

She nodded slowly, following Ethan as he beckoned her over to the couch. She hesitated, clearly unsure whether she wanted to commit to staying long enough to sit down. Ethan knew he needed to finish his conversation with Levi, but Amelia was here for a reason, and Adam's rudeness was only the tip of the iceberg. There was still so much that lay unsaid between them.

"So...the other day—" Amelia started.

Ethan cleared his throat, fighting off his blush. "It's okay, really. I know it's a weird thing, and I don't blame you if you don't believe me. Or if Adam doesn't..."

The last bit was harder to get out, although he didn't feel he knew Amelia well enough to tell her what he really thought of Adam or his behavior. But if Amelia didn't believe him at least a little, surely she wouldn't be here now? If she only wanted to apologize, she could have left a voicemail on his phone or sent a text.

"Still it was—" Amelia frowned, pulling a face and changed tack as she finally took a seat in the battered old armchair adjacent to the couch where Ethan now perched. "I wanted to talk to you about Elle, but I should have known it wasn't a good time. Adam gets so jealous sometimes, and he shuts down or gets mad if anyone mentions Elle these days."

Ethan thought back to the coroners report. He wasn't good at this kind of thing, trying to be tactful. He didn't know how to ask what he really wanted to know. It didn't help that he wasn't sure exactly what that was beyond the obvious—how Elle fell down the stairs in the first place.

"She...was already dead when you found her, right?" He watched her face intently for any reaction, so he immediately noticed the tears spring to her eyes.

She blinked them back before answering.

"Yes, for a couple of hours." She swallowed several times before she could continue. "I don't remember everything. It feels like so long ago now, and I was..." She frowned, her eyes drifting towards the staircase before bouncing back to his own as if repelled. She couldn't hold his gaze for long, though, and dropped her eyes to her hands clasped on her lap.

Ethan thought he understood. They'd been out together that night, but Elle had come home alone well before Amelia. How much more had Amelia drunk before she got home that morning?

"I remember the moment I saw her. It was dark, but I knew something was wrong. I didn't realize until I saw it, but I could smell the blood." Her lips pursed. "As soon as I found the light switch and saw her lying there, I could tell right away she was dead."

"I guess, being a nurse..." Ethan started, but Amelia interrupted, shaking her head.

"No, it didn't take a degree to work that out. There was so much blood, but head wounds are like that. It doesn't mean as much as you think. But she was so still, and...her neck was broken."

It was obvious from the way Amelia's head kept twitching that she was having trouble stopping herself from looking at the stairs.

"Her body lay on the floor, but her head was on the bottom step, almost like she was resting it there, but the angle was so wrong, although at least her eyes were closed." Amelia closed her own eyes as she continued to speak. "It was surreal. Shock does funny things to a person. Even though her eyes were closed, and I *knew* she was gone, it felt like she was staring at me."

Ethan's mind whirled. The breeze tickled the back of his shoulders again, but he couldn't afford to take his eyes off

Amelia to check if Elle was there. He wished he hadn't sat with his back to the staircase.

They spoke in quiet voices, leaning in towards each other. It was the type of subject that lent itself to hushed tones and quiet confessions, but they were also both conscious of the eight-year-old boy in the next room. A sound from the kitchen brought them back to themselves. Was that Levi laughing?

Amelia cleared her throat. "I guess this isn't the best time to be talking about this," she said, brushing imaginary lint off her lap as if she was about to stand.

Ethan reached a hand out to forestall her. "Wait, you're right," he said, glancing over his shoulder to the kitchen as he could just make out Levi's high-pitched voice.

He swallowed nervously. Was there one voice, or too? He turned back to Amelia. An air of impatience settled around her now, one he recognized from their earlier encounters. Oh, dear.

"I just need to know one thing," he said as he held his index finger up in front of his face. They both looked at the finger as if unsure what it was doing there. He flushed, putting his hand down before continuing. "Did she die straight away?"

The coroners report was inconclusive, but as a nurse, she might have been privy to information that didn't make it into the report.

Amelia shook her head slowly, but her air of uncertainty was unmistakable. "They didn't think so from the swelling of her brain, although they thought it likely she was unconscious, especially with the broken neck."

She sighed. "Even if I'd come home earlier, it probably wouldn't have made a difference. They deemed it an unsurvivable head injury. They might have been able to keep her alive for a while on machines, but it's unlikely..." She didn't finish, but she didn't need to. Some head injuries people never woke up from.

"It sounds terrible, but part of me was relieved that it didn't come to that. It would have been horrible to have to make that decision if..." Her hands, which were loosely spread in her lap, clasped each other until Ethan saw her knuckles turning white.

Amelia stood but didn't immediately make her way to the door. She fidgeted with the shoulder strap of her leather satchel as she watched Ethan.

"They told me there would have been no hope so many times, and I know it was true, but I still blamed myself for so long for not being here. Maybe it never would have happened if I was." She looked away, tension radiating from her entire body.

"I know it wasn't my fault, but...maybe you could tell her..." She gave a self-deprecating laugh as Ethan stood hastily. "Tell her I'm sorry I wasn't here. Just in case she really is still here. Lord knows I said it enough times after it happened, hoping she could hear me somehow." She took a deep breath and looked Ethan in the eye. "And tell her I'm sorry I wasn't a better friend. I didn't understand what she was going through." She turned her head away with a sigh. "I guess I still don't."

Ethan couldn't stop himself from looking over his shoulder this time as the sounds of laughter drifted in from the kitchen. Two distinctly different laughs. His stomach churned as he turned back to Amelia.

"Is she..." Amelia asked. Her face showed her trepidation, but she was unable to finish speaking the words as she stared at Ethan's uneasy face with wide eyes before her gaze drifted past him to search the space behind him.

Ethan understood. Sometimes saying the words made it too real. She shook her head before he could open his mouth to answer. "It doesn't matter."

"She doesn't blame you. For anything." Ethan was torn. He knew Elle wasn't listening to their conversation as Amelia seemed to assume. No, he was pretty sure she was having her own with Levi in the kitchen.

He didn't know why he was surprised. Two mediums in the house, plus Amelia showing up, added up to a lot of energy to draw her out. He wanted to ask Amelia about Adam being at the house that night, but he *needed* to get back to the kitchen.

He took a step towards the front door. "Ah... I should probably check on Levi," he said as he noticed Amelia also looking towards the kitchen with a slight frown on her face.

Ethan winced a little. As far as she knew, the kid was in there giggling to himself.

Amelia nodded, hitching the strap of her bag again as she made for the door, only for yet another knock to stall her, causing everyone to go silent.

"Are you expecting anyone?" Amelia asked with a worried glance at the door. She fetched her phone out of her bag and unlocked the screen in one quick movement.

Ethan frowned at her reaction. The stress coming off her now was palpable, but she was leaving. Why would she be concerned about them being interrupted?

"My sister," Ethan responded as he stepped to the door.

At least he thought it was Julie. It hadn't even been two hours, but it made sense she'd try to finish work early to deal with her wayward son and his playground incident. Hopefully, she'd calmed down a bit more. She wasn't pounding on the door this time. That boded well for Levi.

Ethan wasn't facing Amelia anymore, but he still caught her relieved sigh when he opened the door and greeted his sister.

Julie smiled at him. That was a good sign. He took a step back to let her enter, holding the door out wider for Amelia as she stepped forward.

"Oh, you must be Ethan's sister," she said warmly, holding her hand out in greeting. "You have a lovely son. You must be so proud."

She smiled widely as Julie took her hand. His sister flushed slightly, taken off guard as she shook Amelia's hand and made the appropriate polite responses.

Amelia looked Ethan in the eye as if trying to impart some meaning that was lost on him. He blinked helplessly. She smiled again, but unlike the business-like one she'd directed at his sister, this smile seemed genuine. His own lips curved in response.

Amelia nodded. "I'll see you in class next week," she said over her shoulder as she took her leave.

Ethan called out his goodbyes as she hurried down the driveway. He stepped back as he swung the door shut and came face to face with Julie, eyebrows raised and a questioning tilt to her mouth. Ethan had no idea what his face looked like at that moment, but it only took Julie two seconds before she broke down in laughter.

"Is that the girl who has you so distracted? I wouldn't have thought she was your type."

Ethan frowned at the repetition of Dean's earlier comments. Was it that hard to believe a woman like Amelia could actually like him?

His lips thinned. "You mean you don't think I would be her type."

"No, not at all!" Julie's face softened as she laughed fondly at her little brother. "She would be lucky to have you."

Ethan couldn't help the faint blush that rose to his cheeks.

"He doesn't like Amelia," Levi interrupted, coming from the kitchen to stand next to his mother. "He likes Elle."

Ethan's cheeks flamed, and he couldn't help scanning the room for Elle before it hit him just how revealing his nephew's revelation was.

Ethan stared at Levi, who watched him with a smug little smile that, if Ethan wasn't mistaken, contained a challenge. Ethan swallowed hard. Well, that took care of the blush. Ethan's sudden light-headedness left him certain the blood had drained straight out of his face. His mind was so chaotic that he almost missed Julie's delighted exclamation.

"And who's Elle? A girl from school?"

Ethan sputtered. "For god's sake Julie, I'm studying medicine at university. This isn't high school!"

Julie only giggled in response. Ethan's eyes widened. His sister did not giggle. At least not since *she* was in high school.

"So this is more than a crush, then!" It wasn't so much a question as a pronouncement, which, unfortunately, was far more characteristic of the Julie he knew (and loved). He really hoped the blush wasn't coming back.

"Elle is a friend," he stated, perhaps a touch more firmly than warranted. "And that's all she'll ever be. All she can be," he finished on a quieter note that caused Julie's smile to slip. Ethan almost felt guilty. His big sister only wanted him to have someone special, even if she touched on more nerves than he knew he had while trying to help.

"And Amelia is engaged," he added for good measure.

As Julie attempted to formulate a response, Ethan looked down at his nephew again, who seemed to have lost interest despite his cheeky comments setting his mother off. He had half turned away. Ethan took a step closer so he could follow Levi's line of sight into the kitchen.

Elle was definately back. Ethan's eyebrows shot up towards his hairline as she gave a little wave.

Levi waved back.

Chapter 16

What a cute kid. Well, okay, perhaps he was a little weird. He could see ghosts, after all. Elle wondered if Ethan had been like Levi as a child.

"I don't understand why you're so surprised. He is your nephew. Clearly, this thing," Elle waved her hands in a vague all encompassing gesture at Ethan, "runs in the family."

He nodded in an absent fashion, but the poleaxed expression on his face remained even when the bright red leather made an unfortunate noise as he slumped further into the couch.

"Like your grandfather, right?" Elle continued.

Ethan straightened a little at that and dragged his eyes away from the ceiling to meet Elle's. He stared unblinking at her for several seconds before responding with a slow nod.

"You must have known—" her brow furrowed as she sat down in the armchair facing Ethan, "—you definitely suspected. I heard you talking about it in the kitchen."

Ethan continued to stare, but the blankness was gradually replaced by intensity as his eyes widened and then narrowed. It gave her the creeps.

"Elle?" Ethan leaned forward, one hand grasping his knee and voice strangely quiet. "You're sitting in my chair."

Elle's brows drew together, and her mouth opened and closed. She stared back at him for several seconds before looking down at the heavy leather recliner that had been Ethan's main addition to the lounge room. Her breath caught and held as she reached out and lightly brushed the armrest with her fingertips. In her preoccupation with Ethan and Levi, she had bypassed Amelia's solid old armchair without a thought.

"Oh my god," she whispered, eyebrows shooting upwards.

Before she knew what she was doing, she had stood and sat back down again. Twice. She didn't fall through the chair, but what did it mean? Had she become strong enough to interact with the world around her, even the parts that had changed since she died?

She grinned at Ethan. A euphoric glint shining in her eyes. She stood again. Ethan swallowed as she stepped towards him. His breath drew in sharply when she stopped directly in front of him.

His hand clutched at the armrest now, fingers white from the strain. Elle stared at them in fascination before raising her own hand in front of her face. She had *felt* the chair beneath her fingers. It wasn't the same as she remembered feeling things while she was alive, but it was still something. Something more than she had before.

She avoided Ethan's wide-eyed gaze and focused solely on his hand. The armrest was a little worn, and gray flecks showed through the red leather in several places, unnoticeable until she was this close.

Hand hovering above Ethan's, she hesitated.

"Elle..." It was barely a breath.

She swallowed but still couldn't bring herself to look at his face. Her hand inched towards his, index finger outstretched further than the others. Ethan turned his hand over, palm up. Her eyes shot to his at the movement, she couldn't help it.

His Adam's apple bobbed as he swallowed hard. He was the one to pull his gaze away this time and focus on his hand. Elle found it easier to keep her eyes on his now that he wasn't watching her face. She reached down to touch his open palm.

Ethan shivered and squeezed his eyes shut tightly.

Elle couldn't feel anything.

Reluctantly, she lowered her gaze until she could see her hand. Or rather *their* hands. Fingers entwined, but not in the way two living humans would hold hands. She wasn't entirely sure if she felt disappointed or relieved. What would it mean if she could actually touch Ethan?

She shifted her fingers around until they looked more natural. Well, except for the fact that her fingertips were disappearing into the red leather.

Ethan drew in another breath. It was slow but had a raw, almost ragged edge. She watched his face. Deep lines creased his forehead that she'd never noticed before. He kept his eyes closed. She moved her fingers again, just a little. Fascinated, she watched his mouth tighten and a quick breath huff out his nose.

Slowly, she drew her hand back. Ethan finally opened his eyes. They were dark as he stared up at her, mouth slightly open, but whether to speak or in surprise, she couldn't tell. Either way, he seemed lost for words as he closed his mouth, but his eyes said it all. She couldn't touch Ethan, but *he* could feel her...somehow.

Elle didn't want to turn away from those eyes, but she needed to sit down before her ghostly legs gave out on her. She backed up until she hit the armchair and sunk into the cushioned seat. It was far more comfortable than it looked, and that was a hell of a lot more comfortable than the god dammed bottom step.

Ethan's eyes softened as she retreated back to his chair and a small smile quirked up one corner of his mouth. Elle couldn't help the smile that curved her own lips in response, and before she knew it, they were both laughing. Not a snickering laugh because someone burnt their toast or made up their own dance moves to Lady Gaga. Real, genuine laughter. The kind that two people shared, the kind that created bonds. It felt good. It felt real.

As their hilarity gradually died down, Ethan started shaking his head. A few last giggles escaped Elle while he caught his breath.

"I really need to do more research," he said.

Elle couldn't stop another laugh from escaping. Talk about the understatement of the year.

"What I don't understand," Ethan began, "is what happened last night in the bedroom." He wiped his eyes, tears from their laughter moistening them.

Elle stilled, her gaze drifting past Ethan's face as her eyes lost their focus.

"You said you couldn't hear...but you weren't talking to me, were you?" He looked away, pulling his lip between his teeth.

Elle nodded once. Her fingers twitched, and she stared down at them, recalling the lack of sensation when she 'touched' Ethan.

"It's hard to explain," she said with a shake of her head.

The truth was she wasn't sure what had happened herself, but that wasn't the only reason for her hesitancy. It had been hard enough for Ethan to accept her presence. She was worried about scaring him off if he thought something *else* was in the house. Not that it was *in* the house, not like she was. At least, she didn't think so.

"I could still hear you. It was just like you were far away. Other sounds that were louder." She looked at Ethan now. "Other sounds that were distracting."

"What kind of...sounds?" Ethan asked.

Elle forced herself to hold his gaze as she registered the unspoken fear in his eyes.

"My name...maybe."

"Maybe?" Ethan asked, voice rising along with his eyebrows.

Elle shrugged, but that only caused Ethan's brow to draw down, eyebrows nearly meeting above his nose, and she knew she had to give him more.

"Not my name exactly. It wasn't that clear." She looked away, unable to face the fear she could sense growing in his eyes. "But something...calling to me."

"Calling you from where?" Ethan asked faintly. "The other side?"

"I don't know," Elle replied, but what she really meant was, 'I think so,' and she was pretty sure Ethan could tell.

"Has this happened before?"

Elle nodded. "Yes, although I wasn't always sure at the time. Since you moved in, it's been stronger, more like a pressure, but even before, it felt as if sometimes I was being watched."

"Do you see anything?" Ethan asked, an urgent tone creeping into his voice. "A light?"

That brought Elle up short. She straightened in the chair and met Ethan's gaze with a wide-eyed one of her own.

"There has *never* been a light." She shook her head for emphasis. Tears sprang to her eyes, or at least they felt like tears to her. She wondered if Ethan could see them or whether she was just remembering how it felt to be on the verge of tears.

"What about the handprint on the window when I passed out? That was this *other* presence, wasn't it?"

Elle bit her lip. "Yes," she whispered. "But it feels different now."

"Different, how?" Ethan asked, one hand coming up to rub at his eyes.

He leaned toward her on the couch now. She hadn't even noticed how close he'd come. His eyes felt like they were trying to bore into her own. She struggled to find the words.

"Less forceful. It doesn't feel like it's trying to come between us anymore, more like it's taking advantage of whatever it is between us to..." She bit her lip again. She didn't know how to say the next part without scaring him, but Ethan was already ahead of her.

"To come through?" he asked. He perched on the edge of the couch now, elbows digging into his knees as he stared intently at her. "It's pulling energy from me, from both of us probably, to try to come through from...where? The other side?" His voice went up too high at the end, even for a question.

She leaned forwards and reached out, intending to touch his knee, giving in to the instinct to comfort him. He looked down as she hesitated and started to withdraw her hand, but a thought made her stop. He had been able to feel something when she touched him before. She reached forward the couple more inches needed to rest her fingers lightly on his knee.

She wanted to watch his face, but she didn't want to risk putting her hand through him, so she kept her eyes focused as she shifted to the very edge of her chair and held her hand just above his knee. She heard him release a slow breath as his shoulders relaxed, and she smiled as she sat back.

She folded her hands in her lap and raised her eyes to his face once more. That look was back, not the scared one. No, the look almost of wonder. Her imaginary heart flipped in her chest. She wasn't sure anyone had ever looked at her like that while she was alive, but she wished they had.

"It feels like everything's getting closer now, and maybe this presence is something...or *someone*...from the other side. It doesn't scare me anymore, but...I'm not ready to go yet."

Ethan nodded slowly. He released another long steady breath, but a stiffness remained in the way he held his shoulders.

"Perhaps I'm not the only one who is trying to help you move on."

***

Intense orange light captured Ethan's attention as he reached the top of the staircase a few hours later. He blinked as he paused to watch the sunset. The small balcony off the upstairs landing boasted the best view in the house.

He'd watched the changing colors of the sunset from his bedroom window more than once since moving in, but from here, you could see it set over the ocean. The beach wasn't close, but the house was on the high side of the street, and the whole area sat well above sea level. If the house had actually been in decent condition, it would have been well out of his price range.

Elle had disappeared not long after their disturbing conversation downstairs. Not that she seemed to find it as unsettling as Ethan. At least he didn't believe that was why she vanished this time. He was pretty sure she drifted off when his rumbling stomach prompted him to finish the last of his and Levi's lunch. Apparently, cold pizza wasn't appealing to a ghost.

After finishing his third lot of pizza for the day, he grabbed a beer and headed upstairs to study. Perhaps not the best study beverage, but between Levi, Amelia *and* Elle's revelations, he definitely needed a drink.

He took a swig now as he reached out to flip the lock on the sliding door and cautiously ventured out onto the balcony. He tested his weight with one foot and then the other. The wooden boards looked sturdy enough despite the paint peeling away in large patches. No, the warped railing was the real worry.

"You should be careful out there. That railing is as rickety as it looks." Elle's voice drifted out from the still-open door.

He spun around to see her hovering right at the edge, unable to pass the threshold. While her voice had been calm, the frustration showed clearly on her face as she gazed past him to the horizon. The sun was almost touching the water now.

Ethan bit his lip, a reckless impulse welling inside him. The balcony was a part of the house, after all. He stretched his hand out to Elle but not to beckon her forward. His fingers closed around hers.

It looked right, like they were holding hands, but it felt like he had a hold of something far more insubstantial than the woman he could see standing before him. Swallowing his doubts, he forced himself to focus on Elle's hand. His fingers closed more surely around hers, and he gently tugged her forward.

She stared at him now, the sunset forgotten by them both.

"Come on," he whispered with another tug. His heart tripped as he drank in the expression of wonder on her face.

She drew in a deep breath and took one hesitant step onto the balcony, then another, until she stood right next to him. The setting rays picked out highlights in her hair, but her eyes were bright from more than the reflected light.

Suddenly the air was filled with her laughter. She pulled her hand away from Ethan's as both of hers shot up to cover her mouth and rapidly widening grin. Her eyes shone almost as brightly as the sun.

Ethan's breath came shallow but fast. The sunset no longer captivated him, not with Elle here—outside—and more radiant by the second, like her skin absorbed the light of the sun and reflected it back to him. He took a step back to get a better look at her face. The breeze blew his hair into his eyes, but he brushed it away. Elle's hair didn't move at all, and her dress lay in perfectly still folds against her body.

She reached out to take his hand again and pulled him forwards.

"Can you feel my heartbeat?" she asked, tone excited but hushed at the same time.

She placed his palm over her chest just above the low neckline of her dress. He swallowed hard, his eyes could see her chest rise and fall with each breath, but he couldn't feel the movement. He spread his fingers out carefully, thumb brushing her collarbone. Her skin was smooth and cool, but he couldn't help the disconcerting feeling that if he pressed too hard, his hand would go straight through her. He bit his lip and shook his head.

Her face fell, but only for a moment. She studied him for a few seconds, a slight smile tilting one corner of her mouth before she turned to the setting sun.

"It's enough." She nodded her head.

Ethan's hand fell away to hang by his side. His fingers tingled, and he rubbed them with his other hand.

Elle turned back, her expression calm once more until she caught sight of his face. Her mouth drew down into a frown.

"Ethan? Are you all right?"

He blinked. Why was it still so bright when he wasn't looking at the sun anymore? He shook his head. The pain between his eyes was back. He reached up to pinch the bridge of his nose.

Elle stepped closer to him, hand outstretched. "Ethan?"

The light was so bright now, but he didn't think it came from Elle. It felt more like it burst from behind his eyes. He needed to get back inside. He started towards the door, but his foot caught on an uneven board, sending him stumbling into the railing.

"Ah!" he yelled as it broke away under his hands. He hovered for a tense moment, off balance as he stared over the edge of the balcony before he felt something grasp him around his middle and pull him back. He turned to find Elle right in front of him, arms encircling his waist. Her face, no longer bright, but stark with worry.

"You need to go inside—now!" she urged, pulling and then pushing him as he grappled with shaky hands to slide the door open. His feet tingled now too.

A sudden gust of wind made the balcony groan, and another section of railing fell away as Ethan finally slid the door open. He hurried through and turned to reach for Elle's hand only to grasp air as her eyes widened, and she, and the section of balcony she stood on, both disappeared. A short high-pitched scream rang in his ears for a brief instant, and then there was only the groaning of wood in the wind.

"Elle!" he screamed, but she was already gone.

The shock paralyzed him for several long moments before he steadied himself enough to peer over the edge of what remained of the balcony. Broken wood littered the garden bed in front of the house, but there was no sign of Elle. He leaned out as far as he dared.

Darkness was descending quickly now, the sun having dropped below the horizon, but the red dress should have stood out amongst the wreckage and thorny rose bushes. His mind whirled. He paced up and down the landing, hands in his hair. His head was clearing, but the numbness faded slower. Elle couldn't leave the house, but what did that mean now?

He hurried to the stairs and dashed down them in such a panic he nearly couldn't bring himself to a stop when he saw her. She turned her head slowly to look up at him. Her eyes were still wide, but a laugh escaped, much like the one she'd given when she first stepped out onto the balcony.

Ethan froze, staring blankly at her as she sat there on the bottom step. He opened and closed his mouth wordlessly, and then he did it again. That elicited another round of laughter from Elle. She stood and climbed the couple of steps between them until she came to a stop just below him.

"Don't look so worried, Ethan. A girl can only die once."

She gazed down at her feet and wiggled her bare toes. "I don't think I even hit the ground!"

He stared at her for a few more tense seconds as it finally sank in. Before he knew it, they had both doubled over in hysterics.

Thank god Dean wasn't home yet.

Natalie Pearce

Chapter 17

Ethan couldn't be sure, but he had a strong suspicion that Amelia was avoiding him the following week.

She skipped Neurology on Monday morning, then canceled the study group she was due to host on Wednesday with a vague message about a family emergency. By Friday, he was worried.

Avoiding him was one thing. He could understand her feeling awkward after their last encounter, but neglecting her studies in order to do so seemed out of character. Amelia was the dedicated type.

Ethan knew nothing about her family (except for her unfortunate engagement), but he sent her a quick message wishing them well and offering his notes when she returned to class. When he received no response, he decided to get creative.

Amelia didn't owe him any explanation about her whereabouts, but somewhere along the way, he thought they had started to become friends, and they were few and far apart in Ethan's experience. His nagging doubts about Elle's death also wouldn't let him leave it alone.

It was Elle who came up with the idea in the end after Ethan returned home the following Monday only to report that Amelia missed another Neurology lecture. They discussed several carefully worded versions before settling on a very simple message:

I hope you're ok. Elle wants to talk to you.

"I'm not sure if I'm comfortable with this," Ethan said as he put the phone down on the coffee table. He folded his arms across his chest and leaned back into the couch as if distancing himself from the act of sending the message. "Isn't it a tad manipulative?"

Elle huffed. "Why? It's true enough. I do wish I could talk to her. And I know exactly what I would say—don't marry Adam."

Ethan squirmed. "I can't tell her that! What if she doesn't think it's really coming from you?"

"So what if she doesn't? I know you've been thinking the same thing." She shifted slightly in Ethan's armchair, which had fast become her favorite spot in the house. Her eyes unfocused as they drifted past his shoulder and to the staircase behind him.

Ethan cleared his throat. "So does that mean you think he was here when you came home the night you died?" He kept his voice pitched low and his words careful as he drifted into dangerous territory.

Her brow furrowed, but her eyes didn't return to him. She worked her mouth for a few seconds, but her only response was a shrug.

Ethan bit his lip, gaze dropping to the coffee table. "Well, first, we need to wait and see if she replies."

Elle appeared to gradually came back to herself, blinking at the phone resting on the table between them. She leaned forward as if to catch a glimpse of the screen, even though the phone remained silent.

Ethan, relieved the talk of her death hadn't sent her back to wherever she went when he couldn't see her, reached down and scooped the phone up. He held it in one hand, which he rested on his thigh in an effort to stop his leg from jiggling up and down.

Elle watched with her head tilted at a slight angle.

"I don't think I've even thanked you." She bit her lip as Ethan raised his head, surprise evident on his face. "You can't possibly understand what it means to me after all this time to feel like a real person again. Even for a few moments."

Ethan stared at her as he searched for a response. Her earnest expression made his heart ache, but he honestly had no idea what to say.

Elle was right. He didn't know what she'd been through, and he dearly hoped he never would. He remembered her face when she told him there had been no light. The pain in her eyes touched him in a way he couldn't explain, and he promised himself that when his time came, he would be on the lookout for any sign—even the slightest glow or ray of light.

The prospect of being left behind like Elle was disconcerting. His mind drifted to Levi's little ghost friend and how confused she must be. How many more were out there, like Elle and Charlie, stuck on the wrong side of death for reasons they couldn't understand?

Ethan blinked. Elle was still talking. He'd been the one tuning out this time, so distracted by his revelations that tears stung his eyes.

"It's been amazing," Elle continued, "talking to you, being with you. Don't get me wrong, I'm so grateful you moved in," she shifted closer, although they sat too far away to reach out and touch without standing, "but now it feels like I'm in a holding pattern, poised between the living world and whatever comes next. Like I'm waiting for the penny to drop. I *want* to remember. I *want* to know what happened to me." She paused to take a deep breath before finishing in a whisper. "So I can move on."

The now familiar chill ran up Ethan's spine as those last few words seemed to hang in the air. Elle felt it too, or whatever the equivalent was for her. He could tell from the way she straightened, her gaze drawn to the staircase again but without the vagueness of before.

A sharp bell tone rang out. Ethan started and nearly dropped the phone he still held loosely on his leg. He fumbled to unlock the screen before reading out Amelia's simple and direct reply.

I'm on my way over now.

***

Talk about awkward.

Ethan braced himself on the couch against the silence that hung between him and Amelia. She stared at him from the old armchair, which Elle had helpfully informed him once belonged to her former housemate.

Amelia had made some vague apologies for being out of touch when she arrived, and thanked him for his concern in a perfunctory manner that made it clear further explanation would not be forthcoming. Which was fair enough. A family emergency (or anything else) that happened in Amelia's life was none of his business.

"Is she here?"

Ethan automatically looked at Elle, who perched on the edge of Ethan's armchair.

His gaze returned to Amelia only to find her eyes fixed on the empty (to her) chair. She swallowed visibly.

"I'm still not sure about any of this, you know."

Lips pursed as her gaze returned to him. Her nostrils flared, causing Ethan's heartbeat to kick up a notch.

"I don't know what you'd have to gain from any of this, but..." she trailed off, her face screwing up slightly as she struggled to express a skepticism that Ethan thought she didn't really feel. At least not anymore.

He wasn't sure why, but as Amelia's eyes drifted back to the chair Elle sat in, he felt confident that whatever she tried to tell herself (or whatever Adam had told her), she did believe.

"Tell her I'm sorry about her heels," Elle said in a quiet voice that shook a little on the last word.

"Ah..." he started. Amelia's eyes shot across to him, blinking rapidly as if it was difficult to focus on him. He wished he and Elle had made a proper plan of attack here. This was too important to 'wing it'. Maybe a few episodes of *Ghost Whisperer* would have helped.

"She's sorry about your shoes."

Elle huffed as Amelia continued to blink at him, slower now but somewhat blankly.

"Not *shoes*, her Jimmy Choo stiletto pumps. She saved up for them for ages." Elle corrected.

"The Jimmy Choo...um...pumps? She says they were expensive."

Amelia didn't make a sound, but her eyes bored into his in a way that made him feel like there was a physical pressure behind them. It was an effort to maintain eye contact. There was no blinking now as her eyes shone with unshed tears.

"The thing is," Elle said, standing in between him and Amelia now, "I think I took them off when I got home, so I don't understand how the heel broke."

Ethan froze, eyes widening as he continued to stare into Amelia's. But he couldn't repeat Elle's words yet. If she was remembering anything from that night, he didn't dare interrupt.

Amelia's gaze finally relented, and she looked down at her lap for several seconds. Ethan took the chance to slant his eyes sideways. He didn't want to chance distracting Elle, but she wasn't looking at either him or Amelia. Her eyes were on her feet. Her bare feet.

"I had blisters. I hardly would have put them back on again to go upstairs. So why did the coroners report say I was still wearing the heels?"

Ethan's mouth dropped open. Apparently, she'd read more of the report than he'd thought. He couldn't help but tilt his head a little to look at her feet now. The bright red nail polish was metallic and caught the light.

"She's sorry they got broken, but..." Ethan faltered, unsure how to continue.

He'd read the report. He knew her left ankle had been broken, and so had the heel of the shoe on that foot. It was noted as a possible contributing factor. That the heels, combined with alcohol and fatigue, might have caused her to trip. Or they could have broken in the fall itself, although neither option made sense now.

His mind spun so fast trying to fit everything together that he almost missed the soft sob from Amelia. He swallowed hard as he looked up to see her face slowly crumple.

His heartbeat thudded double time in his chest. His instinct to comfort Amelia fought with the doubts nagging at his mind. Even if she had nothing to do with Elle's fall, she'd still stayed with Adam all these years.

A single tear ran down each side of Amelia's face. Elle stood right next to him now. He didn't look up at her, but he knew she was watching Amelia as well.

"I wouldn't have put them back on," Elle repeated. "Because I was worried about waking Adam up."

Ethan couldn't hold in his reaction to that. He shifted closer until he could look up at Elle's face. She still watched Amelia, but the earlier emotion on her face had disappeared, wiped clean and replaced by a strangely intense but dispassionate gaze. It made him uneasy.

"What's wrong?" Amelia asked with an intensity of her own. She shook her head and continued before he had a chance to answer. "I don't care about the shoes. What is she saying?"

"She said," Ethan started as he dragged his gaze away from Elle to meet Amelia's pleading eyes, "she took the heels off when she got home."

Amelia's brow furrowed. "No, that's not right. She was wearing them when..." She breathed in and out several times before she could get all the words out. "She was still wearing them when I found her."

"But Adam was here that night, wasn't he?" Ethan asked carefully.

"What?" Amelia exclaimed. "How do you know that?"

Ethan automatically looked at Elle again. Her face was completely blank. She'd drifted away a few steps, but she turned her head slowly to look at him now. He ran a shaky hand through his hair and shot Elle an apologetic glance before turning back to Amelia, who watched him with eyes that glinted with more tears. Ethan tried to keep his expression neutral as he faced her.

Amelia relented, gaze dropping to her hands as she folded them tightly in her lap. "Yes, he was here."

Ethan ducked his head until he caught her eyes again and gave a quick nod to encourage her to continue.

She took a deep breath, bracing herself as her fingers flexed repeatedly. "They argued while I finished getting ready. He knew we were going out, but he still came over." She shook her head, lips pursing. "He always does things like that, passive aggressive crap."

Ethan nodded even as he bit his lip, wondering what other crap Adam 'always' pulled. Both then and now.

"Why did he come over, then?"

"He said he wanted a quiet place to study. He had loud housemates," she added as Ethan's brow drew down in confusion.

She shook her head, a frustrated sigh escaping. "I think he was worried because he wasn't invited. Elle was my plus one." Amelia turned her head, avoiding his gaze.

Straight brown hair shielded her face from his view. "He's always been the jealous type, even of our friendship."

"It was a presentation dinner, right? You won an award?" Ethan asked, trying to sort the scant details from the coroners report and Elle's vague memories into some kind of order.

Amelia nodded. "It was the annual Nursing Awards dinner. I won Young Nurse of the Year..." Ethan watched her face as she trailed off, and his heart went out to her as he recognized that the achievement was forever tainted in her mind.

"Was Elle angry?" Ethan asked.

"Yes, although by the time we left, she was the one saying sorry to *him*." She huffed out a short, bitter laugh as she shook her head. "He has a way of turning things around. He doesn't always get worked up like he did at the bar. Most of the time, he stays calm while *you* get agitated until you end up feeling like you're the one being unreasonable. It's so frustrating!"

"That sounds like gaslighting," Ethan said quietly. He tried to keep his tone even, but he felt as though he was treading on broken glass.

Amelia's head shot up, a defiant fire in her eyes, although once she saw the carefully neutral expression on Ethan's face, the fierceness faded, and she hung her head. She tucked some loose strands of hair behind her ear as she stared at her knees.

"He can be manipulative..."

Ethan recalled Elle telling him how Amelia claimed Adam was exactly that—manipulative. It didn't sound like he'd changed much over the last four years, so why was it so hard for her to see it now?

"But he never did anything violent? I mean...was he ever violent towards Elle?" Ethan asked, careful to refer to Adam and Elle's relationship even though a large part of him wanted to ask about her own relationship with Adam.

"No, of course not!" The fire rekindled, and Ethan felt the need to look away this time.

The instinct to apologize was strong but also frustrating. He couldn't imagine Amelia being with someone who would hurt her. It was also hard to imagine Elle in that position, but she ended up at the bottom of those stairs either way.

Amelia perched uncomfortably on the edge of her chair. Ethan looked at Elle, still standing to the side and not quite looking at them, the vagueness of her expression at odds with her tense posture.

He sensed her struggling. As he well knew by now, anything touching too close to her death caused her to retreat. Considering how strong she'd become since Levi's visit, he'd been hoping that might have changed, but now he wasn't sure.

Amelia was shaking her head. Both hands gripped the armrests of her old chair as if holding on for dear life. The intensity coming off her was palpable.

"Elle was distracted all evening. I'm sure that's partly why she left after the dinner finished rather than going out on the town with the rest of us like we'd planned. It was so hard to get her out of the house back then, except for work, but she was excited about the awards. Excited for me, anyway."

Ethan frowned at that. Elle certainly wanted to get out of the house now. He couldn't imagine her being a homebody by choice. He looked at her again, but he felt uncomfortable speaking to her in front of Amelia in case she was still on the fence about whether he could really see Elle or not.

Elle stared at Amelia, her brow drawn down. Her expression was still hard to read, but what looked like confusion warred with the blankness.

Amelia lowered her voice, but the intensity only deepened with her quieter tone. "Adam told me he wasn't here when she came home. He said he left after a couple of hours studying because he didn't want to be woken up by us coming home drunk."

Ethan waited for her to continue, sensing more, that the real reason she had come over tonight was yet to be revealed. She took a shaky breath, hands clasped together as if to stop them from trembling.

Ethan felt his own fingers twitch in sympathy. He wanted to reach out to her, but he was too tense, waiting for whatever she would reveal next.

"The truth is, I don't really know if he was still here." She deflated visibly at the confession, eyes dropping again to her lap where her hands now lay limp and lifeless on her knees.

Ethan couldn't think of a response. The sound of their breathing was loud in the otherwise silent house.

Elle shifted, disappearing in a flash from his sight. He stood before he had time to think about what it would look like to Amelia. Ethan turned and surveyed the room until he found Elle standing at the bottom of the stairs. He made a small sound of surprise, but Elle paid him no mind as she stared straight up the staircase.

Amelia came to stand behind him. "Even if he was still here...there's no way he would have pushed her. He loved her." Amelia continued, but the words didn't hold the conviction Ethan thought she intended to convey.

He released a breath he wasn't conscious he'd been holding.

"How can you be so sure?" he asked without turning to look at her.

"I don't know," she whispered. Her lips pursed, and she continued more strongly. "No, it was an accident."

She walked around the couch until she could see his face and gazed into Ethan's eyes. A desperate light shone in her own, but he wasn't sure what it meant. Was it really him she needed to convince, or herself?

"I don't remember everything from that night, but I remember screaming after I found her. As soon as I saw her, I knew she was dead, but I couldn't touch her. I don't know how long I screamed for. I called out for Adam, thinking he must be upstairs in bed, but he wasn't here."

Ethan swallowed hard, his throat tight. And not because of Elle this time. Or not just because of her. He glanced back at the staircase. Elle still stood at the base, her back to him. She seemed less substantial than she'd been in weeks.

He looked back at Amelia. The misery on her face was hard to see. He cursed himself for ever thinking she could have hurt her friend and ever thinking she was cold.

"You really can see her, can't you?"

Ethan bit his lip, heart beating a mile a minute. He couldn't tell if horror or wonder made her words sound so strangled.

"What happened next? She needs to know."

"I called him right after I called the ambulance. I don't remember what I said on the phone. I don't know if that's because of shock or the alcohol." She shook her head. "He got here before the paramedics, looking like he'd rolled out of bed, wrinkled clothes and all. I'll never forget his face." She shook her head back and forth several times and had to clear her throat. "He was devastated—horrified—there's no way…"

Privately Ethan thought he might have been horrified at what he'd done, but his heart ached for Amelia, the pain spilling out had been repressed for far too long. She looked like a lost child, still shaking her head from side to side slowly, eyes unfocused.

Ethan stepped toward her but froze when she looked up, and their eyes met. Silent teardrops rolled down her face. He ached to reach out to her, but he'd never been good at comforting anyone.

The sound of a car door slamming interrupted them. Ethan caught movement through the front window and gasped at the sight of Adam marching toward the house.

He swung back around to Amelia but didn't have time to warn her before a booming knock sounded on the front door, causing them both to flinch.

A series of sharp knocks followed, each louder than the last.

"Amelia!" Adam yelled through the door after neither of them made a move to respond.

Her car sat in the driveway, there was no denying Amelia's presence, but Ethan didn't understand how Adam knew where she was in the first place. He may have spent a lot of time at the house in the past, but that was years ago. He certainly hadn't been here since well before Ethan moved in.

Amelia had her phone out, frowning at it. Ethan had heard several texts come through while they talked. It seemed clear enough now that they were from Adam, but she hadn't even checked them.

Amelia's whole body revealed her tension, and her fingers flexed around her phone until her knuckles turned white. Another shout sounded, and she let out a huff of air as she strode to the door and pulled it open.

Adam's hand was raised for another strike in a manner strangely reminiscent of his sister last week. Except for the ugly snarl on his face. Amelia was having none of it, though, cheeks flushed as she pushed her phone in front of her fiancé's nose.

"Have you been tracking me?" she accused incredulously.

Adam's still raised hand reached out to ward off the phone before he registered her angry words. His face, already red, flushed further as he snatched the phone out of her hand.

"I don't know what you're talking about! What are you even doing here? With him!" He pointed accusingly at Ethan with Amelia's phone clenched in his fist.

She drew herself up as Ethan hesitated behind her. She held her hand out, nostrils flaring. Ethan noticed a slight tremor as she turned her hand palm up, but her voice remained steady as she demanded her phone back.

Adam worked his jaw for several tense seconds, shooting a glare at Ethan for good measure before he slapped the phone into Amelia's waiting hand. She closed her fingers around it and stepped back. She crossed her arms over her chest in a defensive manner, jaw flexing as she ground her teeth.

Ethan stood slightly to Amelia's side as he watched Adam work his own jaw while he attempted to stare down his fiancé. Ethan edged a couple of steps closer to her and raised his chin. He tried to straighten his shoulders as Adam's narrow-eyed gaze shifted to him. This was one of those moments in life where Ethan wished he were taller.

"Can't you see he's only causing trouble?" Adam accused, pointing his finger at Ethan even as his gaze swung back to Amelia. "He can't talk to Elle. He's just trying to get in your pants!"

Amelia let out an irritated huff as she glared right back at her fiancé. Even so, Ethan didn't miss the sideways glance she shot him.

He opened his mouth to defend himself, utterly at a loss about what to say, when suddenly Elle appeared in his peripheral vision. He sputtered for a couple of seconds as he forced himself not to turn to her fully.

Now both Amelia and Adam stared at him.

"Is she here?" Amelia asked, almost in an undertone, as if she was trying to ask him without Adam hearing.

Ethan looked from one of them to the other. Adam's face had turned a worrying shade of red. If he continued at this rate, he would either blow his top or pass out. Ethan forced himself to look only at Amelia. He opened his mouth to respond but ended up giving her just a simple nod.

Adam shot Ethan a dark look and moved closer to Amelia, attempting to edge Ethan out. He spoke to her in an angry undertone, trying to convince her to leave.

Out of the corner of his eye, Ethan saw Elle watching him. They stared at each other for several tense moments before, with an abrupt turn, she began to climb the stairs. He somehow managed to close his mouth as he watched her disappear into the shadows at the top of the staircase. A chill breeze floated down in her wake.

Amelia and Adam's 'discussion' had started out hushed, but quickly increased in volume. Ethan tried to turn his attention to them but found himself struggling with a dissonant note, as the sounds of arguing seemed to accost him from all sides.

Adam stood directly next to Amelia now, his hand on her elbow as she stared at the ground, biting her lip. He took a step backward toward the door, trying to draw her along, but she pulled her arm free.

Ethan stepped forward, his instinct to intervene, but he found his gaze drawn back to the staircase, his eyes searching the darkness on the landing. He thought he could make out Elle's form, her back to him.

"Let me go!"

The sharp cry ringing in his ears caused Ethan to jump into action.

"Leave her alone!" He strode forward as the words left his lips, only to be confronted by two confused faces. One hostile and the other a little embarrassed.

Ethan froze. It hadn't been Amelia crying out.

He backed away, moving several steps closer to the base of the stairs before something clattered down and landed with a sharp crack. Ethan spun around, his throat constricting with dread at the thought of seeing Elle's body, even if it was insubstantial. But the stairs remained clear of ghostly bodies.

Ethan's eyes shot to the top of the staircase, where Elle's faded face stared down at him. No, not at him, slightly to his left and lower. He followed her line of sight and saw it—a single Jimmy Choo lying on the floor. With a broken heel.

He swallowed hard, his mouth suddenly dry as dust. When he spoke, it sounded like someone else's voice, even to his own ears. "Were they silver?"

"Silver? What on earth are you on about now?" Adam asked with a heavy note of contempt. "You can't possibly believe any of this!" That part was directed at Amelia, but she wasn't paying attention to Adam. She was staring at Ethan with wide frightened eyes.

"The heels?" she whispered. Ethan nodded, but he was still staring at them. They had been metallic and shiny but were quickly fading, much like the sounds of the argument at the top of the stairs. He looked up at the landing, but he could no longer see Elle. The fight still continued in a small corner of his mind, but the words grew indecipherable as the pressure in his head mounted.

He turned to Amelia as she touched his arm. He stared into her bright eyes, trying to focus on the here and now. Elle was already dead. This was the only way he could help her now. He squeezed his eyes shut as the sound of a distant scream tapered off in his head.

"Someone threw them down the stairs."

Complete silence met his words, both in the room and in his head.

"Is that how they broke?" Amelia asked in a whisper. She held herself at an unnatural angle, watching Ethan while avoiding Adam's gaze or looking at the bottom step.

Ethan nodded as he glanced to the side where the broken heel had rested, if only to his eyes, moments ago.

"They were arguing." His head rose now, gaze lifting to the staircase and up to the now empty landing.

Amelia's face underwent a tense transformation, but Ethan couldn't read anything besides pain as her expression crumpled and a gasp escaped.

A strained noise of frustration alerted Ethan before Adam moved. He swiveled his head just in time to see Adam advancing on him, fists and jaw clenched.

"Just because we had a fight doesn't mean I pushed her down the stairs!"

Ethan took an involuntary step backward, making a less than dignified sound before steeling himself as Elle drifted into view. Her presence gave him the confidence to raise his chin, push his shoulders back and fight off the flush that threatened to turn his entire face crimson.

As Elle approached Adam, his aggression eased, and a look of confusion came over his face. She circled him slowly. Ethan couldn't quite tell if her bare feet touched the ground. She came to a stop off to the side a little, but between the two men. Her blank expression fixated on her old flame.

Amelia's breath came fast and hard. Her eyes shone with unshed tears as her gaze swung between Adam and Ethan before settling on her fiancé.

"You told me you weren't here when she got home!" A single tear escaped from each eye, leaving two wet tracks down her face.

That brought Adam up short. He reeled back from his looming stance over Ethan and turned to Amelia. His hands came up, palms out in a placating gesture at odds with his harsh tone. "I wasn't here. We fought before you went out, you know that."

"I don't *know* anything!" Amelia exclaimed. Her hands came up to cover her face, and she shook her head repeatedly. She wrenched herself away as he reached out to grab her arm.

"She didn't break the heel while she was out...and if she wasn't wearing them when she fell...if they didn't break when she fell..."

Ethan's heart ached for her as she trailed off each time without voicing the obvious, if painful, deduction. Those heels were on Elle's feet when Amelia found her body. If she wasn't wearing them when they broke...

"They blamed the heels in the coroners report," Ethan interjected, rounding on Adam. "That they could have caused her to trip. But that's not what happened, is it?"

"I don't know what you're talking about!" Adam protested. "It was an accident. How would you even know that her shoes broke?"

"Oh god, Adam, don't you get it already?" Amelia exclaimed. "He knows because Elle told him, because he can see her, because she's—still—here!"

"That's impossible!" Adam protested even as he turned his wide-eyed stare to the staircase, apprehension filling his face.

"He was here," Elle said. "He threw them." She didn't look at Ethan as she spoke the simple words, her eyes still fixed on her ex.

Ethan's throat tightened at the confirmation. It wasn't hard to guess what happened next. He'd already suspected Adam's involvement, but suspicion was one thing, confronting the man at the scene of the crime was a whole lot more than he'd bargained for.

He edged around Adam until he stood by Amelia's side.

"He lied to you," he told her in a quiet but firm voice.

Adam's gaze swung wildly between the two of them. Anger distorted his visage as he glared at Ethan, and a kind of desperation overcame him when he looked at Amelia.

"Okay, so what if I was here when she came home? She was drunk. She kicked me out before..." His face blanched as a shiver seemed to take him over. He rubbed his arms briskly as he glared at Ethan. The subtle signs of fear became more obvious as his fast breathing took on a rasping note.

Ethan just shook his head. He didn't need to look at Elle to know Adam still lied. He'd heard Elle's replay of voices arguing on the landing, heard the scream.

"You were here that night." He drew himself up as straight as he could and forced himself to hold the other man's gaze. "And you were still here when she fell."

Chapter 18

Elle felt both focused and insubstantial in a way that differed from all of her ghostly experiences to date. She couldn't pull her gaze away from Adam. He didn't react to Ethan's words beyond a sharp exhale. Instead, he ignored Ethan and focused solely on Amelia.

Elle had heard her gasp, heard Ethan move, perhaps to comfort her, but Elle blocked them both out as she drew closer to Adam.

It was a strange disconnect, staring so intently at someone who couldn't see you, although this wasn't the first time she'd examined him like he was a stranger. It had been easy to put it aside after Amelia moved out, but now she remembered the confusion she'd felt as she watched him after her death, and it wasn't just because he started making the moves on her friend.

But it wasn't only memories from after her death that troubled her now. Her mind whirled, trying to make sense of the earlier memories that flooded through her since he stepped foot inside the house. She stared into his eyes, wondering how she'd been so blind while she was still alive.

Standing on the landing had felt like being battered by storm winds. The memories came thick and fast, crashing into her in waves. Not just the argument and her death, but other things that came before. Hindsight really was twenty-twenty.

Some memories still confused her. She remembered the argument, but she couldn't make sense of it all. Why had he been angry about her mother? She couldn't even remember introducing Adam to her mother, but that didn't make sense. They were together for nearly a year. She must have introduced them at some point.

Something else pushed at her mind, a flash of her brother's face, but it was too bright and painful. She pushed it back along with the other older memories. She kept them at bay as she embraced the sense of numbness settling over her being.

***

Amelia's eyes shot straight to Ethan's as he challenged Adam's whereabouts the night Elle died. As he stared back at her, her hand came up to cover her mouth, stifling a shallow gasp.

He wished he could see Elle's face too. She still stared at her former boyfriend, her back to Ethan. He didn't understand how someone who had become so insubstantial could radiate so much tension.

Amelia's hand lowered from her pale face as her eyes bored into his. Ethan tried to keep his expression calm as he moved closer to her side to offer what support he could, but his thoughts were likely clear on his face.

Adam had lied about being here and arguing with Elle. He'd thrown the shoes. Elle didn't need to tell him what happened next.

Amelia drew in a sharp breath as she spun around to face her fiancé.

"You did do it, didn't you? You pushed her!"

The accusation seemed to reverberate in the air, breaking the tense silence as they all froze, even Elle. Amelia's mouth hung open for several painful moments before slowly closing as though even she couldn't believe the accusation she'd thrown at her fiancé.

"No..." Adam protested, mouth dropping open in shock. "It wasn't like that!" One hand stretched out to Amelia, only to retreat and clutch at the back of his head as she hurriedly backed away.

His eyes moved desperately from Amelia's face to Ethan's and back again.

"I grabbed her arm, just to stop her—to make her listen—and she pulled away! That's why she fell. She lost her balance..." he trailed off, his face crumpling in on itself, but whether from guilt at what he'd done, or shame at having to face it in front of Amelia, Ethan couldn't tell.

A single heartrending sob broke the heavy silence. Amelia pressed both hands to her middle as she hunched forward and drew in rapid shaky breaths.

Elle moved to Amelia's side but continued to watch her former boyfriend with a dispassionate expression that Ethan struggled to read. She turned her head just slightly to look at the bottom step. Did she remember now? Was Adam finally telling the truth?

Ethan felt as tense as a drawn bowstring, but the other occupants of the room, both living and dead, had forgotten him.

Adam fixed his desperate gaze on Amelia. "I would never deliberately hurt Elle. You know that...I loved her."

It would have been more believable if not for the telling pause before those last three words. Regardless of whether Elle's fall was an accident, Ethan doubted Adam truly knew how to love anyone besides himself.

"I was only trying to help her. You know what she was like then, how hard it was to get through to her after the accident. She made me so frustrated sometimes!"

Amelia shook her head, but whether in denial or purely from grief, Ethan had no idea. She wouldn't look at Adam anymore, but that didn't stop him from reaching for her. She backed up quickly, just as Elle would have done if what he said was true. Backed away from him until she stood at the edge of the staircase.

Ethan's gaze sought Elle now, but she still didn't seem to be listening. She moved further toward the stairs, but wasn't looking at them either.

"She didn't even want to go to that award dinner. You're the one who made her get all dressed up and wear those goddamn slutty shoes! You think just because she planted that bloody rose bush she was better? Of course, she ended up drinking too much—she was still grieving!"

"Grieving?" Ethan asked, unable to keep the startled tone from his voice. Elle never told him she'd lost someone. He stepped back so he could keep her in his line of sight. He couldn't quite tell, but he thought her form was becoming less distinct again. The panic that rose in Ethan now had nothing to do with Adam turning his focus back to Ethan.

"This is all your fault!" The other man accused as he advanced on his perceived rival. "Everything was fine until you went and brought it all back up. You really are trying to be some kind of pathetic ghost whisperer, aren't you? But you don't even know about the accident? That's some pretty shoddy research there. Why pretend to only see one ghost when you could have had your pick of ghosts!" The incredulity in his voice was almost as insulting as the finger that practically poked Ethan in the chest.

"It doesn't matter what I am," Ethan replied tersely as he tried to cover his confusion.

He didn't want to give Adam any further edge over him, but his mind went straight to the other presence he'd felt. The one that made him pass out. Something had been trying to get to Elle—through him—and this must be why. But who had she been grieving, and why hadn't she told him?

He shook off the distracting thoughts and focused on keeping his back straight as he tried not to lean away from the taller man.

"What matters now is what you are and what you did!" And whether he was a murderer or not, although Ethan wasn't game to say that part out loud. The look in Adam's eyes was barely controlled as it was. He vibrated with angry tension, and the hard glint in his eyes only added to the image of a man at the end of his rope.

Ethan dared to take his eyes off Adam for a split second to check on Elle. She was watching the two of them, but still seemed distant, unfocused. Ethan had to force down his frustration—why wouldn't she speak?

"Whatever else happened with Elle," Ethan continued, keeping half an eye on her while somehow mounting the courage to push Adam's finger away from him, "you left her there!"

The accusation roused Amelia, who straightened beside Ethan, a fire lighting her eyes.

"All night." Her voice was tight, but the words were quiet as she fought for control. "For me to find her." Another deep breath. "Was she even dead?" The last was a whisper, tears straining her voice.

Ethan's throat tightened, angry tears pricked at his own burning eyes.

Adam reared back as if the question was a slap in the face, eyes wild as he attempted to defend his actions. "It wasn't like that! I don't know why I left. I panicked. She was *dead*." He nodded once, then continued nodding as if that would give his words more conviction. "She died instantly."

Ethan felt sick. The remains of his dinner roiled in his stomach. Elle stood directly next to Adam now. Ethan hadn't seen her move again. A visible shiver ran through the man causing him to gasp. The breath he expelled turned to fog.

Elle finally met Ethan's gaze. Amelia watched him now as well, eyes wide and shining, tears dripping from her chin. And Ethan knew. Elle hadn't died right away. It might not have been for long, he'd read the coroners report after all, and Amelia had told him it was an unsurvivable head injury, but Elle had still been there, however briefly, alive, scared and suffering. And Adam's first thought had been to cover his tracks.

Ethan met Amelia's eyes, and all he could do was shake his head, just the once. Her lips thinned, turning white as her chin trembled, and she swallowed visibly.

Ethan reached out to steady her, but she was stronger than he gave her credit for. She turned back to Adam, half stepping in front of Ethan, head held high and shoulders set.

"Since you're so goddamn good at leaving, you should go—now!"

Adam drew himself up as well. "I'm not going anywhere without you!"

Amelia shook her head, hands clenching and unclenching at her sides. "Wrong. You're not going anywhere *with* me. Not ever again."

Adam let out a huff of breath that sounded almost like a whine, his own head shaking as he continued to protest. "You can't leave me—we're getting married!"

Amelia's laugh had an ugly edge. She didn't reply, just tore that huge diamond off her finger and held it up in front of his face.

"This?" Her tone was incredulous. "Do you really think a ring makes up for what you've done? For lying to me? For leaving Elle like that!" Her eyes squeezed shut at the last. Her left fist clenched so tightly around the ring that her fingers started to turn white. "There was so much blood…"

The light above them flickered once and then blew with a loud bang. They all jumped. Amelia dropped the ring as she gasped, hands shooting to her face. It made a dull chink as it fell on the worn rug and bounced against the front door.

"For fuck's sake, woman, that's a three-carat diamond!" Adam exclaimed, advancing on Amelia. The fog of his breath forming in front of his face, gave him pause, as did Ethan stepping forward to place himself between the former couple.

"Take your precious ring and leave before I call the cops!" Ethan threatened through clenched teeth, hands curling into fists at his sides.

Adam scoffed. "And tell them what? Elle's death was ruled an accident. It *was* an accident!"

"I could start with trespassing for one thing. You're not welcome here, and I think we've all made that pretty clear!"

Ethan's breath puffed out in front of his face now as well. That and the now familiar pounding in his head told him Elle's patience wasn't going to hold much longer.

Adam needed to leave—fast. Ethan wouldn't be any good to either Elle or Amelia if he passed out on his own goddamn doorstep.

Adam got right in his face trying to intimidate Ethan with his larger size, but Ethan stood his ground. Suddenly Adam didn't seem quite as tall as Ethan had first thought.

"What the hell is going on here? Are you messing with the air con to try to pass off your bloody ghost story?" Adam accused.

"And the electrics too, I guess!" Ethan retorted just as Elle backed him up, and the lounge room light went out with an even louder bang. The tinkling sound of broken glass hitting the floorboards followed.

The air in Ethan's lungs felt icy now, and Amelia shrunk away, eyes darting around the now dimly lit space, arms clutched tightly around herself in a futile effort to keep in some warmth. It wasn't just cold now. There was a distinct breeze.

Ethan watched Adam's head swivel as he stared into the shadows in growing disbelief. A hand shot to the side of his face as the ends of his hair fluttered.

"You're doing this!" he accused, nostrils flaring at Ethan.

"No, this is because of *you*." Ethan was the one pointing his finger now at Adam. A burst of adrenalin shot through him as the other man took a step backward.

Adam spun around to face the staircase as a frigid gust blew down and passed Adam to slam into the front door. It rattled on its hinges.

"I think that's a pretty clear message, don't you?" Ethan asked as he reached for the door. His fingers barely grazed the handle as another blast made it shudder alarmingly.

He wrenched it open as Adam let out a choked scream. His head swiveled madly, trying to take in the whole interior of the now dark house. He stumbled as he backed into the doorway. A shaky finger pointed at Amelia.

"You know what?" he shrieked. "You're not worth it!" And he was out the door.

The wind ceased with his departure, although the chill lingered. Amelia darted forward and snatched up the engagement ring from where it glinted weakly in the moonlight just inside the doorway.

"Don't forget you're bloody ring!" she screamed after Adam as she pitched it out the door so hard it probably ended up in the street. Ethan strained his ears to listen for the clink of it landing, but if it made a sound, he didn't hear it over the exhausted sob that came from Amelia.

He wasn't sure if Adam stopped to look for the three-carat diamond or not, but he wasn't taking any chances. He slammed the door shut.

The change in the room's atmosphere was immediate. The pressure in Ethan's head cleared as Amelia deflated, sinking to her knees as the tension drained from them both. Wide-eyed, Ethan stared at Amelia, and she stared right back, panting.

The only thing holding Ethan up was the solid door behind him. Belatedly, he turned around and flicked the handle lock even though he could hear the engine of Adam's car disappearing down the road.

Elle was nowhere to be seen. Ethan had no idea when she'd disappeared.

He took one deep breath, then two. He closed his eyes tight and slowly counted to ten—something he hadn't done since he was a teenager in therapy. It never helped him back then, but strangely enough, he found his equilibrium returning. Almost.

"I don't know about you," he said to Amelia, "but I need a beer."

Chapter 19

Ethan wordlessly popped the top off a second beer and offered it to Amelia. She made a face but took it from him and didn't hesitate to tilt the dark bottle to her mouth.

"I don't think it's so much that I believed him," Amelia struggled to explain after a couple of deep swigs of beer. "But that I chose to believe him."

As she looked at Ethan, he saw unshed tears still caught the light in the corners of her eyes.

"It was too painful to question it—I couldn't face the thought of what it would mean if he was lying."

Ethan reached for her hand and was surprised when she grasped his back and threaded her fingers through his own.

"That was the whole problem with the two of us. I believed what he said and not what he did." She sighed and let her head hang as she stared at the scuffed floorboards in front of the fridge.

"I think it was the same for Elle. She tried to break it off with him once, but he could talk his way out of anything, and she was so lonely. I was all she had besides Adam. I just didn't want to believe he could do something like that, even if it was an accident."

Ethan shifted as he leaned against the kitchen bench, his own beer clutched in his free hand. He was still uncomfortable with the details of what had happened that night. He was half tempted to call the police despite the lack of evidence, but he knew that should be Elle's decision.

"What did he mean about her grieving? What accident was he talking about?" Ethan asked.

Amelia shook her head, dislodging a few of the tears that had never really stopped. They ran down her cheeks and fell on the kitchen bench after she released his hand and turned around to brace herself against it. She took another swig of beer. Ethan couldn't tell if the face she pulled was from the painful memories or because she didn't like the taste.

"It was horrible," she started, her gaze fixing on the wet splashes in front of her as she hung her head. "Seth was only thirteen."

"Seth?"

"Elle's little brother. It was a car accident. He was in the back seat. He lingered in a coma for nearly a week, but..." She shrugged as her words trailed off. No more needed to be said.

Ethan took several deep breaths. "I don't understand. Elle told me her mother and brother lived on the other side of the city. I thought I might write them a letter..."

Amelia shook her head. She rested her beer on the bench as she wiped at her eyes. "They used to."

"What happened to her mother?"

"She was in the passenger seat. It was Seth's birthday. Elle picked them up to go out for lunch. Her mother died instantly. Elle was barely injured." Amelia let out a shaky sigh. "I think that's what made it so hard for her—survivor's guilt."

The last was said with such a bitter note that it jolted Ethan out of the confusion his mind had fallen into. If the accident happened while Elle was still alive, how could she have forgotten?

"Wait, when did this happen?"

"About six months before Elle died." Amelia looked up. The pain shone in her eyes.

But they weren't the eyes he wanted to see now. How on earth was Elle feeling after somehow repressing this for the last four years? Was she still here? Had the confrontation with Adam drained her energy so much that she couldn't manifest, or was she gone now that she knew the truth about more than just how she died?

"Elle blamed herself because she was driving, but the accident wasn't her fault." As Amelia shook her head, two more drops hit the bench top. Ethan reached out to touch the largest splash, shifting closer to Amelia as he did so. They both stared at his hand between them until Amelia slowly raised her head.

"I think she would have broken it off with Adam if it hadn't been for the accident. They weren't serious yet.

They'd only been together a few months, but Adam was…" She made a face, and suddenly Ethan remembered Elle telling him that Amelia didn't like Adam back then.

She shook her head and started again. "After the accident, he was really there for her. He comforted her, said all the right things, helped with the funeral arrangements, and talked to the nurse manager at the hospital. He even called her uncle and cousins. He did everything he could, really."

She exhaled heavily, face downcast after the rush of words as though they'd drained the energy from her, and suddenly Ethan understood Amelia wasn't just talking about what Adam had done when Elle's family died, but also what he did when Elle died. He released a shaky breath of his own.

"The problem was, he didn't stop when she started getting better. He kept making all the decisions." Her tone had become so flat it sounded void of all emotion.

Amelia shifted around until her back leaned against the bench and held her right hand in her left, up to her face. It was such a strange position that it didn't register at first that she was staring at the space on her finger where her engagement ring had been.

Ethan cleared his throat and pushed himself away from the bench. He pulled one of the kitchen chairs out and made an awkward sweeping gesture with his almost empty beer bottle. Amelia didn't seem to notice the awkwardness and sat in the chair, putting her beer down in front of her a little too far away to easily reach.

Ethan was about to sit too, but thought better of it and grabbed a glass from the cupboard, which he quickly filled from the tap. He placed it gently in front of Amelia and turned away again before returning to present her with several pieces of paper towel.

Amelia raised an eyebrow. The disdainful effect was somewhat diminished by the way her wet eyelashes stuck together. Her eyes still gleamed beneath them.

"There are tissues upstairs..." he offered, but Amelia shook her head with a strained laugh. She took the proffered paper towel and proceeded to mop her face.

"You must think I'm a pathetic wreck," she said with a bitter laugh as he sat across from her.

At least, he thought it was supposed to be a laugh. In reality, it was more of a choked huff.

"Of course not," he replied softly. He nudged the glass of water a little closer to her and felt a warm flush spread over his face as he received a grateful smile in return.

"Adam said something about her planting a rosebush. Did he mean one of the bushes out the front?" Ethan asked.

Amelia's smile turned sad as she nodded. "It's the one closest to the door. Her mother loved roses. Elle spent so long trying to find the perfect variety as a memorial for them both. She wanted to put the blooms on their graves once it reached maturity."

"Maybe I could hire a gardener so we can put roses on all their graves," Ethan suggested as he suppressed a pang of guilt at the thought of the barren bushes out the front. The few leaves on them looked like they were about to die.

The smile Amelia sent his way now was blinding. She reached across the table and gave his fingers a squeeze.

"What a lovely idea, but you don't need to hire a gardener. Elle taught me how to prune them. The older bushes looked pretty bad when we moved in, but Elle had the house full of roses before too long."

Ethan squeezed Amelia's hand in return as he tried to hold back the tears prickling in his eyes. He didn't know if it was only his imagination, but the faint scent of roses seemed to drift into the room.

His beer sat abandoned on the kitchen bench, so he reached for Amelia's half full bottle and took a deep swig. That eyebrow rose again, causing him to fumble. He saved the beer from spilling all over the table just in time. He laughed as he settled it on the table between them, then started to choke and nearly knocked the bottle over again. Before he knew it, they were both laughing.

***

Everything was dim. Elle watched Amelia and Ethan as they continued to laugh at the table. They were the ghost equivalent of black and white. It felt -like watching a TV on the fritz.

The laughter gained an edge as their adrenaline wore off. She remembered what that was like, being alive and feeling like all you could do was laugh, or you would cry.

She'd been listening while Amelia spoke about her brother and mother. At first, she had strained to hear, their voices indistinct in a way she'd never experienced before. But then she didn't need to listen as it all came rushing back. But it didn't hurt anymore. Nothing hurt now.

She wandered to the front window. Elle remembered planting the rosebush. An Eternity Red Rose. The perfect tribute to her mother. She should be able to see it through the window, but the glass blurred towards the edges, and the moonlight transformed it into a glowing gray rectangle to her eyes.

She wished she could pull the curtains closed.

The argument with Adam was clear in her mind now too. He'd accused her of being drunk and waking him up. But that wasn't true. As soon as she saw his car still in the driveway, she knew he would be waiting up for her.

He wasn't even supposed to be there. It was Amelia's big night, and he knew they'd be out late. Elle had come home before Amelia, but it was still close to midnight. The alcohol in her system affected her enough that she just wanted to climb into bed despite Amelia's urging to let her hair down and forget her troubles.

In truth, she didn't want to forget her troubles. She didn't think she deserved to. Survivor's guilt, as Amelia had said. But Elle didn't feel the guilt anymore, just the sadness. Maybe because she wasn't a survivor anymore.

Adam hadn't trusted her. He just had to check up on her. Maybe he started the night with good intentions, but she had smelt alcohol on his breath as soon as he came out of her bedroom. He'd probably had more to drink than her.

He couldn't handle not being the one in control. The only one in control. She'd resisted him moving in because she knew if he did, he would force Amelia out. He might have even managed to be subtle about it. And it probably would have worked. But she'd needed her best friend. Unfortunately, she'd thought she needed Adam too.

"Elle was depressed." The sound of her name drew her away from the window.

"Sometimes I thought she was coming out the other side, but something would set her back." Amelia took a deep breath. "But she'd been doing better. It hadn't even been that hard to convince her to go out that night. Usually, she stayed in and, yes, sometimes she drank too much. But not that night. I was the one who got drunk." She shook her head. "I can barely remember the cab ride home, but I'll never forget the sense of wrongness as soon as I opened the front door."

Ethan reached across the table and took her hand. Amelia, who had been staring at the glass of water as she spoke, raised her head and locked onto Ethan's eyes. She took a deep breath as if to brace herself.

"Was he telling the truth? Did she die right away?"

Elle drifted back to the kitchen. Everything seemed to brighten as objects gradually came into focus.

Ethan hadn't answered yet. Elle moved forward until she could make out his expression. He looked torn. Amelia's wide eyes were uncertain, scared, like she didn't actually want to know the answer to that question.

Ethan finally looked up from the table. He didn't so much as glance at Elle, who now stood at his shoulder, just shook his head minutely. She could tell from his tormented eyes how hard the denial was for him, and from Amelia's tearful gasp, she felt the same way.

She hadn't been dead, not right away, but it hadn't taken long. Just long enough for the last thing she saw to be Adam's panicked, tear-stricken face. She hadn't been able to speak, but he had. Apologies, excuses, so many words running together that they barely made sense through his tears.

She didn't remember being in pain. She didn't remember him leaving either, even now there were still gaps. Apparently, more than just a body could go into shock.

It was Amelia who drew her out of it, hours later. That's when she became a 'ghost'. Her body must have been cooling by then, but Amelia begged, and Elle had stayed. But why hadn't she moved on before then? Her mind still shied away from that. It was easier to think about Adam and Amelia, rather than Seth and her mother.

Amelia was crying now, soft sobbing. Ethan held her hand in both of his as his own eyes filled with tears. They'd been talking about her again, but she had stopped listening. The dimness was moving in, the edges fading.

Was this how it happened? She knew there was another side now, one that had been reaching out to her, but she'd been trying to hold on. Not only to her old life, but to the memory of a life lost to her even before her death. Or rather, the memory of two lives.

She pictured their faces now. Her little brother had been a happy kid, quickly transforming into a moody teenage boy. But it wasn't the image of a little boy or a teenager she remembered now. No, it was Seth in a hospital bed, eyes closed, a machine the only thing keeping him breathing. Her little brother, who had grown almost as tall as her, looking so small. A broken boy. No one would want to remember that.

Her mother's face came easier. She'd never seen the body. Elle's injuries had been minor, but she'd suffered a concussion and only regained consciousness in the ambulance. Her mother had died at the scene.

The ache in her chest was sudden but familiar. The grief. The guilt. But more than grief gnawed at her mind now. Fear, uncertainty, anxiety, they all vied for space.

Had her mother's spirit remained on earth like Elle, or had she moved on? The thought of her stuck haunting that patch of highway was cruel.

And what about Seth? Had he still been there, trapped in his body, unconscious in the hospital for weeks, or had his soul already moved on? The idea of him not making it to the other side was painful, but Elle didn't think that was the case.

Because now that she could picture Seth's face, she remembered his voice. A child's voice, but one fast changing. And one Elle had been hearing for weeks.

Suddenly she understood it hadn't just been her name being called. No, there had been more, and it spoke to her again now, loud and clear.

"We're here. We've been waiting for you."

Elle looked up, but it wasn't the room Amelia and Ethan were in that she saw. The features blurred so much that she could be anywhere. She breathed out, almost expecting to see her breath turn to fog, except, of course, there was no breath, not anymore.

She heard the voice again and turned her head from side to side, searching for the source, but she felt like she was at the bottom of the ocean, so disorientated she couldn't tell which way was up.

"It's time, Elle."

She spun, convinced the voice came from behind her that time, but she was still alone.

Time for what? To move on to the other side? But she wasn't ready!

She turned back to where she thought Amelia and Ethan still sat. She tried to focus, to picture their faces, the chairs they sat in, their joined hands stretched across the table. Elle wanted to go, she did, but she couldn't leave without saying goodbye to Ethan, without thanking him.

The gray surrounding her receded, points came back into focus, then sounds—Amelia, still crying. The two figures gradually resolved into recognizable forms. Ethan had shifted his chair closer and held Amelia in his arms. Her sobs were quiet, muffled as she tucked her head into his chest. Elle couldn't see his face, but she thought she heard him crying too.

It hurt to watch, to see the tears and know they were because of her. But the pain hit her in an unexpected way. Was this history repeating? Except Ethan had never been hers. Never could have been. Watching them together didn't feel wrong like it had with Adam and Amelia. They were so alive, everything Elle felt dulled by comparison.

The voice was right. It was time. Soon.

Natalie Pearce

Chapter 20

The house had been silent for some time now.

Over the last couple of hours, events continued to come in and out of focus for Elle.

At some point, Dean came home, surprised to find Ethan with his supposed crush, who had clearly been crying. Amelia was asleep in the spare room now. In her old room, in fact.

Ethan had taken his time getting ready for bed. Elle caught his darting eyes searching for her more than once, but somehow she couldn't cut through to reach him. She wasn't sure she was trying hard enough, but everything felt numb now.

But it wasn't only Ethan she wanted to say goodbye to. She sat with Dean in his room for half an hour, marveling at the goofy smile on his face as he texted Jenny.

Maybe she was putting off talking to Ethan. She could feel him calling to her with his extra senses. If she could just reach out and 'touch' them, she'd be there with him. It had never felt so clear before. She could still sense the other presence too—Seth—but he was quiet, waiting, but not impatiently. Like he was giving her space.

She made her way to Ethan's room and held her 'breath' as she passed through the door. It didn't feel as strange now as it always had before. Perhaps because she truly accepted she was dead now. Not that she would have denied the fact before, but still, somewhere deep inside, part of her had clung to this sad semblance of life as if the real thing was something she could get back.

Ethan sat in bed, the covers drawn over his legs and a book in his lap. It was very late now, well after midnight. As she drifted towards the bed, the way he wiped at his eyes gave her the distinct impression he hadn't actually been reading.

His head came up, mouth open to speak, but his gaze passed over her, and his eyebrows drew together as he cocked his head and squinted.

"Elle?" The uncertainty in his voice startled her. She watched him for several long moments before she finally reached out. His eyes widened as he repeated her name with a note of wonder.

"What happened? Where have you been?" Ethan asked as he sat up straighter, book discarded to the side.

"I've been here," Elle replied. "Listening."

"You have?" Ethan swung his legs over the edge of the bed. "Do you remember now?"

She nodded slowly. Everything felt slower now.

"I remember enough."

"Adam..." Ethan started, lips pressed together in a thin line as he struggled to find the right words.

Elle screwed her face up in turn. "We were arguing. He grabbed me."

"Did he push you?" Ethan asked, the tension filling his voice also visible on his face.

"I...pulled away..." It was difficult to say it out loud, but finally, her head was clear. And she was still here. "We were arguing when he grabbed me, and I'd already backed away from him..." She shrugged. "I guess I didn't realize how close I was to the top of the staircase."

Ethan swallowed. Elle watched his throat move. He opened his mouth and closed it again before he managed to ask. "So it was an accident?"

Elle shook her head, but it wasn't a denial. She looked down as she spoke. "I pulled away from him, and then everything dropped away. It happened so quickly. I screamed." She raised her head, eyes widening. She could almost hear her own cry echoing in her ears now.

"I reached out to him. I think he tried to grab me, but I only caught the banister." She shook her head. "I was already falling. It wasn't enough, it broke."

Ethan leaned forward, arms reaching towards her before he faltered at the last second. Elle's heart clenched. How she would love to be held close now. She shook her head and then shook it again. Tears fell down her cheeks, but they were only a ghost's tears. When she touched them, her fingers weren't wet.

Ethan scrubbed away his own tears as he watched helplessly.

"He didn't mean to," she whispered. "I can remember his face now, the horror in his eyes as I started to fall. He wasn't trying to kill me."

Ethan huffed.

"I don't remember the pain, the shock maybe. But that feeling when I lost my balance, that terrifying rush of adrenalin, I saw that same terror in his eyes when I reached out to him, but it was too late. He yelled my name too, although maybe that was after."

At some point, as she spoke, she started pacing alongside the bed. She only registered what she was doing when she noticed Ethan's head move as he tracked her.

"Adam was a controlling jerk. I would have broken up with him after that night if..." She took a deep breath. "But that doesn't make him a murderer."

"I don't understand. If he grabbed you, the coroners report should have shown something—"

"Fingers don't leave bruises most of the time, and there was alcohol in my system. I've seen enough intoxicated people coming through the ER to know what judgments get made."

"And the shoes?" he asked.

Elle stopped her pacing and turned to Ethan.

"The report said they were a contributing factor," Ethan added when she only continued to stare at him. He pointed at her bare feet. "But when Amelia was here, you said you took them off, and I saw..."

She clenched her eyes shut, trying not to remember Amelia's pleased grin as she presented Elle with her favorite heels while they got ready to go out.

Elle blinked at him, blanking for several seconds before her mind caught up.

"I took them off. As soon as I got home. I had blisters, and I was trying to be quiet because I knew Adam was upstairs. I was holding them when we started arguing."

She turned away, her back to Ethan and the bed as she moved towards the bedroom door. She heard him make a startled sound as she stepped through the door and onto the landing. The scene of the crime, so to speak.

She'd come here earlier, while Adam was downstairs, to try to remember. It helped, but everything had still been slotting into place. She could picture it more clearly now. Herself at the top of the stairs, with sore feet and heels dangling from her hand. And Adam, where she stood now until he got mad and advanced on her.

He'd grabbed the shoes first before he grabbed her. She remembered the crack of a heel breaking when he threw them down the stairs. She'd been so mad.

The bedroom door opened behind her, breaking the memory. She stepped further into the hall to make room for Ethan. She didn't want to look at him now. If she was wearing the heels when Amelia found her, that could only mean Adam put them back on her after.

After she died.

Such a cold and calculated move. Whatever shock or panic he felt when he saw how injured she was, he had chosen to cover all traces of his presence in the house when she came home. And worse, it had worked. Her ankle, broken in the fall, only served to make tripping on the stairs all the more plausible.

She didn't want to tell Ethan, even though he must have come to the same conclusion, but she found herself staring at the closed door at the end of the hall. Amelia's old room, the one she slept in now. After the scene earlier, she couldn't imagine Amelia taking Adam back, but she had to be sure.

"I need you to do something for me," she said as she turned to Ethan.

He nodded wordlessly. She watched him carefully for a few seconds before turning to drift down the stairs. She stopped on the bottom step as her eyes fixed on the hall rug Adam had bought to cover the floorboards. After.

Ethan swallowed hard when he saw what she was staring at. She didn't look at him, just asked him to move it aside for her in a dispassionate voice.

Ethan edged around her insubstantial form and bent down to slowly roll the rug back.

Even by the dim moonlight streaming through the front window, she could tell the boards were more worn at the base of the steps compared to the surrounding floor. Whether that was due to foot traffic over the years, or Amelia's desperate scrubbing, Elle couldn't say.

"There's nothing..." Ethan breathed as he leaned over for a closer look.

He stood to turn on the overhead light, but nothing happened. No one had changed the globe after Elle blew it earlier.

She didn't need to bend down to check for any traces. Now that she could see beneath the rug, it didn't seem important. How many times had she stared at that damn rug—a fraction too big and always bunched up a little towards the step?

The memory of Adam stopping Amelia from varnishing those floorboards came to mind now. Elle was pretty sure they hadn't been varnished in at least the preceding decade, if not actually since the 70s, but Amelia had been ready to do the whole house so they wouldn't look out of place. She'd even bought all the supplies.

Elle remembered Adam calming her down, returning the varnish and the applicators and coming back with that ugly hall runner. That was when Amelia agreed to move out.

"You need to make sure Amelia understands," she urged as she stared at Ethan intently, holding his gaze as his eyes tried to slide away.

"That there's no stain?" Ethan asked, eyebrows lifting even as his brow creased in confusion.

She blinked at him several times. It was becoming harder to focus on the here and now. She'd taken the first metaphorical step on the path to the other side. She was nearly ready, but this was important.

Ethan had seen the shoes and knew the heel was broken before she fell, but now she told him about how Adam, tear-stained, had fitted the broken heels back on her feet after she died. The memory returned to her in fragments as she spoke. Confusion that she couldn't feel his hands on her feet, followed by worry that she'd been paralyzed, and finally disorientation because the angle she watched him from wasn't quite right. She didn't remember him leaving.

Ethan's lips thinned as she spoke, his hands clenched spasmodically. She didn't think he was aware of it.

"You'll tell her?" she asked. He gave his head a slight nod, but the anger and confusion coming through every pore on his face showed he didn't understand what she was truly asking.

She took a small step towards him, hand outstretched for a brief moment until she realized the futility of trying to touch him. She wasn't supposed to be here anymore. Amelia was the one who could comfort him now.

"Adam's not just a liar. He's a narcissist. I might have paid the ultimate price, but Amelia suffered because he wouldn't even admit to being in the house when I fell. He couldn't stand the idea of anyone questioning his involvement. He cares more about his reputation than he could ever care about another person."

She shook her head again. "I'm sure she knows how important image is to him, but she stayed with him all these years..." Elle took a deep breath. That part was still hard to accept. "She cared about him. I don't want her thinking I blame her."

"I'm sure she doesn't think that..." Ethan started before trailing off as he recalled Amelia's apologies the day Elle was busy befriending his nephew.

Elle nodded. "Of course she does." She averted her gaze for several tense moments as parts of Ethan and Amelia's conversation after Adam's dramatic exit, replayed in her mind.

"I can't imagine she'll go back to him after this, but you need to make sure. Even if he didn't mean to hurt me, he'll never genuinely put someone else's needs before his own. I don't think he even knows how."

Ethan stared at her. "You actually think she would take him back after what he's done?"

Elle watched the slightly panicked look on Ethan's face turn into one of embarrassment as she gave him a small smile. "No, I don't think she would now."

Ethan nodded, a quick up and down of his head that kept going for slightly too long.

As Elle turned her face away, her smile took on a pensive aspect. Ethan was the type of man she should have been with. At least Amelia might have the chance to rectify her own mistakes.

"But what about you? Don't you want vengeance or something?" Ethan asked. His face twisted as he practically squirmed in place. "We could ask the coroner to reopen the case..."

Elle raised an eyebrow, but in truth, her mind was already drifting, seeking out the now comforting voice of her brother. She forced herself to focus.

"I don't think Adam is the reason I'm still here." She shook her head. "Even if you could convince the coroner to reopen the case, unless Adam admits what happened, it would be your word against his."

Ethan nodded but averted his eyes as he did so. Elle could see him struggling to find another way to help her, but he couldn't give her the kind of help she needed now.

"I think it's time," she said.

"Time?" Ethan asked, a nervous edge to his voice. "Time for what?"

Elle watched panic creep across her friend's face as she failed to respond, but she hadn't been talking to him. She descended from the last step onto the now bare floorboards. The other presence had been strongest in the bedroom before, just like her, but she sensed this was the right spot now. Here, where it should have happened in the first place, four years ago.

"Seth?" she called in a soft, almost reverent tone.

Ethan froze, mouth half open, eyes comically wide.

Elle forced herself to meet those eyes. She still needed to thank him, to find the right words.

"I'll miss you," she whispered instead, even as her eyes were drawn to a lighter place in the darkness developing halfway up the staircase.

Ethan hadn't noticed yet. He was too busy watching her, his back to the unfolding miracle behind him. But she was sure he would be able to see it as well, and she wanted him to.

She stepped closer to him. Her hand reached out for his as it hung by his side. Just a loose intertwining of fingers. Her heart jumped at the sensation, but it was still a shadow of what it would have been when she was alive.

Ethan drew in a sharp breath at the contact. His eyes, full of questions, sought hers.

"What you have, what you can do, it *is* a gift. I hope you can see that now. Feel it." She pulled her fingers away from his and rested her palm gently on his chest, over his heart.

"I would never have come this far without you," she turned to face the staircase, "and Seth would never have been able to reach me."

Ethan's brow drew down as he turned his head to follow Elle's gaze.

Chapter 21

Who knew—there really was a light!

Elle thought Ethan gasped next to her, but she was too distracted by the now brilliant starburst of light radiating out from the center of the staircase.

With no further thought, she began to climb the staircase but halted on the bottom step—her step—as a silhouetted figure resolved in front of the light. She couldn't make out any features, but she didn't need to. She could feel him, and she knew this was her little brother.

She wondered if Ethan could see him too, but before she could turn her head more than halfway look back at him, Seth drifted down the stairs and touched her wrist.

The first actual touch she'd experienced since her death was so shocking that her head snapped back around, Ethan forgotten for the moment. She didn't even look at her brother's face. She could only stare at their hands as he slid his fingers through hers. She flexed her own fingers as he did so, marveling at her ability to do so. There was warmth too, actual warmth, and as she tightened her own grip on his, she could feel the heat travel up her arm.

These new feelings were so distracting that she completely missed the other presence that had appeared in the middle of the light.

Absently, she heard another gasp from Ethan, but the warmth now enveloped her shoulder, and she could feel it spreading across her chest. She finally looked up from their joined hands.

Seth stood a step above her, leaving them face-to-face, his youthful features now clear despite the glow emanating from him, which she could now feel spreading throughout her entire body. His wide smile seemed all the warmer for it, and she found tears forming at the corners of her eyes. She tried to blink them away as her vision blurred. Seth wasn't looking at her now, but she felt the tug on her hand as he turned towards the light.

'Mom?' Elle asked faintly. The figure in the light didn't move, although the silhouette gained more definition the longer she stared.

"Seth, what's happening?" she asked, rising anxiety warring with the encompassing light.

Her head swung around to find Ethan. He still stood in the entry hall behind her, one hand covering his mouth and eyes so wide she could see the blue despite the distance between them.

He lowered his hand as their eyes met, and she felt a pang in her heart. It wasn't just her imagination now either. She could actually feel her heart hurting. The warmth had almost completely enveloped her now, and a tingling sensation spread through her whole form, making her feel simultaneously heavy and light.

"You're glowing, Elle."

Ethan's voice was faint. She could see his lips still moving but couldn't hear what else he said. She hoped he could still hear her because there was one more thing she needed to tell him before she moved on. She wanted to say it earlier, but it had still been too painful. A part of her had still wanted to hold on.

Now she gazed into his eyes one final time. "I'll miss you, Ethan, but you have Amelia now. You have each other. I know you'll be better for her than Adam ever could be."

"It's time." That was Seth. Elle's head swung back to him, eyes still blinking away her tears. He was right. Elle didn't just know it, she could feel it in every fiber of her being. She didn't think she could stay now even if she wanted to. The time for second-guessing had passed.

The distance she felt growing between her and Ethan wasn't anything new. It had always been there. That they managed to bridge it for a little while was something special, but it could never last, and it shouldn't. It wasn't good for either of them.

She felt another tug on her hand. Seth had turned away from her and taken a step towards the light. Her gaze gravitated again to the figure inside the light. Was it closer now or further away? She couldn't tell, but it was her mother. She was sure of that much, even though her features remained indistinct.

Part of her wanted to call out that she was sorry, but a bigger part of her, a warmer part now, knew that she didn't need to. The figure didn't move or speak, but she could feel the acceptance coming from her.

Amelia had been right. There had never been anything to be sorry about. Sometimes an accident was just an accident. Or maybe it just didn't matter anymore. They would be a family again.

Her brother gave her hand another tug as he ascended one more step.

"I love you, Seth," Elle said as she squeezed his hand and stepped forward with him. He turned his head back to her, the calm smile still on his face.

"Back at you, big sis," he said. "Come on now, you'll see."

"See what?" Elle asked as she took another step with him.

Seth's smile only widened, although how Elle could tell when the light shone so bright, she had no idea.

Her answering smile was just as brilliant as they ascended one last step, and she felt another hand reach out and take hold of her empty one.

***

Ethan blinked. The sudden absence of the light disorienting. It wasn't so much that the light had been bright but that it had been all encompassing as if it lit up every dark corner of the room while at the same time obscuring those who stood within it. Because they had been within it—Elle and her brother.

Ethan knew she hadn't looked back. He didn't know how he knew when he could barely distinguish her figure from her brother's as they moved closer to the source of the light, but he guessed that was a part of moving on. Truly moving on. Ghosts stuck on this side were always looking back or holding onto something, even if that was pain or guilt.

Ethan shook his head, surprised to feel the motion dislodge more tears from the corners of his eyes. He drew in an unsteady breath as he wiped them away, only for them to be replaced by more, slowly dripping down his cheeks. Silent tears, but not sad ones. How could he be sad when Elle had finally gotten what she wanted—what she needed?

And Ethan? He had just received a glimpse into the greatest mystery of life—death truly wasn't the end. Something more waited for all of them, and it was beautiful. He understood now why his grandfather never came back.

Elle and Ethan might have said their goodbyes, but that didn't mean he wouldn't see her again someday. The abilities he was only just beginning to explore were only the tip of the iceberg.

"Ethan?" The quiet feminine voice drifted down the stairs.

He looked up to see Amelia descending the staircase that only minutes before had been a stairway to something else entirely. He rubbed his eyes again, thankful the tears had stopped.

"What happened? I was asleep but..." Her mouth twisted, and her brow furrowed in confusion. "Something woke me up."

Her eyes searched the dimly lit room before returning to his. Her arms crossed in front of her breasts, and she rubbed at her bare shoulders. Abruptly, Ethan noticed she was only wearing a thin camisole and the boxer shorts he had lent her didn't cover much more than Dean's shirt, which Jenny continued to wear around the house in the mornings.

"Ethan, are you all right?" The concern in her voice drew his attention back to her face. "You're shaking."

She reached out and cautiously took his hand. Ethan didn't think that would help with the shaking.

"Why is it so cold down here?" she asked as she continued rubbing her upper arm with her free hand. It proved more than a little distracting.

Several responses ran through Ethan's mind as he realized he hadn't spoken at all yet, and Amelia was looking worried. But all he could manage was a quiet, "She's gone."

Amelia gasped and reached out to take both of his hands in hers. "Are you sure?"

He could only nod once. The tears might be dry on his cheeks, but he couldn't stop himself from clutching at Amelia's hands. Elle's last words returned to him, and he felt a rising flush as he wondered whether he could give Amelia something to cover up. Or rather to warm up. He could just make out the goosebumps rising on her arms in the weak moonlight filtering through the thin curtains.

"I think I felt it," Amelia whispered.

Ethan's mouth opened, but he didn't know how to respond to that. His own mind still raced. Every nerve felt like a raw ending.

Would Amelia have seen the light if she'd been downstairs with him and Elle?

He thought she had sensed more than she let on during the confrontation with Adam. She had always been more willing than he expected to believe that Elle was still here. At least after her initial attempts to brush him off. Maybe he wasn't as different as he thought.

"Seth came for her." He barely whispered the words. That was all he could manage at the moment, but Amelia deserved to know.

She gasped as she stared at him with something between horror and wonder widening her eyes

"Hey, it's all right," Ethan murmured, drawing closer to her.

He gently freed one of his hands from hers, which now clutched at his as if at a lifeline. He reached up to brush his thumb under her right eye. Her tears glistened in the faint moonlight.

"They were happy, I think. It felt…" Ethan trailed off, unsure how to put the overwhelming power of the light into words.

"Peaceful?" Amelia asked in a hopeful whisper.

Ethan nodded.

"Thank you. For helping her. I still can hardly believe…" She shook her head. Ethan's hand brushed against her face again. "I've been so blind." More tears followed her words, and Ethan raised his other hand to wipe them from her face. He ignored the wetness dampening his own cheeks again.

"You didn't know—" Ethan began, but Amelia shook her head as tears continued to fall from her eyes. She squeezed them shut and hung her head, lips pursed tightly.

Ethan took her face in his hands and tilted it back up to his, determined now.

"You didn't," he said with more conviction. "And maybe that's partly because you didn't want to, but Adam manipulated you—"

"I don't want to talk about that bastard anymore," Amelia interrupted, a harsh edge to her voice despite her tears.

A fierce spark lit her eyes now. Ethan didn't know what to make of it, but he knew she was strong. He would never understand how she'd let Adam manipulate her for so long. The Amelia she showed to the world was such a tough, take no prisoners woman. That toughness came from an inner strength she somehow didn't know she possessed.

The hardness in Amelia's eyes softened, and Ethan suddenly realized he still cradled her face in his hands. He flushed as he drew his hands away.

"Elle knew you loved her," he stated with quiet intensity.

He tried to hold her gaze but failed as the heat spread from his face and down his neck.

Amelia stayed quiet for a few moments before reaching out to touch his cheek with the tips of her fingers.

"I don't want to talk about Elle now either," she whispered as she slid her hand into his hair and drew his face towards her own.

The kiss was brief, little more than a gentle brush of lips. Ethan froze, but the flush that had already traveled down his neck seemed to spread to every part of his body.

As Amelia tentatively pulled back, Ethan sprang into motion, reaching out to cradle the back of her head. He didn't pull her in for another kiss, though, he pulled her even closer until her forehead rested against his own.

She breathed out, and he breathed in. It felt right.

His other hand made its way around her lower back as hers did the same. Amelia's head dropped to his shoulder as Ethan tightened his hold. Her warm, unsteady breaths tickled the hair on the back of his neck.

Ethan didn't know if he would be good for Amelia or not, whatever Elle thought, although he would do everything in his power to be. But he knew one thing for sure. She would be good for him.

Natalie Pearce

Chapter 22

"So Levi told you what really caused the fight at school?" Ethan asked as he watched Julie fiddle with her takeaway coffee cup at the kitchen table.

His sister, with her son in tow, had shown up at his door first thing this morning. While tension radiated off Julie in waves, she also came bearing fresh coffee, so Ethan couldn't really complain.

She cleared her throat and took a small careful sip before nodding once.

Ethan nodded too, but only as an automatic response. The sound of Levi giggling over the blare of Saturday morning cartoons, drifted in from the lounge room. Amelia's laugh followed shortly after.

"Amelia seems nice," Julie said, head tilting in the direction of the noise.

"She is," Ethan replied, almost surprising himself.

Once Amelia relaxed, the harsh edges started to round out, at least towards him. She certainly had some uncomplimentary things to say about her ex-fiancé. But it had been almost a week, and the thing developing between the two of them was new and tentative but promising.

"I think she'll be good for you," Julie added, a small smile twitching her lips. Her shoulders released some of their tension at her change of subject.

Ethan had filled his sister in on Elle's departure and Adam's involvement in her death (the short version, anyway), but that wasn't why she'd stopped by this morning before dropping Levi off at school.

"The prospect of having someone who understands and accepts me is more than I ever thought I'd have," Ethan said, trying to bring the conversation back to his nephew without pushing his sister too far.

He took a final sip of his fast-cooling brew and pushed the cup away.

"Even Dean isn't worried about the ghost thing. I mean, I'm pretty sure he still doesn't believe any of it, but he only gave me a few weird looks before deciding it didn't matter either way as long as I thought the ghost had moved on now."

He was careful to catch his sister's eyes as he spoke, and he could tell his meaning wasn't lost on her. Levi needed to know that his mother had his back.

She rubbed at her eyes before leaning back in her chair. "I do believe him. Of course, I do."

Ethan's face must have shown doubt because she shook her head before she conceded. "Ok, maybe when we were kids, I didn't totally believe *you*—" She held a finger up to ward off his protests, "—not all the way, but it *didn't* matter. You were still my brother, and what mom did wasn't right. I would never do that to my son." The last was said with such quiet conviction that Ethan found himself relaxing back in his chair with a long sigh.

"What are you going to do, then?"

She took a steadying breath. "Beth called last night. She's still angry. She's going to take Jimmy out of the school. I tried to change her mind but...I have to admit, part of me is relieved."

"Because if Jimmy's not around, Levi won't see Charlie anymore?" Ethan asked.

Julie nodded. "I know it's a copout, but it's not my decision."

Ethan squirmed in his chair. "I could try to talk to Beth..." he offered.

Julie's eyes widened. "What? No, no!" She took a breath and continued. "That's the last thing she needs. Trust me. She's not ready to listen." She glanced away. "I'm sure she knows it's more than misplaced grief from Levi, but Charlie was sick for a long time." She paused for several moments as she folded her hands tightly around her coffee cup. "She told me she promised her little girl that she'd go to heaven."

Ethan sat back. He hadn't known Charlie, but he could sense the grief coming from his sister as well. "How did she die?" he asked in a subdued tone.

"Leukemia."

"And Levi?"

"I haven't told him about Jimmy moving schools yet."

"Do you want me to tell him?" Ethan asked, craning his head around in the direction of the lounge room. He could hear voices. Levi and Amelia.

"No." She shook her head, shifting in her chair until she caught sight of the back of her son's head as he bounced on the couch. "I'll tell him before I drop him off, but..." She took a last sip of coffee and crushed the cup between her hands, seemingly unaware of what she was doing. "It won't just be Charlie, will it?"

Ethan watched her with sympathy in his eyes. He could only shake his head in response. It hadn't really been a question after all.

"Perhaps you could come over for dinner tomorrow night. Talk to him about...all of it, I guess."

"Of course." Ethan nodded his head with true enthusiasm. He smiled reassuringly at his sister as waves of relief coursed through his body.

Julie stood, an answering smile on her face, although it was a little less bright.

"You should bring Amelia. Levi and her seem to be getting on like a house on fire." Her smile ratcheted up a notch as she extended the extra invitation.

"That would be nice," Ethan responded as he rose.

He pushed his chair neatly under the table. A pang ran through him as he remembered Elle telling him off every morning until it had become a habit.

"There's one thing I don't understand," Julie said as she gathered her handbag. "Shouldn't you call the police about Adam?"

"I don't know," Ethan replied as he picked up both empty cups and deposited them in the bin. He paused at the kitchen bench, eyes lingering on the spot where Elle used to perch next to the coffee maker.

"Elle wasn't angry. It was Adam's fault, but he didn't actually push her." He shook his head and turned back to his sister. "There's no way to prove anything unless he confesses."

"But he didn't call an ambulance," Julie insisted. "What if they could have saved her?"

Ethan shook his head, even though he'd wondered the same thing. But he'd read the coroners report and knew it was impossible. He remembered Amelia's guilt that she hadn't been home when it happened, even though it was deemed an unsurvivable head injury.

A few days ago, he'd gone with Amelia to pick up some essentials from the apartment she shared with Adam. Her ex-fiancé wasn't supposed to be there, but he came home before they finished loading the car. Ethan didn't think that was an accident.

If looks could kill, Ethan would have been fried on the spot, but Adam had held his tongue while Amelia asked Ethan to wait in the car. He had been ready to jump out at the first sign of an argument, but Adam remained surprisingly calm as he and Amelia talked on the steps of the building.

After they got home, she'd been quiet for the rest of the evening. Ethan found it hard to stop himself from questioning her while they watched episode after episode of some reality show that neither of them paid much attention to.

As the silence stretched on, he started worrying that she might go back to Adam, but he didn't feel he had the right to ask her. They hadn't even talked about what they were.

It was too new, even though they were now technically living together.

It wasn't until the following morning that Amelia put him out of his misery and told him that Adam had apologized for his part in Elle's death and for leaving her body for Amelia to find. She hadn't met his eyes as she confided the thinly veiled subtext—if she let it go, then he would let her go.

"It might sound harsh," Ethan told his sister, "but if it means he'll leave Amelia alone, then I think I can live with it."

Julie nodded, but she didn't look convinced.

"I don't even know what they would charge him with besides failing to render medical assistance." He took a deep breath.

"He was a medical student, wasn't he?" Julie asked. At Ethan's nod, she continued. "Surely he wouldn't have left her there if he thought there was any hope?"

"I don't think he would have," Ethan answered slowly.

He remembered the expression on Adam's face as he waited in the car for Amelia. He couldn't hear their conversation, but the pain on both of their faces had been clear. Of course, Adam may have been more worried about what Amelia would do now rather than suffering from genuine remorse.

"And she's definitely...moved on?" Julie asked, jolting Ethan back to the present.

He could only give a weak nod in response. His suddenly tight throat prevented him from explaining further. The memory of Elle literally going into the light still took his breath away. He hadn't even tried to describe it to Amelia. Instead, he held the memory close, like something precious he needed to protect. Maybe one day he could talk about it with Levi.

Ever since that night, the whole house felt different. Ethan found himself missing the hum of energy Elle emitted, even when she was weak. The house was truly quiet now in a way that had nothing to do with its mortal inhabitants.

Ethan had no idea how to stretch his rudimentary abilities to the other side, but Seth coming through for Elle had proved it was possible. If the celebrity medium shows Amelia had taken to binge-watching held any truth, he should be able to communicate with spirits on the other side left right and center.

At least those that wanted to make contact with someone here on earth. He hoped he would see Elle again one day, but even if he never managed to contact her, he knew he wouldn't try to hide from another spirit again.

Something of his thoughts must have shown on his face as Julie, in an uncharacteristically affectionate move, stepped forward and threw her arms around him. The familiar flush rose to his cheeks, but he beat it down and embraced his sister in return. They held each other for several long moments, only parting at the sound of Levi's giggle as he and Amelia entered the kitchen.

Amelia stood behind his nephew, hands on his shoulders and a smile on her lips as she watched the siblings. Ethan's answering grin lit up his face as he sent a wink his nephew's way.

Levi stepped forward and pulled a red rose from behind his back. He presented it to his mother with a shy smile and a glance upwards at Amelia.

Ethan's eyebrows shot up as he too sought Amelia's gaze. "Is that from the rosebush you were pruning yesterday?"

Her smile widened as she nodded, and a delighted laugh escaped her as she swept one arm behind her to indicate the small vase full of blooms sitting on the coffee table. Ethan stared at them as he realized their scent had filled the room.

"Amelia showed me how to cut them properly while you were talking," Levi piped up. "That's all right, isn't it? There are loads of them."

"There are?" Ethan asked as he raised a shaky hand to his brow.

He could make out more than just red roses in the vase. There were a couple of barely open pink blooms too. He swallowed hard as a light-headed feeling came over him. He'd given no thought to the color of the roses in the front garden before Amelia told him about the bush Elle planted. None of them had flowered since he moved in.

Amelia laughed again and stepped forward to take his hand. "Come and see," she said as she closed her fingers around his and drew him toward the front door.

The four of them all crowded out the door. Ethan breathed in deeply as a cool breeze brought him the full scent of the roses. He didn't know where to look first. The bush to the left of the front door that had previously looked so sad was now a riot of red. The garden bed on the other side contained several bushes with pink and white buds and barely a dead or yellowing leaf in sight.

"This is the one Elle planted," Amelia said as she bent down to smell a large red bloom. "The other bushes were here when we moved in."

"Ethan..." His sister's uncertain voice interrupted him as he bent down next to Amelia to smell the same rose. He straightened to see Julie staring at each of the bushes in turn and then at the single red rose she still gripped tightly.

When she raised her eyes to Ethan's, he saw wonder mixed with fear. "There were only a few roses blooming when we got here."

"And none at all yesterday," Amelia added, but she didn't look the least afraid. Nor did Levi, who grabbed his mother's free hand with a giggle that prompted Ethan to start laughing too.

"I asked her if I'd ever see her again right before she disappeared, but if she answered, I couldn't hear her." Ethan looked around at the roses, then at Amelia smiling by his side and finally at his sister and nephew. Julie clearly shaken, but putting on a brave face.

"I asked her too," Amelia said as she took his hand again. "While I pruned the roses."

Julie looked from one of them to the other while she grasped the red rose and her son's hand. "Well, I think she has answered you both."

It was hard to believe that only a few short months ago, Ethan had felt as if his life was unraveling. Who would have thought a haunted house held the key to opening his mind and his heart in more ways than one.

THE END

Natalie Pearce

Acknowledgments

Thank you to my wonderful husband, Huw Pearce. Without your support and unwavering belief, I would still be dreaming about writing my first book.

Thank you also to all the wonderful friends and family who have encouraged me and provided valuable feedback. Especially my wonderful beta readers.

And a huge thank you to all my readers! If you would like to read more about Elle, make sure you check out *Ghost of a Chance,* a fun novella featuring Elle and Dean that takes place a couple of months before Ethan moves in.

Ethan, Amelia and Levi will also be back in another ghost story coming in 2023!

If you would like updates on my future books and author journey, follow me on Amazon, Goodreads, Facebook or Instagram. Or subscribe to my newsletter at www.nataliepearceauthor.com.

Finally, if you enjoyed *Don't Fade Away*, please consider leaving a review!

Natalie Pearce

Ghost of a Chance

Ghost of a Chance is a novella set before *Don't Fade Away* and can be read either before or after.

What's a girl to do when the guy of her dreams doesn't even know she exists? Literally.

Elle's been stuck haunting her share house for the last four years. Being dead is frustrating enough, but when her newest housemate sets her sights on Elle's longtime crush, Dean, she reaches her limit.

She needs to get her ghost on and break these two up before she becomes the ultimate third wheel!

Or worse, Dean moves out...

Natalie Pearce

About the Author

Natalie loves writing almost as much as she loves reading and believes all stories should contain at least a little romance and a dash of humor!

Natalie has worked in a number of government office jobs but finally decided to ditch the cubicle to follow her dream of writing full-time.

She lives in South Australia with her supportive husband and loves spending her free time with her pets.

When Natalie is not busy procrastinating, she can be found working on her next book!

www.nataliepearceauthor.com

Printed in Great Britain
by Amazon